MW00639687

Editing by Studio ENP

Proofreading by Paige Sayer Proofreading

Cover Design by TRC Designs

For my loyal readers,
Thank you.

Playlist

Chlorine - Twenty One Pilots

Euphoria - bülow

Ribcage - Plested

MonyOnMyMind - UPSAHL

Bloody valentine - Machine Gun Kelly

Way With Words - The Wrecks

Lies - Ivy Adara

Save Yourself - KALEO

Introduction & Warning

Hello dear reader!

<u>PLEASE NOTE</u>: Stolen Crown is a **continuation of Savage Prince**. It won't make sense unless you've read the beginning of Gemma and Aiden's story.

Also, our hero and heroine behave questionably at times, so reader discretion is advised.

I recommend reading Ruthless Saint prior to Savage Prince and Stolen Crown, although it's not necessary to enjoy Gemma and Aiden's story! There *are* spoilers for Ruthless Saint, though.

xoxo,
Sara

CHAPTER 1
Gemma

I march into the bar with my head held high. Colin shadows me. Like we're kids again, I reach back and capture his fingers. He gives me a short squeeze, then drops it.

And I'm alone again.

The faces staring back at me suggest differently, but that's because I've got my mask firmly in place. The one that says I've only ever been a West. That I hurt like they do.

But really, my heart is being pulled in two different directions.

My father wanted me to marry Aiden. I was so close to doing just that...

"I'm sorry for your loss, Gem," someone murmurs.

We're in my parents' pub. One that ran without a hitch until four days ago, then shut down with news of Dad's death. It hasn't reopened to the public. The building has been in my family for generations, and I'll run this business on my own if I have to. Until I can hire someone who knows how to maintain a bar, anyway. The sense of legacy just walking into this place is powerful.

It's a familiar place, too, only a couple of streets over from where Colin and I grew up. There are a thousand pictures on the wall. Celebrities or random people, it doesn't matter. Have a drink at the bar, take a picture on our Polaroid camera, and tack yourself to the wall.

Tradition.

It gives West Bar a homey feel, like you can walk in and immediately belong. That's the mood my parents strived for, and the tone it conveys unapologetically.

The crowd of Wests—friends and family alike, their actual last names discarded at the door—parts for Colin and me. As is tradition, we step into the middle of the gathering. Hands touch my shoulders and Colin's. Those in the outer circle touch who they can, creating a web of support. We all bow our heads.

It's been two days since my wedding. Two days since Colin's hired hands yanked me out of Aiden's grip. *Two days* to reconcile in my heart and brain what I need to do.

We're waiting for something—and then I realize they're waiting for me.

I lift my head and take a deep breath.

"He died trying to protect me." I look around at the familiar faces, and the loneliness punches my chest again. "My father was the strongest man I knew. Intelligent. Resilient."

I pause. I've had two days to think of what the hell I was going to say to everyone who wanted answers.

"My father wanted to keep us safe. He wanted to avoid the trauma that a war would bring—but the DeSantises found us anyway. They exploited our hurt and anger for one thing, and one thing only. Power." I meet their gazes and take in their expressions.

Confused.

Angry.

Frustrated.

"This family is the most important thing to me. That's why my father and I devised a plan that, at the time, we thought would work."

Colin's breath hitches. Yesterday, I told him our father's true motivation. I doubted I should, but after everything? We can't have a lie between us. He was stunned... and then accepting. Dad had tried to get him out of the city, too. Something he stubbornly refused to do.

"I gave myself up to the DeSantises, in hopes that I would be enough to stop the war."

Some gasp. Other mutter curses.

No one raises their hands or breaks our embrace.

And that, in its own way, is satisfying.

"It didn't work," I continue. "The war was never going to end just because I stood in its way as a sacrifice. But I hope this proves to you that I'm willing to do *anything* for this family."

"Hear! Hear!" Marius calls.

"For blood," Turner yells.

The rest echo it.

"For family." Colin raises his fist.

We automatically mirror him. A warrior's salute.

"Let's take our goddamn city back," I finish.

Agreeing. Cheering.

"Now let's celebrate a life well-lived." I step forward. Hands slip off me, and our trance is broken. Drinks are passed around, music started. Someone hung a giant, poster-sized photograph of my parents on the wall. A small table below it has tea candles and a box of matches, ready and waiting. Flowers on either side.

Other than this memorial, we're here to be strong together. To celebrate and commemorate. Later, when everyone is drunk, they'll share stories. It's meant to be a beautiful thing.

Yet my eyes burn.

3

"You asked to see me?"

I glance over. The coordinator of my rescue has managed to slip through the throng and end up at my back. His bright-blue eyes see too much, and his gaze softens.

"Don't," I snap.

He shrugs. "Don't what? Feel sorry for the girl who's lost both parents inside of two years?"

"Yeah, don't do that." I face my parents' photo again. "I did ask to see you, Xavier Eldridge. You're a hard man to track down."

He stiffens. "I don't go by that name anymore."

"Right. You're just X, a gun for hire." I scoff. "Easy enough for my brother to track you down—"

"He was unaware of who I am. As is anyone I work with." He glowers at me.

It has nothing on Aiden's glare.

Unfazed, I smile at him. "Well, I'm not anyone. And your guy shot my fiancé."

He grunts.

"Which wasn't your mission." I gesture for him to follow me. I try not to hold it against him. I probably would've been inclined to shoot him, too.

I grit my teeth and force my thoughts away from the image of him lying on the altar. He can't be dead—Amelie would've found a way to tell me. *Someone* would've heard. But there's just been radio silence, and I can't help but think that's for the best.

There's a set of stairs in the back that lead up to Dad's office. Of our many bars and restaurants in Brooklyn and Manhattan, this is the only one where he kept an office.

And now it's mine, I suppose.

Xavier climbs the steps behind me, almost too close for comfort, and I remind myself that I'm armed. I won't let anyone catch me off guard again.

I unlock the door and circle the desk.

He eyes me, then finally allows the door to swing shut behind him.

The noise from downstairs abruptly cuts away.

"Okay, Gemma West, you've managed to get me alone. Now what?"

I drum my fingers on the worn wood. Mom used to do the same thing when she was about to say something important, and the unexpected connection has me pausing again.

"You aren't friends with the DeSantises," I state.

There's bad blood between the families. As in, Jameson took personal issue with the Eldridge family and did his best to wipe them out—and he succeeded. The Eldridges were conquered and ground into dust. I thought they were all gone, either dead or in hiding. The fact that Xavier stands before me is a testament to his... what? His tenacity? His anger? His need for revenge?

Either way, I can use it.

"Clearly." His voice is dry.

"Which is why you didn't hesitate to shoot Aiden." My fingers still on the wood.

He quirks his eyebrow. "As you said earlier, it wasn't me. One of my guys. And if he had listened to orders, he would've been just fine... But you seemed upset by what happened."

Amelie would've told me if he was dead, I remind myself. She... Well, I suppose she wouldn't if Luca went all protective beast on her again and locked her away.

I really need to stop thinking of worst-case scenarios.

They're bad for my health.

"I'm upset because I'm trying to prevent unnecessary death," I say instead. "But I'm curious about your family. Are you the only one who remains?"

"Me and my merry band of mercenaries," he answers cheerfully.

I narrow my eyes. He knows he's attractive, and that's half of the issue. Xavier Eldridge has probably relied on that too much in his life. A way to charm clients and women alike. A way to slip in and out with whoever they're paid to abduct. *Or rescue*, I allow.

"They're family," I repeat.

He lifts one shoulder. "I'm not sure why I should be telling you any of this. You're a DeSantis lover."

"That's a pretty little line. Did you practice it in the mirror?"

He leans back and finally smiles. "Yeah, did it sound okay?"

"It could've used a few more adjectives to spice it up." I roll my eyes. "Listen. I think you know as well as I do that the West family is ill-prepared for a war against the DeSantises. They outnumber us."

By a lot.

In two days, I've learned more about my own family than I could've imagined. And that boils down to a body count: there are at least five times more DeSantises living in the tower than there are Wests in total. And that's not even counting the DeSantises who are loyal to the family that reside elsewhere.

We have solid allies in Brooklyn. Our drug trade gives us easy access to money, and the legal operations clean said money. Our expenses are lower because we're spread out, and we don't have a whole fucking skyscraper. That has to cost a lot.

But the DeSantises have the billionaire Pages acting as bankers. They've been preparing for this for far too long, stacking the deck against us.

Xavier straightens. "They do outnumber you, just like they outnumbered us."

"And they wiped you out because...?"

He presses his lips together, and maybe he remembers a

conversation between our fathers from a few years ago. He was there, after all. And so was I. One teenager invited to participate in the conversation, and the other eavesdropping at the door.

"We should've accepted your help," he says tightly.

"See, that wasn't so hard to admit." I grin.

He grunts.

"Now's your chance to make up for past mistakes. Help us. Help *me*. Everyone downstairs trusts me to make decisions to win this war the DeSantises are bringing to our doorstep. The truth of the matter is that they'll wipe us out in weeks if they put their minds to it. Up until now, Jameson has been toying with us." I slide a piece of paper across the desk toward him. "Our families were on good terms when our fathers ruled. If you need more reason to help me, I'm willing to pay for your services."

They aren't cheap—but trained security?

Even if they're patrolling our establishments under the guise of patronage, they can stop us from bleeding out.

In theory.

He doesn't touch the paper and instead stares at me like he's never met me before.

Hell, he hasn't. I'm not sure I've even had time to meet the new me.

The angry Gemma.

The betrayed Gemma.

"I want one thing," Xavier says.

I raise my eyebrows and wait for him to go on.

"When this is over, I want to be the one to kill Jameson DeSantis."

My stomach rolls. *This is a negotiation*. Of course he's going to ask for something ridiculous—I just naïvely thought it would be more money.

"You know he killed my father, too," I point out.

7

There will be many people who want to have Jameson's blood on their hands. Me. Colin. Hell, maybe even Aiden. Not only adding Xavier to the mix, but ensuring he gets to be the one to pull the trigger?

Tricky.

So many moving pieces, guaranteeing *anything* at this stage is a risk.

"I can't guarantee it," I finally say.

He shrugs. "Then I can't guarantee my help."

Fuck, fuck, fuck.

He strides to the door, and I let him get halfway down the stairs before I yell out, "Okay!"

I'm seriously going to regret this. It feels like a deal with another devil—one I'm not sure I can trust. Once he's back in his chair, staring at me with a cocky expression, I list out my rules. He can kill Jameson, *but...*

When I'm done, he nods. "Deal."

"You and your five friends who rescued me are included in this agreement," I push.

"Yes, Gemma."

I rise, and he does, too. "If you double-cross us, I will hunt you down and make you wish you were never born."

He chuckles and moves back toward the door. "I'd expect nothing less."

I give him a head start, then go back downstairs.

Xavier is gone.

Colin climbs up on the bar and stomps his feet until the whole place goes quiet again. "The DeSantises are going to pay for taking my father."

I narrow my eyes. There's a bottle in his hand, the sloshing liquid already below the top edge of the label. The crowd doesn't have any such worry, though. They murmur their agreement. The sound rushes through me like water.

"They took Lawrence West, the greatest leader this family

has seen in a long time." He raises his hand in a fist. "They took my cousin, Kai."

Angry hisses and jeers.

My skin crawls.

Colin's attention lands on me. "They almost took my fucking *sister*."

Everyone is moving now, restless.

But he's not done. "Gem. It's your job to lead this family into war. It's your job to *win*."

"Do you have a plan?" someone calls.

"What are we going to do?"

I force my emotions down, down, down. The panic, the worry. My family might want me to lead now, but that doesn't mean they won't turn on me if I show weakness. And I'm afraid I'm full of weaknesses.

Colin is stoking the fire, but I can't tell if it's intentional or drunken frustrations. He watches me from on top of the bar.

I make a snap decision and walk through the crowd— people leap back to avoid touching me—and climb up beside my brother. I slide my hand down his forearm and relieve him of the liquor, quick enough that he doesn't realize that's my intention.

"It is my job," I say quietly.

Dad used to say that speaking quieter would draw attention to you. It showed a confidence you couldn't fake. Loud people were often desperate to be heard.

On the other hand, crowds are desperate to hear quiet people.

Power. He knew it. My mother knew it.

Now I've got to figure it out.

"Do you want war?" I ask them. "Do you want to ride through the streets and spill DeSantis blood?"

They agree—it's on their faces. Devils, every last one of

them. I'm almost tempted to join us, but as I told Xavier earlier: we're outnumbered.

The hate is not their fault.

It's not my fault, either.

"Who killed my father?" I ask, then wait.

"Jameson," Turner calls.

I meet his gaze and incline my chin, and he mimics the movement.

"Jameson," I repeat. "Jameson lured my father to a restaurant in Queens, then shot him in front of me. He disguised it as a choice, but there was no choice at all. And you want to take out his army? An army of soldiers thirsty for *your* blood— but they overpower us." I'm getting angry, and I let it seep through my voice. "And you want to poke the bear? Cut down our family with senseless attacks?"

I've got their attention now. Their faces are pale, still, horrified. Family. Men I was raised around, who dealt with my parents, who ruffled my hair when they saw me.

"That isn't how we win. We are underdogs—believe it or not. Hate it or accept it. We need to start fighting *smart*." I smirk. "Lucky for you, I'm used to being underestimated. Used to being seen as the weaker counterpart."

Colin flinches.

"I have a plan," I say. "But now isn't the time to discuss it. Now, and this week, is the time to mourn my father and Kai. We need to collect ourselves. Regroup. Heal. And most of all?" I meet as many eyes as I can. "Stay off the fucking radar."

I step down onto a stool, and a hand reaches out to help me down. I let them, then blink up at Marius. One of the two who almost killed Aiden after crashing into our bike—one of the scarier members of the family, honestly. Tattoos crawl up his chest and neck. A snake curls up his jawline, ending at his temple. I wouldn't want to be on his bad side.

He releases my hand and nods to me. "I'd like to help with protection," he says. "If you'd allow it."

I glance around, then nod. "Knock yourself out."

I slip away, to the edge of the room, and sip on the alcohol I took from Colin. The whiskey burns on its way down my throat. The flavor is smokey and lingers in my nostrils. I take another sip, then set it aside. Heat unfurling like wings in my chest.

Someone pulls out a guitar, and people retake their seats. And sometime later, the stories begin. Marius takes his place at my shoulder, leaning against a wall, and I allow myself to close my eyes.

I won't cry—not here. But soon, I'll mourn my father and Kai and Aiden and every other tragic loss in this pointless war.

CHAPTER 2

Gemma

I cross the street and unlock my car door by hand. I just snuck out of my house like a teenager—although back then, I had two parents who gave a shit, a better security team, and less risk. Now I have an empty house.

Colin was asleep on the couch, so I guess there's that. He'd freak out if he knew where I was going. Unbeknownst to me, he's been staying in the Manhattan house while I've been with the DeSantises. But that isn't good enough anymore, and he's sticking close to lend his support.

For a week, it's felt less like support and more like suffocation.

I love my brother, I remind myself.

We're just... different. Our childhoods were almost opposites. If Dad knew what he was doing by leaving me everything, he sure had Colin and me fooled. I would've bet money on Colin being Lawrence West's perfect heir, regardless of the fact that I'm older.

I navigate into Manhattan, down semi-familiar streets. They're quiet, but I know better than to assume I'm alone. There's always someone watching. If they know to look out

13

for me or my car is another mystery. I don't drive much—
never have a good reason to, not in Brooklyn and certainly not
in Manhattan.

The interior of the car smells faintly of cigar smoke, a
remnant of the last time Dad and I drove together—to Mom's
funeral. I forced him to let me drive, because I didn't want to
give up that piece of control. He sat stoically beside me until
we reached the cemetery, then looped my arm through his and
guided me to where she'd be buried.

After, he rode with me to West Bar. Someone else drove
my car home from there, I think. I certainly wasn't fit to drive
it once I snuck into the alcohol.

Now, my new phone's GPS helps me figure out the right
way. I haven't been in this area since I was younger. Eventually, it beeps that I'm approaching my destination. I park on
a deserted street and climb out. My nerves are constricting
my throat, and I take a deep breath before I continue
forward.

The warehouse takes up the whole block. There are huge
bay doors halfway down, and a glass one that leads into an
office on the corner. I try the office one, but it just rattles in
place.

I should've expected that.

Instead, I circle around and find an alleyway that cuts
behind the building. Trucks would probably come this way to
deliver. There's a dock back here and another metal door that
says, *PRIVATE PROPERTY*.

Yet, it swings open under my gentle tug.

I hold my breath and click on the flashlight, then step
inside.

In a way, it doesn't feel like I've been away from the
DeSantis tower for a week. Five days have passed since my
pretty little speech at the celebration of life. The Wests'
patience is wearing thin. They want action, and I've been

plagued by *inaction*. I know what I need to do, but I don't know how to do it.

Xavier's men have been in and out, but the man himself has pulled a disappearing act.

That's fine.

He wants Jameson's head on a silver platter, and the last thing I need is him breathing down my neck to make it happen. He's providing an additional layer of security, and so far, it's working. By his report, three attacks have been cut off before they've begun.

Now, I only have to believe that...

Word on the street is that the Wests rescued me because a larger attack is coming, and they didn't want me in the crosshairs. Xavier delivered that piece of news, grinning as he kicked his feet up on the desk. He enjoyed that—both my expression and the rumor itself.

We've put out a rumor of our own: that after Lawrence died, everything was left to Colin. Including my care. The thought turns my stomach, but we're setting the stage for a misdirect.

Anyway, now I'm here, exploring what I hope will be an empty warehouse. My flashlight's beam catches on cobwebs and old, leftover machinery. This place used to be a hub for West imports, but it was shut down almost a year ago.

My father knew its location had been compromised and quietly sealed it off.

The leak was plugged, but the damage had been done.

I step through into the main room of the warehouse and blow out a breath when I don't see anything. Just dust and the remnants of faint memories. Still, I aim my flashlight all around and try to figure out what the hell happened here.

How a shipment was delivered with none of us the wiser.

There are muddy tire treads on the concrete that might be fresh... or they could be a year old. There's a thick layer of dust on most of the machinery, but some of it could be disturbed. I rub my eyes and try to make sense of it. Again.

Why would someone use an old West storage warehouse to stash the stolen contents of the DeSantis shipping container? If it was still in use, it would look active. There would be guards. People in place to protect against breaking and entering, even if the B&E was to leave something here, not steal.

But anyone with a brain could watch this place for two, three days and see that it's abandoned.

"It doesn't make sense," I mutter to myself.

"This is the address Rubert gave us."

I wheel around, and my heartrate kicks up. My flashlight beam illuminates Aiden's face, and my eyes lock on his face. He doesn't move to block the light. Doesn't move at all, really.

Something in my chest loosens. I hate that my body has this response—immediately nervous and *relieved*. It's because he's alive and nothing else. I have to believe that.

Because immediately following the relief is a surge of anger.

"I—" I snap my mouth shut, because I don't know what the hell I was thinking coming here alone. Or in the middle of the night. What if it wasn't Aiden who found me, but someone worse? "Did you follow me?"

He strides forward and stops just a few feet away.

I click off my flashlight and contemplate reaching for my knife. It's strapped to my thigh, just out of sight, and my fingers itch to move toward it.

"You're stunning," he says.

I glance down at my body. The road rash on my arm and leg is healing well, the scabs dark red and shrinking daily. It's too hot to wear anything other than a loose dress. The last few days have been scorching, carrying over into the night. It's the kind of heat that makes you feel like you're swimming.

"I'm nothing worth stalking." I remind myself that he doesn't know what I know.

He never bothered to ask me—he was too focused on punishment.

His fucking brother is alive, and he's still hell-bent on our destruction. Shame on me for not realizing how deep his hatred goes. He fooled me so easily, I'm almost more disgusted with myself.

I eye his black t-shirt—his trademark—and jeans. Boots. He seems unaffected by the weather. The yellow glow of streetlights stream in through the giant windows, but most of the place is in shadow. It's cooler in here, but barely.

"Don't fucking put yourself down," he practically growls. "A week. I haven't seen you in *a week*."

I shiver—and it's not because I'm chilled. "What would you have wanted me to do? Come knocking at the DeSantis tower?"

His eyes narrow. "Yes."

"You wouldn't have let me leave."

"I still might not."

I back away, folding my arms over my chest. "You promised you wouldn't—or have you forgotten?" I want to touch him as much as I want to run. My emotions are jumbled.

But I get the feeling I'm dealing with the killer Aiden, not the side of him that strokes my hair in the morning or kisses me softly. It only took seven days to erase that version of him. This is the man who would throw me in the trunk of his car. The one who would kill my cousin or his if either got between us.

"I haven't forgotten anything." His voice is low. "You haven't been sleeping?"

And of course he brings that up. I haven't—nightmares have plagued me every night. Visions of him dying in front of

17

me. And then they'll transform into vivid scenes of my brother's head exploding, or Kai coming back to life and screaming at me to save him. Wilder looms over me in others, his hand wrapped around my throat. And in every single one, I can't move.

Over and over, until I've just about given up on ever closing my eyes again.

But Aiden isn't dead. He's here, in front of me.

I almost don't believe it.

I ignore my trepidation and close the distance between us. I put my hand on his chest, surprised at how solid he is.

"You got shot."

His expression softens just the slightest. "I was prepared. I planned for the worst and hoped for the best."

I press my hand harder into him, but he's unmovable. "Hope is dangerous."

"And you fought for me."

"I—"

"No." He traps my wrist to keep me from pulling away. "Whatever excuse, whatever denial, I don't want to hear it. You *fought* for me."

I did. I shouldn't have, but I did. And if my family found out... I *knew* Aiden was withholding knowledge, knew it all by the time I walked down the aisle, and I was still distraught when he was shot.

Why?

Questions I can't answer.

"We haven't used this warehouse in a year," I tell him instead. "Whoever's trying to frame us has bad information." Or they want us to think that.

He clenches his jaw. "And who might that be?"

I dig my nails into his shirt. "I think you know."

"Gemma. Don't be irrationally afraid of danger."

"Why, because I'm not forthcoming with my secrets?" I shove at him. "Takes one to know one."

He laughs, unbothered. "Okay, princess. Keep your secrets. But I can't go another second without kissing you." He hauls me in without giving me a chance to reply, and his lips find mine.

All at once, that hollow feeling trapped in my chest gives way to butterflies. My anger dissipates into a deep ache. I hate it as much as I need this moment of reprieve. Our tongues slide together, and I throw my arms around his neck. He runs his hands down my sides and under my ass, lifting me.

I don't need more prompting than that. I lock my legs around his hips. He nips my lower lip, and I whimper. I missed this, even when I didn't want to. And that lust comes roaring back, mixed with something deeper.

It doesn't have to mean anything.

I tear my lips away from his and kiss his jaw. His stubble tickles my lips. I work my way lower, down his throat. He groans and shifts me, and then we're moving. I nip his skin and soothe the spot with my tongue as he walks toward the closest wall.

His erection grows against my thigh.

And then my back touches metal, and his fingers brush my skin. They skate up my legs, sliding my dress up. He stills at the thigh holster he gave me for my knife, the leather sheath. And he seems to fall into a trance for a moment, struck dumb by the sight of it.

"Armed and beautiful," he says.

He resumes touching me like he didn't just rob my lungs of air. I mirror his frantic movements. He rips my panties off just as I free his erection. I turn around, but he stops me.

"I want to see your face." He cups my cheek.

I almost twist away, but then my stomach flips. A sickening feeling crawls up my throat. *Let's see how good of a liar he really is.*

I let him lift me higher and resume our position with no barrier between us. I put my hands on his shoulders. Watch his face. Absorb everything.

His gaze flicks down. He slides the head of his cock through my folds, over my clit, and I let out a low moan. I'm drenched, and he knows it. My pussy pulses with the need to feel him.

I was fine, and now I'm burning from the inside out.

"Fuck, I love that noise."

He pushes into me slow enough that stars burst behind my eyelids.

"I missed you," he says, kissing my cheek.

I let him trail more kisses down my jaw, to my throat. His teeth on my skin blinds me—in a dangerous way. My morals are hanging by a thread.

He pulls almost all the way out and thrusts hard and slow. I tip my head back. My body shudders with effort. I thought I'd experienced sex in all the ways that mattered—fast and slow, upright or in a bed. But this is something entirely new. I didn't want this to be intimate, but he's dragging us there.

His fingers pinch my chin, forcing my head down to make eye contact with him. I grip his shoulders and meet his eyes—and the challenge there. He strokes a spot deep inside me, and the muscles in his neck stand out at his effort.

We stare at each other. I hope he can't see the anger behind my eyes—or my desperation for everything between us to be real. I shouldn't even travel down that road. I shouldn't hope that he's on my side.

And then he releases my face and touches my clit, and it doesn't matter what he sees in my eyes because pleasure takes over. His fingers rub quick circles, at odds with the tempo he's set. I grit my teeth.

His expression is intense, focused on my face. He seems angry, too. Angry and sad.

"Good girl," he says. "A little more."

His words are going to be the death of me. I shudder at the burst of wetness between my legs, but he only smirks at my expression.

"Aiden, I need to come."

"Hold it, princess."

He speeds up—both his fingers on my clit and his thrusts inside me.

"Now," he demands. His eyes are hooded, gaze glued to my face.

I clench around him, gasping as my orgasm wrenches through me. I grip his shoulders, digging in my nails. My eyes flutter shut. A second later, he pushes even deeper inside me.

I tense again, and he comes, groaning through his teeth. It's hot as fuck.

"Run away with me." His teeth snag my earlobe.

"I can't." My answer is immediate. But I tighten my hold on him, because I know my reaction might drive him away, and I can't bear that. I'm experiencing emotional whiplash—pull him close, shove him away. Love him, hate him. Fuck him coldly, then bare my soul.

If anything, the opposite happens. He bands his arms around my back and hugs me tighter, until we're flush from where we're still joined up to our shoulders.

"Fuck this city, Gem. Fuck our families. I love you."

Lie.

I wonder if he notices my slight flinch. His words are papercuts in my skin—*death by a thousand cuts*. Has this just been a game to him?

"This war is bigger than us," I say. "And I'm not going to let you hurt any more of my family."

21

I lift my hips, sliding him out of me, and drop my feet to the floor.

He catches my hand before I can back away completely. His finger runs over the ring he gave me, and I can't decipher his frown.

"I should've taken it off," I mutter. But it was my mother's, and I can't bear to part with it. Even if it's to shove it in a drawer. And... I was scared Aiden really was gone. Scared like the naïve girl he took to the pier.

"No." He raises my hand to his mouth, kissing my knuckles. "You might not be under my roof, but you're still mine, Gemma West. Don't forget it."

I yank away. I don't know how he does it, lying to my face like this whole ruse is still carrying on. I'm not strong enough to keep up the charade. "I'm not."

His eyes narrow, but he doesn't refute my words.

"I'm not yours, Aiden." I ignore the wet sensation between my legs. The fucker didn't return my underwear, either. "This whole thing was a con."

His jaw tics, and fury washes over his features. He strides forward and grabs me by the back of the neck, hauling me into him. I gasp and free my knife before I can contemplate otherwise. Will he overpower me? Probably. Do I *actually* want to stab him?

Well, actually...

"Go ahead and do your worst." His eyes flick to the blade in my hand. He doesn't try to disarm me, just wraps his other hand around my throat. His thumb presses just under my jaw. "A con, hmm? Did your newfound freedom give you confidence? Is my cum dripping down your legs not enough of a sign that you're mine?"

I shiver. And I still haven't raised the damn knife.

"Answer me," he demands.

"Fuck you."

He sneers. "This again? You know how this ends."

I grip his wrist with my free hand. "Do I?"

"You across my knee, perhaps." His voice invokes heat to spread through me like wildfire. "Perhaps I would spin you around and take your last virgin hole. Would you like that, princess?"

He tilts his hips forward. He's hard again—from the thought of fucking my ass? I struggle against him, suddenly afraid. I don't want him anywhere near that—

"The only con I'm running is convincing my father not to kill you. Because he would. He blames you for the stunt at the church."

I can't help it—I snort. "Ridiculous. He missed the bag over my head, did he? Like I asked for that?"

"Didn't you?"

I stay silent.

"Tell me they wouldn't have listened to you if you told them to stop. Tell me you had no fucking idea anything was coming."

"Even you knew something, Mr. Kevlar Vest," I snap.

He eyes me like he doesn't know me. *Good.* I want to be a vicious thing. Something the DeSantis men should be afraid of.

"Do you have a plan?" he asks.

"I plan on taking this city by its balls," I retort. "Don't stand in my way."

His fingers tighten on my throat.

"Squeeze harder," I whisper. "Go on, show me what you really think of me."

He blinks and jerks away from me.

"Gemma."

I shake my head, and tears fill my eyes. I spin around, giving him my back. Dangerous, given what I know about him —and what he just threatened to do to me.

"I came here for answers," I say to the wall, "and all I'm going to leave with is more questions."

"Look at me."

He's got to be kidding.

But all that anger is gone when he rotates me back to him.

"One month," he decides. He drops my hand and kneels before me, carefully running his hands from my hips, down the outside of my legs. My dress falls back into place. He doesn't need to adjust it—the fabric is loose. But then he takes my forgotten knife from my fingers and pushes the hem up again, to slide it back into the sheath. He leans forward before I can stop him and presses a kiss to my thigh. His lips touch just above the straps.

I stare down at the top of his head, those weird butterflies fanning their wings in my chest. If I was peeled open, that's all you'd see behind my rib cage: thousands of wings.

He smooths the fabric again and meets my gaze.

"One month to sort this shit out, Gem, then I'm taking you out of here. With or without your permission." With him on his knee, it feels more like a promise than a threat.

I shiver.

He rises, his expression pained. But he does it. He walks away from me. I have to bite my lip until I taste blood to keep from shouting after him. I hug my stomach and pretend he's not taking my heart along with him.

Damn him. I shouldn't have kissed him. Or had sex with him...

Then again, I wasn't supposed to do a lot of things.

If I can believe him, I have a month to solve the city's mysteries and save my family.

After that...? No fucking clue.

CHAPTER 3
Aiden

"You could've driven yourself," Luca grumbles.

I shrug. "I wanted company."

"You wanted to make sure someone would stop you from hauling Gemma out of there."

True.

I rub my chest where her hand was. The bullets were caught by the vest I wore under my shirt, but the close range was too much. Deep muscle bruises are spread out across my chest. If Gemma had seen my skin, she might've lost it.

As it is, she's looking like a ghost girl. An angry ghost girl. Never in my life have I been more worried about leaving her with her own goddamn family. I've been able to convince her of a lot of things, but my feelings for her? Never thought I'd have to go out of my way to get her to believe that.

"You're worried?" he asks.

I grunt.

"Naturally," he continues. "Why else would you follow her in the middle of the night?"

Her car slips past us, and Luca automatically starts his engine once she's made another turn. I pull out my phone and watch the blinking dot that is Gemma West travel back toward Brooklyn.

I planted a tracker on her car months ago—before Wilder's death, even. She was newly nineteen, and I was hearing rumors that her father wanted her married off. The tracker was a way to make sure she wasn't going to do anything rash, and then I never removed it.

Handy little thing.

"She's going home?" Luca asks.

I zoom in. "I think so."

But then she makes a turn that she shouldn't, and I pause.

"What?" Luca asks.

"Not home," I grit out.

I should've asked more questions, *then* decided whether or not to throw her over my shoulder and abduct her for real. Knowing her, she'd probably be into it... after the hate sex, of course. After she went limp from coming on my tongue, over and over.

She felt different tonight. There was a barrier between us that wouldn't fall. Her guard was up and fortified. She was surprised to see me, but *surprise* didn't keep her from being happy to see me.

Something else did.

The men who raided our wedding and spirited her away may as well have been phantoms. They left no traces except for the crushed bullets we extracted from my vest, and the three smoke canisters they deployed.

Everything was military grade, and that's as far as that information went before it dead-ended. There are too many places to get your hands on that equipment. It wasn't like the bullets the coroner pulled from the customs officer, which led us to Rubert's little gang.

Six men working in fluid precision—a highly organized and trained team.

Even Hart wasn't able to get eyes on them until it was too late.

I hate mysteries.

I'm sick of them.

Wilder's killer, the shipping container's theft, the councilwoman's anonymous donor, and now Gemma is acting weird.

Family duty has sunk its claws into her and probably compounded since she's been back with them. Rumor has it, Colin brought her home because they were ramping up an attack on our family. And yet, the dumbass let her out of his sight tonight.

Some protection.

It just goes to show that I should've taken her with me.

"What's the play?" Luca asks.

I glance over at him.

Luca is different. He seems happier now that he's been living abroad, traveling all over Europe with his new bride. Where there used to be a weight of obligation on his shoulders, he's been set free. It's not a secret that there's no love lost between him and Dad.

I don't feel nearly enough trepidation as I should when I say, "I caught her in Dad's office the day before the wedding."

He slams on the brakes, stopping us in the center of the road. A car behind us lays on the horn, swerving and flipping us off as they speed by.

"What the fuck?" My brother glares at me. "You waited a week to reveal that?"

I lift my shoulder. "I think she found something."

He stares at me. "Does this mean she was kidnapped on purpose?"

"I don't fucking know." I ball my hands into fists and try to resist destroying the inside of his car. "What if she did find something crucial? I don't know what Dad has in his office that could spook her."

"Crucial to what?" He shakes his head. "We're surrounded by questions. What was she searching for? And you didn't think to, I don't know, *question* her about it?"

I laugh. No, I didn't even think to ask her about it. I was more focused on my own anger and fear of what Dad would do to her if *he* had caught her. All I can do is shake my head, and Luca groans.

"You're an idiot."

I scoff.

"When it comes to that girl? Downright stupid," he mutters.

"You're an ass."

He chuckles. "Well, are we following her?"

I give him a look, and he laughs louder.

Of course we're fucking following her.

CHAPTER 4
Gemma

I park in my father's spot behind West Bar. A sensor light only flickers on after I've climbed out of the car. It buzzes softly, attracting bugs. I glance up at it, then quickly unlock the metal door and stride inside. I take two steps forward and touch the smooth counter of the small kitchen's workspace, then feel my way into the main room.

The only glow out here comes from the neon signs on the walls that no one ever bothers to turn off. The closest one is the outline of a green beer bottle, and it allows me to navigate past the bar and to the hallway.

Up the stairs.

I draw the blackout curtains across the large window that overlooks the street, then click on the desktop lamp. I fall into the leather chair.

Despite practically living in here for most of the week, I've been unable to change anything. Dad had it a particular way— the sleek computer at an angle, the thin keyboard tucked away when he wasn't using it. A framed photo of his family before it imploded. Pens collected in a *World's Best Dad* mug.

He never did business with his enemies in here. That's

why he let pieces of himself shine through—the mug, the photo. The books lining the inset shelves along the far wall, even. Texts on philosophy of war, memoirs of war heroes and old, infamous gangsters of New York City. Back in the eighties, this city was run by five Mafia families.

There was a big crackdown, and now it's just us and the DeSantises struggling for power.

I slide open the bottom drawer and stare down at the safe. I've been hesitant to try more than one code per night, and each one was unsuccessful. Not Mom's birthday or their anniversary. Not Colin's birthday—not mine, either. I reluctantly tried that the other day. The issue is, I can't tell how many digits the code is supposed to be. It could be four or twelve or anything in between.

I bite my lip and tap my fingers along the edge of the desk, then on a whim, grab the photo and pull it closer. There's a little layer of dust along the top that I swipe off with the pad of my finger. I lean forward to set it down, and something at the bottom catches my eye.

Mom's bracelet.

Her arm is wrapped around my front, forearm pressed to my collarbone. Dad has both his hands on Colin's shoulders. But it's the gold bracelet that catches my eye. *Have Faith*. Mom's name. I still remember the day Colin and I spotted it in a store on vacation. We pooled our money together to get it for her.

Tears well in my eyes, and I clutch the frame tighter.

It turned her wrist green after a few days of wearing it.

Where did we get that stupid thing? Some little hole-in-the-wall gift shop on Coney Island.

Coney Island.

There's even the blurred out Ferris wheel in the background of the photo, because it was taken on the boardwalk before we left for the day. Could it be a sign?

What the hell—worth a shot, right?

The keypad has the letters beneath it, similar to a phone, so it makes translating the words easy. I don't hold my breath.

But then the sensor flashes blue, and it lets me twist the handle and pull it up.

"Holy shit," I breathe.

Files. A notebook. A handgun locked in its holster, a full magazine beside it. A ring of keys.

I go for the notebook first, flipping it open. It's full of my father's handwriting, and it chokes me up for a moment. I close it and clear my throat, then open to the first page. It's dated a year and a half ago—before Mom died.

Nope.

Not ready for that heartache.

So instead, I do what any good sleuth would do... and skip to the last page of writing. He filled most of the notebook, but I have to trace back a few pages to actually get to the start of the last entry.

It's a letter...

To me?

My stomach knots, and I bite my lip as I scan it. He congratulates me for figuring out the code, then goes on to list instructions. Who knows what, the people he trusts. Passwords and accounts and how to access them. There's a folded piece of paper wedged between the pages.

I pull it out and gasp.

You're not alone, Gem. Even if it feels that way. And below that, an address. The safe house for the women? I tense and set down the paper. Colin couldn't tell me where they were. It was one of those things that Dad was apparently playing too close to the vest.

I type it into the maps app on my phone. It's only a few hours away.

I shoot a text and set my phone back down, then grab the

key ring. Very few are labeled. There's a house key to both the Brooklyn house and the one in Manhattan. One has a piece of tape on it that reads *Hell's Kitchen Office*. But there are at least ten that I can't place.

My phone chimes.

Frustrated at that dead end, I drop the keys back into the safe, along with the notebook. I keep the piece of paper with the address, and on a whim grab Dad's gun. Better safe than sorry, right? Especially since I don't know what's waiting for me. I find a hoodie on the back of the door and stash the gun in its pocket.

Once the office is shut down and locked, I slip back out the back door.

Amelie leans against the hood of my car. She pats it. "Cute little thing."

I roll my eyes. "Sure."

It's not exactly new, but it's paid off and it's mine. I eye the Porsche that Aiden and I once rode in. Actually, it was the car we took to meet my father and Jameson...

"So, what's the nine-one-one? You're lucky Luca seemed to be out with Aiden."

"Following me, no doubt."

She frowns.

I sigh and join her, kicking my legs out in front of me. "I need to go on a trip, but I think he might be tracking me somehow."

"DeSantis men will do crazy things and call it love," she says.

I elbow her. "Don't."

"Don't what, Gemma? Say he loves you?"

I glare at my shoes. "He doesn't love me. Will you help me, though? It's important." And I need to get back sooner rather than later, before the family chooses a new leader. At that thought, nausea rolls through me. I've only been in charge for a week, and I want to cling to it.

"Of course I'll help you." Amelie eyes me. "You want my car?"

"For starters."

Her brow lifts.

"I also want you to take my phone and car. If you lead Aiden and Luca on a wild goose chase—"

"Wait," she interrupts. "We're talking tonight? How do you know they'll follow me?"

"Because Aiden found me there," I mutter. "And if he didn't physically trail me, I'm sure he's somehow keeping an eye out." He's possessive enough to do that.

"Men." She laughs. "Yeah, I'm down." She takes my stuff and tosses it into the passenger seat of my car, then lifts my keys from my fingers. She hands me hers and grins. "I can't wait to see the look on his face when he discovers me instead of you."

I snort. "Take a picture, would you?"

She winks.

I slide in her car and adjust the settings, then type in the address. We're a similar height, so the mirrors and seat are okay. Amelie leans down in the window and points out some specifics, to which I nod, then she lets me go.

I inch down the alley, my headlights off. If Aiden has followed me, and he sees me in Amelie's car?

Game over.

He'd probably recognize it, too. He's good with cars and seemed familiar with hers. There's no way he'd think it's just another Porsche—not at this time of night.

But then Amelie backs my car out of the spot and goes the other way, zooming onto the street without a backward glance. The engine revs and echoes. It draws attention, that's for sure.

37

My heart is in my throat, watching her taillights disappear.

And then another car, parallel parked on the street, pulls out of its spot.

"Holy shit," I breathe.

The bastard *was* following me.

But now I have no phone, and no way to warn Amelie. Hopefully she'll lead him on a merry chase.

As soon as his car is gone, I take my cue and flick my lights on. And then I get the hell out of dodge.

Paranoia winds through me the farther away from the city I get. I make it an hour, then turn into a rest area off the highway. I pick a spot outside the ring of lights, by a patch of trees, and back myself in so I can see anyone approaching. Then I lock my doors and let out a long sigh. I crack the passenger-side window and kill the engine, letting the rush of wind and following silence soothe me.

I'm bone-tired and itching to just hit the gas—but I can't. If someone is following me, they'll make themselves known.

So I force myself to keep my eyes open and scan the deserted parking area.

Again.

And again.

I remove the gun from the hoodie I had taken from the office, then slide the warm material over my head. I draw the hood up, letting it cover most of my face. The shadows will protect me.

A few cars filter in and out, and I try to note anything about them that will help me remember. Color, make, bits of license plates. But soon my eyes are sandpaper, and I can't help but close them.

CHAPTER 5
Aiden

"I think Gemma is leading us on a wild goose chase," Luca says at one point.

She's slow-crawled through dangerous parts of the city, gunned it onto the highway, bounced from one borough to the next. We're in Queens now, close to where her father was killed. I can't imagine she would want to revisit *that*.

"You might be right, but I can't just—" I can't sleep until I know she's home.

Dawn is coming soon. The glowing clock on the dash is no longer the only light. The sky is beginning to wake up, too.

"Let's just confront her," Luca suggests. "Tell her to go home. You already got your dick wet. Surely you can restrain yourself this time."

I snort. "Asshole."

"Sure," he accepts. He hits the gas, then glances over at the moving dot on my phone. "We'll cut her off."

I grunt my acknowledgement.

The only thing I can think of is that she's trying to drive me crazy.

"Besides, the faster we nip this in the bud, the sooner I can go get my own dick wet," Luca grumbles. "Ames is going to be pissed that I stayed out all night."

"She's probably enjoying not being smothered in her sleep." I laugh at his expression. "What? We shared a room on vacation, remember? Your snoring is horrible."

He punches my arm. "I don't snore. I was twelve."

"Right."

He glares at me. "I don't."

I chuckle. "Just keep telling yourself that, bud."

"Fuck off." He rolls his shoulders back and accelerates down a narrow street. We come out at an intersection, and he slams on the brakes.

Gemma's car's headlights blaze into us, and she slows to a stop.

Satisfaction at catching the cat rushes through me, and I climb out.

Luca grabs my arm. "Remember, be cool."

"Obviously. Just going to tell her to go home so we can all get some damn sleep." I jerk out of his grasp and walk to the driver's side of the car. It's dark inside, and I rap my knuckles on the glass.

She rolls it down painfully slow.

"Game's up, Gem." I lean down—and reel back.

Amelie smiles at me, then raises her phone. A flash blinds me.

"Surprise!" Her voice is way too happy about this.

I have to resist reaching through the window and throttling her. Instead, I plant my hands on the top of the door and lean farther in, ignoring that she seemed to have just taken a picture of me. "Where the fuck is she?"

She shrugs. "Somewhere far, far away. Tell me, what were you tracking? Her phone? Her car?"

I grunt and shove away, going back to my brother. He's

staring at me with concern, and I hook my thumb back to Gemma's vehicle. I can't help but feel smug when I say, "Your problem, not mine."

He climbs out, his expression confused... until he gets up to the window, anyway. Then disbelief. I lean against the door of Luca's car and wait for the show. The yelling, or whatever else might happen.

Instead, he just hauls Amelie out and wraps his arm around her shoulders, cinching her to his side. He guides her toward me.

"You take Gemma's car, I'm taking Amelie," he says gruffly, glancing down at his wife.

She's got that smirk in place, like she knows she got away with something—either that, or she's happy Gemma escaped.

I put my arm out, barring them from passing. "Where did she go, Amelie?"

Her cool expression breaks. "I really don't know, Aiden."

I try to see past what I *want* to be the truth.

"She's not lying," Luca says. He shoves my arm. "You're sleep-deprived and going to drive yourself fucking nuts. Go home. Go to sleep. Worry about Gemma in the morning."

That's not going to happen.

I retreat back to Gemma's car and slide into the driver's seat, grimacing when my knees hit the steering wheel. *Short girls.* I adjust everything, then rest my hand on the gear stick. The interior smells faintly of cigar smoke and the light floral scent of her soap. The rest of the car is spotless, like she was never really in it at all.

It fits with her narrative. She's never got to spread her wings in a way that *let* her drive where she wanted to go. And now she's stuck yet again—*wait.*

With Colin in charge, maybe he'd follow his father's line of thinking. Get her out of the city and join the rest of the women in her family. It would keep her out of the way.

43

And Amelie just helped her escape.

Suddenly, nothing is more important than finding her. Not my father, not the missing shipment or the war that's looming over our heads.

I grit my teeth as new fury washes over me. I inhale sharply, trying not to completely lose my mind. The princess has escaped New York City. But Colin West knows where Gemma is, and I'm going to drag it out of him.

Even if it kills him.

CHAPTER 6
Gemma

When I jerk awake, the sky is lightening.

Fuck.

I start the car and glare at the clock on the dash. It's five in the morning—which means I slept way more than just a few minutes. Try a few *hours*. What was supposed to be a quick resting of the eyes turned into something much longer. I shiver, the car chilled. Dew has collected on the bottom part of the windshield.

I wipe the drool from my cheek and glance around. There's more traffic now, but no cars that I could recognize. I drive over to the front of the building and park at the curb, making a quick pit stop inside the building to freshen up. Fucking Aiden never returned my panties, and I'm extra aware of that fact as I tug my dress back down my thighs. I grab a coffee and pull back out onto the highway.

Two hours later, my GPS is alerting me to the upcoming exit.

Bitterwood, New York.

The highway ramp transitions into a narrow road that winds through a forest. I peer around as I go, my curiosity growing. The smart thing to do would've been to take Colin with me. But my family is here, so it can't be too dangerous... right?

My apprehension grows.

I drive past a *Welcome to Bitterwood* sign that proclaims a shockingly low population, up a hill, and then it dips down and I'm thrown back into society. A small one, anyway. Its main street is quaint, the shops packed close together. Well-maintained sidewalks and storefronts, a single blinking light at an intersection.

I slow automatically. There's a library all by itself up another rise. A courthouse to the right. A coffee shop.

It's still early—too early to go arriving unannounced at the address.

But I don't really have anywhere else to go, and I'm itching to stand up and stretch my legs. So I keep driving until the GPS says I've arrived at my destination: a long gravel driveway that disappears into the trees.

Huh.

I turn onto it and creep down. It seems innocent enough. Eventually it opens up, and a large white farmhouse comes into view. It has a wide wraparound porch scattered with plants and chairs. The sun has made it into the leafy part of the trees, casting dancing shadows on the side of the house.

It seems... *nice*.

Which is weird.

I park and double-check the address on the paper, questioning my father's handwriting.

But then the front door opens, and a woman appears. She waits for me on the porch with her head cocked to one side, just... watching. But she doesn't seem angry that I'm trespassing. Her expression is inquisitive.

I kill the engine and step out.

Now is *not* the time for nerves.

So I stride across the lawn and stop just before the stairs, planting my hands on my hips.

"Gemma?" the woman asks.

I jerk back, my bravado instantly cracked. I didn't expect her to know my name. She looks mid-thirties, her sandy-blonde hair in a braid. Her blue-and-white flannel shirt is open over a white tank top, paired curiously with navy athletic shorts and plastic flip-flops.

She grins. "Gotcha."

"I—"

"Your family likes to talk," she continues.

I stare at her.

A man steps out behind her, gently closing the door. A dog's bark echoes through the house. But the guy... well, he's gorgeous. Probably in his thirties as well, with blond hair and a body that could be carved from marble. Don't ask me how I know—maybe it's wishful thinking. His dark-blond beard is full but neatly trimmed.

"I'm Dalton," the man says, grinning at my narrowed eyes. "Welcome to Safe Haven."

"Oh, gosh. I'm usually the one with manners!" The woman smacks her face. "Sorry. I'm Grace. And we're *not* called Safe Haven."

I raise my eyebrow. "Sorry, what?"

"There's already a Safe Haven." She narrows her eyes at Dalton. "We talked about this. You're copying your friend."

He sighs, rotating to face her. Seems like an argument they've had a few times before. "He's in Florida, and he doesn't give a shit, babe. Is Safe Haven two-point-oh better?"

"No."

"We'll talk about it later." Dalton winks at me. "We've been married for a few years, if you couldn't tell."

My face falls, and I automatically touch the ring still on my finger. I haven't had the stomach to take it off, even now.

"You okay?" Grace analyses me.

I take a deep breath. "Perfectly fine."

Now I just need them to believe it.

"My family is here?" I ask. "They've been..."

"Staying here," Grace supplies. "How about you come in, and we'll explain it? I could use a cup of coffee. Maybe some breakfast."

My stomach gives an untimely growl, and she chuckles.

"Oh," she pauses, her hand on the door. "Are you okay with dogs?"

"Haven't had much interaction with them," I confess. "So, yes?"

"Shooter is a darling angel most of the time," she says. She pulls open the door and gestures for me to follow her. "A devil when there are loud noises—like yelling, or aggressive men. It works out in our favor, since sometimes the families who take shelter here get unwelcome visitors. He scares them off."

"You hide people?" I imagine all the sort of people who might need to hide, and I can't get a grasp on the concept. Hiding people from the law?

"Mostly women and children running from abusive relationships," she confides.

We cross through the open living space, and she gestures for me to sit at the breakfast bar. The sliding glass door in front of me opens into an enclosed porch. There's a path that leads to another house in the distance, almost a hundred yards away. Beyond that, a red barn. It's the definition of seclusion.

She opens the sliding door, and a blue heeler comes tearing into the house. He beelines for me and stops short, head diving down to sniff my boots. His thick coat is blue-gray, with black patches on his head and a white diamond between his eyes. Once my boots pass inspection, he gives my fingers a quick lick and trots away.

Dalton comes in, his fingers trailing across Grace's hip on his way to the coffee pot.

I take a seat and watch them warily. "Why did my father trust you two?"

They move seamlessly together. One pulls the pot free from the machine, the other produces three mugs. The kitchen isn't very large, but it seems efficient for them.

"He knew of me," Dalton says. "For many years, my reputation preceded me. And my retirement was seen as... well, some people weren't happy about it."

"Why?"

He slides me a mug. A jug of hazelnut creamer appears at my elbow.

"I was a sniper in the military, then later for a private organization. My team worked overseas. When we disbanded, our infamy followed us, and I was doing private security in Miami. That's where I met Grace." He loops his arm around her waist and pulls her close. "Mob bosses talk to each other, or know of each other. When I came up here, I was essentially walking into West territory."

"Not the DeSantises?" I raise my eyebrow. I don't want to think about the idea that I'm standing in front of an ex-sniper. And I'm not an idiot—a private organization operating in other countries spells *mercenary* to me.

"They didn't give a shit," Grace says. "Jackson—another of Dalton's friends—met with Lawrence a year or two after we relocated to Bitterwood. He established Bitterwood as a safe zone, because we're out of the life. We protect this town."

We.

"You, too?"

She grimaces. "I know more than anyone how much Safe Haven helps people."

"Catch that, Gemma? She called it Safe Haven."

51

Grace shoves him, then passes me a spoon. "What are you in the mood for? Eggs and bacon? Pancakes?"

My mouth waters. I managed a poor dinner with Colin yesterday evening, but that feels like forever ago. "Anything."

Dalton nods. "Your dad's a smart guy. Although we haven't heard from him in a while. He was calling from a burner phone every few weeks to check in on them..."

I swallow over the sudden lump in my throat.

"He was killed ten days ago," I whisper.

Their faces immediately soften.

Grace puts her hand on top of mine. "We hadn't heard—"

I yank away. Affection will lead to me breaking down, and I *can't* do that now. Not when I'm so damn close...

"I was about to marry Aiden DeSantis," I tell them. "And my brother hired a team to bring me back home. Dad had left everything to me. Not my brother, like everyone thought he would."

I touch the ring again, twisting it around my finger. The loss of Aiden is keen in my chest, but I try to force it away. I don't have permission to feel that ache. I don't deserve it.

"I didn't expect to have a big role in my family." I sigh and lift the mug with both hands. Anything to keep myself from fidgeting. "I was hoping to speak with my aunts and get some guidance. There's a war... It's a long story."

"My father was a mob boss's enforcer," Grace confesses. "And one of my best friends, Delia, was the heir to her family's businesses in Las Vegas. Of course, they didn't take too kindly to that and tried to kill her—"

I gasp, my hand flying to my mouth. "Delia Moretti?"

Dalton groans. "I'll never hear the end of this."

Delia Moretti was a legend, even in New York. Most of the stuff I've heard is probably rumor and hearsay. Still, I'm going to choose to believe that she single-handedly took down her family because they turned against her. She basically staged a coup when someone tried to take what was hers, even after she lost everything.

As I said... probably fabricated. Some stories are too fantastical to believe wholeheartedly, as much as I want to.

"We have experience with Mafia princesses-turned-queens," Dalton adds.

I stare at them. *Is that what I am?*

"Mafia Queen," Grace says, drumming her fingers on the table. "I like it."

I think it doesn't fit me. At all.

Dalton pulls out bowls, then items from the fridge. I watch him for a moment and try to forget about the way Aiden was always the one to cook for me. Especially after my meltdown. He said he'd teach me—

Stop it, Gem.

"Okay, so you created this place as a sort of shelter for people escaping their lives. And you know my father." *Knew,* I mentally correct. "Where's my family?"

"They're in the house out back. Did you bring a bag?" Grace leans down to scratch her dog's back.

"A bag?" I echo. "No. I can't stay long."

Dalton nods like he expected me to say that. "Okay."

My gaze bounces back and forth between them. "Did you think I was going to stay?"

He shrugs, but it's Grace who holds my gaze. "You can stay if you want. Maybe just for a night or two? How about this: you say hello to your family, see that they're okay with your own two eyes, and you can decide later."

I let out a breath. "Yeah, okay."

"Come on."

I shake off my nerves and follow Grace into the enclosed porch, then outside. It's cooler here, surrounded by mountains, and I'm thankful for the hoodie now more than ever.

"Are you armed?" Grace asks.

I hesitate, then slowly nod. "Why?"

She grins. "Girls like us should always be armed."

For some reason, that relaxes me. I return her smile. Her gaze stays on my back as I navigate the path down to the second house. I climb up the shallow steps to the small porch and once more hesitate. There's a screen door and a red wooden door with a peephole and brass knocker. Do I knock? Do I just walk in?

My decision is staved off when the red door is yanked open from inside, leaving just the screen door between Aunt Mary and me.

"Gemma," she cries.

I yank open the screen door, and then I'm in her arms. She crushes me to her chest, peppering the side of my face with kisses. I clutch her back, and the grief of losing my father and cousin surges up in my chest.

"My darling girl," she whispers, "you saw my boy die. This life wasn't meant for you. It's only right that you've decided to join us."

Now I do untangle myself from her and let my gaze sweep up and down her body. She seems okay in peach-colored leggings and a loose white blouse. Her silver-streaked blonde hair is swept up into a bun on top of her head.

"I—"

"Gemma is here!" Aunt Mary booms to the rest of the house.

She takes my hand and leads me inside, down a wide hallway to a spacious kitchen. There's a table with at least twelve chairs around it, plus another card table in the corner with four more seats. The living area is attached, a giant sectional couch seeming like it might be enough space only if everyone piles in together.

My aunt Margaret, Dad's other sister, is the first one down the stairs. She's the youngest and usually the most somber.

Her husband is serving time in prison, and it's made its dent in her personality. Being separated like that...

"Your father let you come?" Aunt Margaret asks. "Last we heard, you two were concocting a plan—" She stops at whatever she sees on my face.

And I can't hide my horror that they don't know.

Of course no one told them. Grace and Dalton seemed unaware that he'd died, too. Maybe he called and told them about Kai, explained the incident in detail... but who would've called about his own death?

It was luck I got into his safe, and luck that he had written down the address.

More people pour into the kitchen. Cousins I had grown up with—albeit, a world apart—and their children. My mother's sisters and her daughters, too. Not strictly Wests, but they operated as if they were. Most look like they were just abruptly woken up. Sleep lingers in some of their eyes, but it fades when they see me.

Excitement replaces any haziness.

"Is the war over?" someone calls.

"Did they find who killed Wilder DeSantis?"

"Gemma!" a young girl shouts.

"We haven't heard from your father," Aunt Mary says. "He's been calling with news, but we haven't heard anything in almost two weeks."

I flinch.

"What is it?" one of them asks.

I feel like I've just walked into the Brooklyn house again, with enough eyes on me that I fear I might fold under the weight. But then I don't. I straighten my spine and deliver the worst news possible.

"My father is dead."

The room goes silent.

I meet Aunt Mary's eyes and reach out to take her hand. "I'm so sorry."

She shakes her head and dashes a tear from her cheeks. "My brother always was trying to look out for us, and he did. To the very end."

I nod.

But her tears are a gateway for everyone else, and the grief in the room is too much. I let someone else take my place and slip out. I catch the door going backward and shut it gently, then bump into something.

That something barks, and I wheel around. My gaze drops lower, to the dog sitting so close, he's practically on my feet.

"Hi," I tell the dog. I've never been a dog person, so I'm not really sure how I'm supposed to act. Do I pet him? Ignore him?

He makes the decision for me.

He wags his tail and nudges at my bare legs with his head.

I hop off the porch and start back toward the main house, but the dog blocks me. I pause and meet his amber eyes, and my own widen when he herds me away from the house— toward the barn.

"Seems like a death trap," I mutter.

He barks again.

Chatty thing.

His tongue lolls out, and he takes off, racing in a huge circle around me. I can't help but smile.

And then we reach the doors of the red barn, which are open.

"Shooter usually knows which direction a person needs to go," Dalton says from the shadows.

I jump. I can't seem to stop flinching lately.

He steps into the open and beckons me inside.

"What do you mean by that?" I walk into the barn. The floor is concrete, and the interior is wide open. There's a floor-to-ceiling metal cage on the left, a whole row of firearms lining the walls inside the cage. There's a padlock on the door.

"We've been at this for the past five years, give or take. He's an intuitive dog. Soft people, he tends to guide toward Grace. Not sure why." He snorts and motions for me to follow him.

I ponder that. They both seem a little rough around the edges, although maybe it's because she's a woman? And if they're harboring women and children who are fleeing abuse, it could only be natural that they trust a woman more. I haven't been able to get a good read on either of them... but I've been here less than an hour.

Directly across from the doorway I came in is a monster-sized sliding door and sandbags on the floor.

"And who does he guide toward you?" I ask.

"Shooter, go home," Dalton says.

The dog runs back to the main house. We watch him go, and then Dalton closes us in. He strides away from me before I can make a noise, and he slides open the other door. It opens up onto a long and narrow field, framed in by giant trees, that slopes down and away from us. It ends at a tall wooden fence, almost too far away to see. Just before the fence, though, are white posts.

He flips a switch, and a red strobe light above our heads flickers on.

"I get the kind of people who need help managing their anger," he says. "Or directing it somewhere. People who want a fight, you know?"

I cross my arms. He picks up a stack of poster-sized papers and motions for me to follow him. I turn his words over in my head and tag along after him without complaint. Am I angry?

"Tell me about this war."

I heave a sigh and quicken my pace to match his. "Did you know Wilder DeSantis?"

"The heir that got killed."

I bite my lip.

He eyes me. "What, not so dead?"

"Right. Somehow. But finding him is going to be the tricky thing. I don't know who in his family knows, but Jameson definitely does. Aiden, probably. They've been instigating a war between our families, and we don't have enough manpower for a straight fight." I grimace as we head up a new incline. My breath doesn't come as easily now, although Dalton doesn't seem fazed.

"Oh, and Aiden is obsessed with me," I add. "So just add that into the mix."

"Has he shot you?"

His question startles a laugh out of me. "What? No."

Dalton shrugs. "I shot Grace. Well, it was sort of an accident. I was mad at her, though."

I stop short.

He faces me. "I got her out of a shitty situation. If he's obsessed with you, he might do the same?"

Ugh. I shake my head and march past him. "I shouldn't have brought it up."

"Right. Okay, so you're here to get help from your family?"

Something like that.

We finally reach the posts. Flat plywood squares, three feet wide by three feet tall, hang at chest height. There are binder clips on each side, and Dalton quickly fastens a paper printed with a bullseye to the board. Then we move down to the next one, repeating until all four are covered with targets.

He gestures to the red flags at either end of the row. "Pay attention to these. They're visual representations of the wind."

"You shoot from this distance?"

He grins. "The best target is a small target."

I think of Dad's gun in Amelie's car out front.

And the gun that Jameson fired at my father.

The one Aiden used to shoot the guy who almost killed me.

No small targets—just big warning signs, begging me to run away from the danger. And what's to stop me from just continuing away? To just leave New York City and everything I've ever known?

The best target is a small target.

And then I think of Wilder DeSantis. Hiding. So small he's practically nonexistent.

"You up for this, West?"

I square my shoulders. When have I ever not risen to a challenge?

* * *

I FIRED the rifle until my whole body ached. My issue was bracing against the recoil—Dalton spotted that after only a few shots. I wasn't coming close to hitting the tiny targets, and I quickly learned that relaxing when I know pain is coming is a hard lesson to learn.

An hour later, my weapon is clean, we've retrieved the targets, and Dalton leads me back to the main house.

"Oh, no," he groans.

I glance at him.

"Do you smell that?"

"Um..."

He kicks at the grass and tries not to laugh. "She burned breakfast." There's an unspoken *again* attached to that sentence.

The faint sound of a smoke detector going off reaches us, and I can't help but smile. We enter the house to find Grace standing on a stool, waving a rag at the offending device. There's the unmistakable smell of charred... bacon, maybe?

The shrieking noise abruptly cuts out.

"How do you burn bacon?" Dalton laughs and grabs her around her middle, flipping her over his shoulder. "It was in the *oven*. Set it and forget it, my love."

She giggles. "Put me down. That's exactly what I did—I forgot about it."

"Uh-huh. How did you survive all those years with your dad?"

She smacks his butt from upside down. "Takeout, you jerk."

My chest hurts, but I can't help the smile that creeps up. They seem like they're happy.

"How about Grace shows you the spare room and I'll make something edible?" He cracks the oven door, and another wave of black smoke drifts out. He quickly closes it and hits a button.

"Good idea." Grace tilts her head toward the stairs. She enters one of the rooms and opens a drawer, revealing a bunch of unopened packages of underwear and socks. "We learned this trick from our friend in Florida. Basic necessities, you know? We had pretty much nothing when we showed up on his doorstep."

My cheeks heat, but I am definitely not about to tell her that Aiden stole my panties after we fucked in a warehouse.

But she closes that drawer and slides open another one holding basic leggings and t-shirts with their tags still on.

"Get cleaned up and we'll see you downstairs, okay?" She pauses. "Did shooting help?"

I look away. "I don't know. I just walked out while my aunts were crying..."

Her smile is sympathetic. "They'll be okay."

"Thank you."

She heads out.

I flip through the packs until I find one my size, then grab a t-shirt and leggings. It'll be nice to be in clean clothes again. I shower and take a few minutes to make myself presentable, including pulling a comb through my wet hair, then return downstairs.

Aunt Mary sits at the kitchen table with Grace and a woman I don't recognize.

I eye them, then it clicks. I slam my hand over my mouth again, because I'm pretty sure Delia freaking Moretti is in front of me.

Be cool, Gemma.

Nope. Freak-out mode: initiated.

It's like coming face-to-face with a legend. Or a myth, maybe.

"Is she okay?" Delia asks.

I probably resemble a tomato at this point.

Aunt Mary manages a laugh. "Gemma, sit. Dalton has made us breakfast, and you're being rude."

Rude?

Me?

"She's just in shock," Dalton supplies, coming over from the kitchen with covered plates. He sets them in the center of the table, then doubles back for more.

"Sorry," I say. "Aunt Mary, are you...?"

"Mourning my brother will take time. But for now, it sounds like there are more important things to focus on—and I promised him I would do my best to look out for you. So, sit."

"Gemma, this is Delia. Delia, Gemma." Grace's smile is way too mischievous, and she glances at her friend. "Your reputation precedes you."

Dalton groans. "You weren't supposed to tell her that."

"I never said I wouldn't."

Delia grins at me. "I'm flattered. Mafia men tend to be the worst sort of gossips..."

Grace snorts. "You aren't kidding."

I find myself nodding along, too. That fits most of the men I know—my father, brother, Aiden...

"So, no offense, but why are you here?" I ask.

"I'm here to offer my services," Delia says. "And to help you come up with a strategy."

Well... I can't deny that I like the sound of that.

CHAPTER 7

Aiden

C olin has disappeared.

Hart stops me outside my house after a day of pointless searching, his expression grim. The whole West family is laying low, apparently. No one is stressed about Gemma's disappearance. No one is acting suspicious at all.

That's the suspicious part.

"Your father wants to see you," Hart informs me.

I raise my eyebrow and resist the urge to knock my friend's hand off my shoulder. "You're his fucking lackey now?"

His brow lowers. "Fuck off. Sam called."

I grimace. That, at least, is believable. Sam is on my side, although he pretends otherwise. I've secured my tight-knit group: Hart, Ford, Breaker, Sam. They're the only ones I trust... and my brother, now that he's back in play. Luca was supposed to go overseas and stay gone. It was safer that way.

My father didn't bring him back—my wedding did.

"You seem..." Hart shifts. "Worried?"

"Me? Worried? About what?" I shake my head.

A total lie—one he sees through easily. He passes me,

jogging up the porch steps. "She'll be back. She knows you love her, right?"

I remember the way she watched me in the warehouse, and I'm suddenly not so sure.

Grabbing my keys, I head back to my bike and slide my helmet on. I wave at Hart and let the roar of the engine under me try to beat back some of my demons. I pass by a construction zone on my way to the skyscraper and idle, watching the yellow tape flutter against the scaffolding.

It reminds me that, besides Gemma, I have another issue: the councilwoman's mystery donor. Never mind Rubert and his deal with the Wests. The last I knew, Breaker had left the son of a bitch alive and in a puddle of his own piss on the front stoop of his house. Never mind the weapons we're missing—and the money our family lost.

I shake away that thought and continue quickly to the DeSantis tower, riding the elevator up to the offices on the twentieth floor. The whole level is dark, with no sign of my father, so I cross to his private elevator and ride it to the penthouse. Thirtieth floor. It's half of the building—the other half is the rooftop pool that's open to most of the family. That side is reachable by most of our elevators. His, however, only goes down to the offices. Extra security, he said. He has a private rooftop above his place, but I've never been up there.

I figured if he takes anyone up to that roof, they're in danger of being shoved over the edge.

The elevator chimes, and I wait. My father has to approve who the elevator releases—and if he doesn't want to see you, well, game over.

It only takes a minute of waiting, my annoyance growing, for the doors to slide open.

"Good of you to join us," Dad says from the other side. His white collared shirt is half untucked, tie and jacket missing. The top few buttons are undone.

His gaze sweeps over me, and he grimaces. "There's blood on your collar."

I shrug. "That's what you get when you summon me in the middle of the night."

He watches me for a moment, then grins. "Good, good. I like that." He pats my shoulder. "Come on."

I follow him through the foyer into his giant living room and stop short.

Elise and Michael Page—Amelie's parents—sit on the couch. There are drinks in front of them, but only Dad's has a dent in it.

"Aiden has so graciously deemed us worthy of his presence," Dad says to them. He glances at me. "Sit."

The order rankles. As I watch, though, he collects his glass and gives himself a heavy re-pour from the wet bar. He drains it in a gulp and fills it again. Whiskey, from the look of it. The dark liquid makes him mean.

So I follow directions and sit in one of the chairs near Elise Page.

Her attention flutters over me, pausing at the blood spot on my shirt, then quickly away. She never did enjoy working with us. Her husband was the driving force behind the deal. I lingered at the back of those meetings, too, when it suited me. How Michael Page quivered as he delivered his offer: money in exchange for protection.

Amelie was never supposed to marry Wilder. That was my father's idea. A way to cinch their purse to our name.

A vague threat, too, although only Michael seemed aware of that.

Wilder was a subtle demon. He would've used Amelie as leverage at some point. More money, more support, or…

"As you know, the Pages have contributed a significant amount to our family and the politicians who support us," Dad says, dropping onto the sofa across from our guests. The liquid sloshes in the glass, and he rests it on his thigh. "They've been happy to help assist us with uncovering the mystery donor."

I don't react. He loves a show, and right now I can't tell if it's meant to intimidate me or them.

"Go on, Elise."

"Councilwoman White has provided her PAC's reports of donations, as well as the charities she supports that have received a few large donations from anonymous contributors," Amelie's mother explains. Her voice trembles. "This puts an expectation on the board that she supervises. You know—"

"I'm familiar with how politics work," I say drily. "They chase the money. They're slaves to it. That's why we're working together."

You're our bank.

She swallows and falls silent.

"The councilwoman is running for governor next year. She's announcing her candidacy this weekend at the Children's Hospital Gala," Dad says. "Needless to say, she expects a donation from us—and public support. This is where Wilder was going to come in, but that option is off the table. It's one thing for a mystery donor to try and sway her, but it's another entirely for them to come out and give her what she needs: public backing. Money only goes so far in this town, especially if they want to sit in the shadows like cowards."

Now that's a stretch of truth.

I narrow my eyes. "Obviously."

A buzz sounds, and Dad hops up. Voices drift toward us, and then he ushers the new arrivals into the room.

Amelie strides ahead of Luca and my father, seeming disgruntled—but it's nothing compared to the expression that crosses her face when she spots her parents.

She stops dead. "What the fuck?"

"Language, Amelie," her mother reprimands. She rises and

goes to her daughter, wrapping her arms around her shoulders. The hug is painfully awkward, to say the least.

Amelie stays stiff, her face pained, until Elise releases her.

Her dad rises, too, and presses a kiss to Amelie's temple.

Luca steps forward, scowling. He pulls Amelie back against his chest and glances at Dad. "Okay, enough. Can you tell us why you had one of your lackeys come to my home and demand we go with him?"

"You've been shirking your duties." Dad circles them and points to the sofa he previously occupied. "Sit the fuck down."

Amelie opens her mouth like she's going to say something —bold of her—but then seems to think better of it. She sits closer to me, eyeing her father across the low coffee table. Luca goes to the wet bar and pours his own drink, then perches beside his wife.

"We were hoping Luca and Amelie would attend," Michael says. "Page Printing is hosting the event, and Jameson has agreed that a show of force would be best."

"Agreed," Dad drawls. "You're back in New York. It's time you stop fighting your family, Luca."

I give my brother a warning look. How many times have they had this argument? The idea of family is so scattered in Luca's mind. I don't blame him for staying away.

Stupid fucking wedding.

I had been eagerly anticipating it, too. Not the ceremony, but seeing Gemma in a dress? Tying her to me forever? The idea that forever could be a good thing...

"I'm not sure why you think that's a good idea, *Mother*," Amelie says. "I was supposed to marry Wilder, remember? How do you think your *peers* would react knowing I married his brother?"

Dad's lip curls. "We'll find out."

I watch my father. He has to have another motive besides

just showing support for Sandra White. Maybe he wants in her pants, or he's after more power, himself. Aligning himself close to her—but to what end? It can't just be about the construction business, or the fact that someone else is encroaching on what he perceives to be *his* territory. It can't just be about money.

What does he want that he doesn't have?

Michael glances my way. "And we're hoping you and—"

Dad's loud laugh cuts him off. "I hope you weren't about to suggest Gemma West attends, Page. That girl is nothing but trouble. She created a disaster at her own wedding. We were held at fucking *gunpoint*."

Ah, yes. My father went on a tear after the botched wedding ceremony, but I thought he might've let it go. He didn't really care that I was shot. He only gave a shit about his reputation, and that a small team had bested his guards and spirited Gemma away. The way he's clutching his glass, though, says he hasn't forgotten. He glares at me like *I'm* the one responsible.

I stand, fighting my own temper. He hasn't said anything about Gemma to me, personally, but now? Fuck that.

"We'll be there." I stride to the elevator and jam my finger on the button. I shouldn't leave Luca and Amelie alone with them, but they should be able to handle themselves. The guilt barely registers, instead frustration and annoyance taking over.

The elevator doors slide open, then swiftly closes behind me.

I slam my fist against the wall.

Fuck, fuck, fuck.

I step off on the twentieth floor and storm through the offices toward the main elevators, then pause. What if whatever Gemma found is still in my father's office? Or a hint of it, at least? Without really thinking it through, I go to his office and push open the door. It's neat, not that I was expecting anything different. He keeps things tidy when he's not actively destroying something.

I circle his desk and yank the first drawer open. Well, I would, but it doesn't budge.

Interesting.

The next drawer is locked, too. The only thing not locked down tight is the one on the bottom left, and it's practically empty.

"He's not wrong," my brother says. I can see their shadows on the floor in front of the door. They walk adjacent to the office, toward the other elevators, and I hunker lower.

"He's not *right*," Amelie counters. "He's insane. And why didn't my parents see that he was just going to keep using them like a yo-yo? There was no one-time payment. It's now familial obligation, and Dad walked right into it."

Luca snorts. I step around the desk and press my back against the wall right next to the door, hoping they won't see me. It isn't really pertinent—I doubt Luca will go crying to Dad that I broke into his office—but the less he knows, the safer he is.

At least, that's my line of thinking until he asks, "Are you going to tell Aiden where Gemma went?"

I clench my jaw so hard, my teeth might crack.

There's silence, then, "I don't actually know where she went. And she gave me her phone..."

A phone I now have.

"You believe me, right?" Her voice is small.

"Of course," Luca replies easily.

Resentment pangs through me, and shame a second later. Their trust was hard-won, and I'm *jealous* that Gemma and I don't have the same? For all I know, this is our battle. This could also be the calm before the storm...

The main elevator pings, and I poke my head out in time to watch them step inside.

"Focus," I mutter. Dad's office is a dead end for now. Until I can get back in there with tools to pick the locks, I'm not going to get anywhere. He'd know if I broke the drawers open. My other option is to return to where I know Gemma disappeared from: her family's bar.

But they'd probably shoot me on sight if I walked in during their operating hours. Tensions are high, even though her family seems to have disappeared from the streets. It's only a matter of time before my father begins to press his advantage —and if they're not around to stop our family, they'll be extinct before they can even blink.

Exhaustion burns my eyes. I don't remember the last time I slept through the night. Part of me wants to shrug it off, but I can't ignore my body any longer. So I go home, to my sanctuary, where Ford and Breaker lounge in the living room, and Hart smokes a joint on my back steps, and I finally try to rest.

I even manage to drift off, my mind settling.

Until a phone rings.

One that isn't mine.

I shoot upright and grab at Gemma's lit-up phone from my nightstand. A number with a New York City area code is calling.

What the hell, right?

I swipe to answer. "Hello?"

A quick intake of breath on the other end of the line, and my heart races.

"Aiden?"

It's her.

"Please tell me you're safe." I'm gripping the phone too tightly.

"I am," she says. "Why were you following me?"

I laugh. "That's what you want to talk about?"

"No." She's quiet for a moment. "What I found in your

72

dad's office... I need to know if you know. And if you do, you need to understand that you and I won't be a thing."

I rear back and stare down at the screen. "You want to talk about *this*? I don't know what you found in his office. Up until Wilder's death, I tried to stay as far out of the politics of it—"

"Meet me tomorrow," she says. "At the—"

"You come to my house," I interrupt. "It's safe. My father doesn't even know I own it. I'll text you the address."

"Okay," she says. "I'll... see you tomorrow, then."

My stomach twists, and I lie back down. "Where are you?"

"I had to see my family," she whispers. There's rustling on her end, too. "They didn't know my father was dead. But this place seems good for them. I'm glad he got them to safety."

"Did you consider staying with them?" That fear springs out of my mouth before I can stop it. The thought of her hiding away—I don't know if I'd be able to find her. I wanted to kill her brother when she vanished last night.

Worry and frustration kept me awake—desperation keeps me on edge, even now.

What would I do to get her back?

"I couldn't," she says. "Your father would bulldoze the Wests right out of the five boroughs."

"So, Colin wants to fight?"

She chuckles. "Something like that. Are you suggesting we give up New York? It's late—I need to sleep. And so do you, from the sound of it..."

"I do."

I wish I could see her face right now. Impulsively, I check the screen and see the FaceTime icon lit up. I press it and wait. My own face is barely lit in a green glow from my clock. She accepts the call, and her face fills the screen. It seems she's flat on her back. A lamp off to the side gives her skin a soft golden glow, and the light catches on the strands of blonde hair fanned around her face.

"Hey." Her cheeks turn pink.

"I wanted to see you," I say. "You're beautiful."

"And you're going to get me in trouble." She sits up, pulling her hair over her shoulders. "I borrowed this phone."

"From..."

She shoots me a look. "From a person."

I laugh. "Okay, princess." My voice lowers. "What made you call your own phone?"

Gemma grins and fiddles with the strap of her black tank top. "I hoped you had it. After Amelie took my car... And I was just thinking about what I'm going to do when I get back. What are you doing right now?"

"Thinking about you. Naked." My dick hardens just thinking about her. "How you feel under me."

Her cheeks are no longer pink—her whole face is red.

"How you taste," I continue.

"Aiden," she whispers. "Why are you doing this? Any of it?"

"I'll never let you go," I swear. "And I'm not fucking apologizing for that, Gem."

Her chest hitches, and she inches her finger lower, between her breasts; she takes the fabric with it and exposes her pale skin.

I bite back my groan.

She tilts the camera down, until I can see from her eyes down to the bottom of her rib cage. She slides her hand into her shirt and pinches her nipple. Her eyes flutter, and her lips part.

"Take your shirt off." I wish I was there. "You're going to follow my directions, yes?"

She nods, sucking her lower lip between her teeth. Then she moves, positioning her phone against the pillows. She backs away from it and kneels on the bed, a plain white wall with a nondescript dresser in the background. Her black shorts leave nothing to the imagination—her long legs are tan and smooth. She drags her shirt up slowly, over her head, and tosses it away. She rakes her fingers through her hair and eyes me.

"What now?"

Her left hand catches my attention—she still wears the ring. It's her mother's, but the fact that it's on the finger a wedding band should sit tells me there's still a chance she's invested in us.

"Your shorts."

She complies, and I get harder. I reach under the waistband of my sweatpants and stroke myself, trying not to let out a hiss of breath. She's just too fucking perfect. She wriggles closer to the screen, parting her knees and giving me a full view of her glistening pussy.

"Your finger on your clit," I order. "Now. Rub little circles."

"What about you?"

I rotate my phone and show her my tented pants, the rough movement of my tugs.

She groans, and I quickly flip it back around to see her face. She parts her folds and rubs at her clit, her head falling backward. I shove my waistband down, freeing my erection, and squirt lotion into my hand. The new sensation helps my palm glide up and down, but it isn't as good as the real thing. *Her.*

"Good girl," I murmur.

She shudders.

"Slide a finger in your cunt."

She parts her knees farther and does as I ask. She whimpers, slowly fucking herself.

My grip on the phone is almost strong enough to crack it.

I want to reach through and touch her so bad, but I can't deny that this show is erotic as hell. I pump myself harder, matching her tempo. Remembering her heat.

"Two fingers. Rub your clit with your thumb. That's my hand on you, Gemma. Slower."

She grits her teeth. "You're killing me."

"I'd be drilling into you hard and slow if I was there," I tell her. "You would be soaking my dick, begging me for it." My movement is jerkier now, my balls tightening. "Let your other hand roam, princess."

Her free hand travels up her thigh, over her belly. She squeezes her breast and rolls her nipple between her fingers.

"Just like that. Ride that edge," I instruct.

She moans quietly, her fingers moving faster. I watch with greedy eyes, keeping my tempo matching hers. I'm on that edge, too, about to explode. I sweep my thumb over the head of my cock.

"Show me," she says suddenly. "Aiden, I'm going to—"

"Easy, baby," I interrupt. The feeling is almost overwhelming, and I hold the phone out so she can see my cock, my bare chest, my face. "Give it to me."

She whimpers and presses hard on her clit, her fingers twisting. Her head bows forward when the climax hits her.

"Eyes," I demand.

Her gaze bores into mine through the screen, hazy with bliss.

A moment later, I come with a grunt. The hot, ropey liquid hits my chest, and my eyes nearly roll back. But I catch the rapt way she's watching me, and it just prolongs my orgasm.

Finally, I relax. She pulls her fingers out with a shudder and flops back onto her side, taking the phone with her. I can see half her face now, eyelids heavy. She shows me her wet fingers, and I groan agony when she sticks them in her mouth and sucks her digits clean.

"Tomorrow," I say. I take her with me into the bathroom, letting her see my upper body as I clean myself off and readjust my sweatpants.

"Tomorrow," she repeats. Her cheeks are red again, embarrassment getting the better of her.

"What is it?"

"I..." She glances away. "Is our connection only sexual? Is that why you said you loved me after you fucked—"

"No." I scowl. "Don't think that way. That this connection is our *only* connection."

She hesitates. She fucking *hesitates*.

"Don't ruin this," I find myself pleading. Me. I don't plead with anyone—but I'd get on my knees and beg her. "Gemma."

"I'm afraid for tomorrow," she admits. "But there's no stopping this train."

I nod, but I'm suddenly exhausted. With all of this. New York and the Wests and my psychotic father, war and death and this stupid game we're playing.

She reaches out and clicks off her light, and the screen goes dark. "Goodnight, Aiden."

"Goodnight, Gem."

CHAPTER 8
Gemma

Delia comes to see me off. Aunt Mary has packed her bags and will be returning with me, while Aunt Margaret plans on staying with everyone else. I've decided to tell Aiden the truth about what I discovered, and then I'll judge for myself his intentions. If he was as blind as I was about Wilder's fake death.

Whether he decides to help me or not is another story entirely.

Aunt Mary will act as a liaison between the women here in Bitterwood and the rest of us back in New York. She and Delia both argued yesterday that I needed support. Someone who has been in the family for decades. A person to bounce my ideas off of, and to potentially stop me from doing something stupid.

Although, Dalton pointed out that even Aunt Mary couldn't stop me if I really wanted something done.

"Just don't paint the streets red," he joked.

Now, he clasps my shoulder and thrusts a box of ammunition into my hands.

"What's this for?"

"That handgun in your car," he replies.

I stare at him.

He shrugs, nonchalant. "I don't like unknowns. But you know how to use it—it's the same as the one we practiced with after dinner."

Extra shooting practice. The sort of information I could've absorbed over a month or six, crammed into less than twenty-four hours. After firearm basics, he had Grace go over some self-defense moves with me. Surprisingly, a few other cousins joined in. We were all sweaty and panting by the time she was done with us. And it helped my confidence—exactly what the lesson was intended to do.

I shake his hand. "Thank you, Dalton. I appreciate everything you're doing here. Bitterwood is lucky to have Safe Haven."

"Good luck with everything, Gemma." He glances back at Grace. "Hear that? The name is sticking."

She rolls her eyes, then hugs me. I squeeze her tight.

"Stay safe," she says.

Delia is next, clasping my hand. "Screw being safe. Take risks—just make sure your priorities are straight."

I nod. They are: I'm focused on my family. I try to pull away, but she holds me tighter.

"Your current goals don't have to take priority," she adds. "I thought my priority was taking down my family, but in the end..."

She told me her story yesterday. Her fight—and the way she ended up closer to the guy who helped her succeed. Her now-husband. She fought for *him*, and isn't that exactly what she's telling me to do?

"It can be the scariest thing in the world to trust another person with your heart."

"Thank you," I tell her.

Aunt Mary waits by my—Amelie's—car. She climbs into

the passenger seat, easily lifting the gun and setting it on her lap. My face heats, but she doesn't say anything. I give Shooter one last ear rub before joining my aunt and firing up the engine.

Driving away isn't as hard as I thought it would be. It doesn't feel like I'm leaving pieces of my family behind—I am, but they're safe here. It feels more like I'm heading back to where I belong.

"Your father made the right decision, you know."

I wince. "Which one? He made a lot of bad decisions, too."

She waves her hand. "Putting you in charge. Colin is too young. Too angry. Look what happened at the mall? Senseless death."

I glance at her. "Do you blame him for Kai?"

"It could've been avoided."

We go quiet after that, because it's true—it was unnecessary.

"I was flounced around like bait," I admit. "And I was too dense to even see it until it was too late."

"Your brother should've seen it," Aunt Mary says. "And he didn't. He rushed in to try and save you, regardless of the fact that it was your choice—and your father's—to give yourself up. You were brave, dear. Don't forget that."

We get on the highway and lapse into silence. I'm bone-tired. I wish I had time to actually have a conversation with my father. I wish I knew he believed in me enough to leave me everything, instead of just assuming I was the spare child. The castaway because of my gender.

"When did he change his will?" I ask her.

She adjusts herself, then fiddles with the temperature control. "Not too long ago," she says. "He did warn me about it in one of the conversations, but it was already done."

The sun is creeping up over the horizon.

I glance over again. There's more gray in her hair than the last time I saw her. Her light hair is pulled back into a braid today, almost completely silvery-gray at the temples and streaked through the twisted tail down her back.

Something occurs to me suddenly—something at odds with everything she's said today. It washes away the positive feeling, leaving only a cold ache in the center of my chest.

"When I first arrived yesterday, you said you were happy that I joined you. That I wasn't meant for this life." I bite the inside of my cheek to keep from saying more.

She sighs. "I did. I assumed your father wanted you far from danger. Naïve of me, in the face of my last conversation with him. If the war was escalating and you weren't with the DeSantises, he probably should've sent you here in the first place. Your mother would've haunted him from Heaven if she knew you were still in the city while they were targeting Wests. And you're one of the most valuable Wests."

I don't know that I believe that.

"But..." She makes a noise in the back of her throat. "If you decide to do something with your life that takes you outside of New York, I would still be proud to call you my niece."

I tighten my grip on the steering wheel. "You think I'd leave the city?"

There's still too much to do.

"Calm yourself," she chides. "I think you should not tie your fate to the family's. It isn't a be-all and end-all."

Interesting.

"It's your world, though," I point out. When has Aunt Mary—and the rest of the family—not lived like family is the most important thing?

"And your parents did everything in their power to shield you from it."

For a reason?

I chew on that.

Soon enough, we're back in Brooklyn. Traffic clogs, and it's slow going the rest of the way to the house. My mind zooms back to Aiden. He had texted the address to the number I called him from—Dalton's phone. Dalton didn't even notice it was missing. At least, he didn't say anything to me about it.

I just replaced it on the kitchen counter in the middle of the night and slunk back to bed.

Easy.

The address of Aiden's house is on the back of a receipt I found and tucked in my sock, and I keep one eye on the clock. I'll have to leave Brooklyn again, traveling as if I were going toward Hillshire County. That's where Aunt Mary's house was, and Jameson's large estate.

"I have somewhere I need to be," I tell my aunt. I make the turn onto our street. "Colin might..."

"Throw a fit?" She chuckles. "You didn't tell him you were going, hmm?"

"It's a long story," I mutter. My bitterness rankles. "Besides, do I owe him that?"

She tsks. "Common curtesy for your younger brother. Manners, Gemma. We raised you better than that."

We, like a group effort. And I guess it was. In a way.

"Just stave him off for a bit," I plead.

She relents as I stop in front of the house. "Fine, but help me with my bags."

I leave the engine running and step out, circling to the trunk. She packed enough bags to completely fill the space in the back. Xavier comes out of the house, bounding down the steps, and grabs my wrist.

"What the fuck?" he barks.

I freeze, my gaze going from his grip to his eyes.

"Get your hand off me," I manage as calmly as possible. Inside, I'm boiling. *No one* touches me. My fingers twitch.

He slowly releases me, but his gaze is just as dark as mine. "You ask us to protect you, then you vanish—"

"I asked you to protect the Wests," I interrupt. "I don't need a personal bodyguard—or worse, someone who thinks they deserve to know where I am and who I'm with."

He sneers. "I'm not a groupie, Gemma."

"You're Rob's son." Aunt Mary appraises him. "An Eldridge."

Xavier's shock has him stepping back. "You knew my father?"

"And mother," she says evenly. "Don't expect me to give you free information, though. Especially after manhandling my niece."

He scowls. "She left a mess in her wake."

"*She* has been gone for a day and a half," I retort. "Tell Colin I'll catch up with him later." I shove Aunt Mary's bags into Xavier's arms and climb back in Amelie's car.

"What's the plan?" he calls. "Still hiding?"

I roll down the window. "No. Things are changing. Tonight."

He nods, immobile in my rearview mirror as I drive away. I shiver, his gaze still following me until I've rounded the turn and disappeared from sight.

A thrill of excitement chases through me, and I sit up straighter. I grow more restless the farther out of the city I get, heading the way I'd go to Aunt Mary's old house. And then Amelie's car's GPS beeps, warning me of the upcoming exit, and I find myself in a quiet, forest-shrouded town not unlike Bitterwood.

A gate bars access. I roll to a stop beside the speaker. It has a call box with a sign that says to dial the house number, then the pound key. There's another keypad, too, without instructions.

I type in Aiden's house number, and it crackles with static. A moment later, his deep voice says, "You made good time."

I frown. "How did you know it was me?"

"Anyone else I might be expecting would know the code. Come in. Pull into the garage."

For privacy? In the most private neighborhood I've ever seen this close to Manhattan? I shrug it off and navigate through the now-open gate and locate his house. The garage door is sliding open, revealing his battered motorcycle against the far wall and my car parked perfectly on one side. There's enough space for me to navigate in, and then I climb out.

I exhale.

What am I doing?

Nerves bounce through me. I cast another glance around, surprised at how much stuff is in here. Shelves of tools and plastic bins, neatly labeled with black marker. Aiden's helmet, plus the additional one, are balanced on the seat of the bike. Unbidden, I walk forward and run my hand along the scraped paint. That was us, too. My skin is still scabbed from sliding across the asphalt, although it looks a lot better than it did.

The door into the house opens, revealing Aiden.

I step forward, then freeze. I can't just throw myself at him —*again*. His eyes are dark, and he takes me in quickly, from my borrowed leggings and shirt up to my hair piled on top of my head. In an effort to be anything other than awkward, I hook my thumb back at my car.

"Glad to see she's still in one piece."

He nods once, then gestures for me to enter.

I slip past him without touching and kick off my shoes in the little laundry-slash-mud room.

"Not planning on using those boots as weapons again?"

His voice sounds right behind me, his warm breath raising goosebumps on the back of my neck.

"Not this time," I manage.

"Knife?"

"In the car." Along with the gun.

I go through the kitchen and into the open living room. The house is beautiful, and so much more of Aiden than I expected.

"My office is upstairs," he says.

I turn back to him. His stance could trick someone else into thinking he's relaxed—legs widespread, hands in his pockets—but the tension is practically pouring off him.

"You want me upstairs?"

He inclines his chin. "Easier to keep you here."

I scoff.

He circles me without touching, and I have to fight to suppress my sudden shiver. "No knife, no phone. No boots to crush into my feet, even."

There's a grin in his voice, even if I can't see it—because I'm too busy focusing on my breathing.

"Are you privy to your father's plans?" I ask, in an effort to stop this whole thing from being derailed. It's either that or I give in to my temptation and kiss him—or worse.

I am on a mission.

Of course, this wasn't part of the strategy Aunt Mary and I talked about with Delia...

"I try not to know everything." He stops in front of me. "And before Wilder died, I just followed orders to protect my family."

From us, among others.

I shudder and back away. "How am I supposed to tell you the hardest thing I've ever had to admit?"

"Why is it hard?" His brows furrow.

"Because if you don't believe me, I don't... I don't know

what I'll do." My back hits the wall, and there I stop. "But I think it's something that you don't know—I believe *that* much."

He tilts his head. "You thought I knew this piece of information already."

I jerk my head up and down.

"Okay, Gem. Time to spit it out."

Rip off the Band-Aid.

I take a deep breath. What the hell, right? I don't know why this is worse than telling my family. Maybe because I knew they'd share my reactions: the shock and horror of it. Aiden is the wild card.

"Wilder is alive." I press my lips together as soon as the words are out, trying like hell to read his mind.

He doesn't move for a moment, like what I just said is still trying to sink in.

"That's what I discovered in Jameson's office. Proof that he's alive. And..." He'd never asked. He'd dragged me down to the DeSantis *brothel* and tried to scare some sense into me, but he'd never asked if I'd found anything.

"Gemma."

I shake my head and look away. "Please, if you don't believe me, don't say anything. I'll just walk out of here—"

"Stop." He catches my chin in his fingers, redirecting my gaze back to him. "I..."

I close my eyes for a moment.

"What's the proof?" He kisses my temple. "Don't try to hide from me. We've been through this. What proof do you have? Show me."

I grimace. "Actually, you've been holding it for me." I slip out of his grip and go back into the garage, popping the trunk of my car. He'd closed the garage door after I arrived, and it seems almost too quiet in here. Just my nervous breathing and the *click* of the trunk's lock disengaging.

Aiden follows me into the garage and steps up beside me. He's about to find my secret hiding place—but I trust him with it.

Weird, right?

Still, I glance at him carefully. He shows no indication that this is affecting him negatively... just a wrinkle between his brows as he waits for my evidence.

I shove the door up and pull out the emergency bag— filled with random tools if my car ever decided to break—and a beach towel. Some sand falls out of it. I haven't been to the beach in ages, though.

Finally, with a small pile of mismatched belongings at my feet, the trunk is empty. The bottom panel lifts, revealing the spare tire. I rotate the stiff board around. There's a slit in the scratchy fabric. And when I slip out a yellow envelope, he chuckles.

"Clever."

I can't hide my smile, but then it drops off. In my hands is the clear evidence that Aiden's brother isn't dead, like he was led to believe. Like we were *all* led to believe.

I mean, Amelie's whole life got tipped upside down because of this. Luca's. Aiden's. Mine. Kai and my father are dead because of it.

"Can I..."

I nod once. "It was in his locked drawer," I say softly, handing it over.

"Sneaky little devil." Aiden flips it open and scans the pages.

It's an email conversation between the chief medical examiner in Manhattan and Jameson. It starts with Jameson's request for Wilder's death certificate. The medical examiner replies that it's hard to forge those documents, and it would take time.

Jameson offers more money, and the man agrees—also

saying he has a John Doe body that's been scheduled for cremation that would work for Wilder's urn, in case anyone asked questions.

I wait, tense, while Aiden reads through the exchanges.

It ends with one last email from the medical examiner, and the death certificate attached. Cause of death: major traumatic injuries. Believable, I suppose.

"Why did he even need a death certificate?" I muse. "Most people won't ask. And if it's a sham, then they'd want a way for it to be reversible."

Aiden's gripping the papers so hard, they tremble like leaves in a hurricane.

I reach out and steady him, my hand on his wrist.

"Because of Amelie," he says under his breath.

His gaze sears into mine.

"Huh?"

"Before the wedding, Amelie and Wilder signed their marriage license. Her father sent it in—I don't think Dad thought he'd move as quick as he did, or maybe my father thought he'd wait until the following Monday. I don't know. Either way, the office processed their marriage, and it couldn't be dissolved until Wilder's death certificate was produced." He sets the envelope on the hood of Amelie's car and grabs my hands. "It's enough proof. I believe you."

A weight lifts off my shoulders. "Thank fuck."

He crushes me into him, his hand cradling the back of my head. I wrap my arms around his waist and hold on tightly, blinking away sudden, intrusive tears. Dear Lord, I didn't realize how much I *needed* him to believe me. And it's more than that, too—I just told him that his *brother* is alive. There's so much more to process than just a secret his father has been keeping from him.

There's the grief and months of agony to unpack, too.

His hands slide down my back and under my ass, lifting

me. I wrap my legs around his waist, and then we're face-to-face.

"Hi." He brushes a loose strand of hair from my temple, tucking it behind my ear.

My cheeks heat. "Hi."

"I'm going to take you upstairs, and we're going to forget about this shit for a few hours." He grins. "And then, when we come back to reality, we can think about what to do next."

I nod my agreement, ducking forward to kiss him. I believe *him*—and that in itself is a lightness I wasn't expecting. He didn't know about Wilder. He was following revenge blindly, and his family, too.

It's Wilder and Jameson who have to pay.

He carries me into the house, but the rumble of the garage door opening stops us. He sets me down carefully and snags my hand, placing a kiss on my knuckles.

"Stay here."

And then he leaves me alone.

CHAPTER 9
Gemma

I don't move as he returns to the garage. He doesn't seem particularly alarmed. Just annoyed at the interruption.

"Sam," he greets his cousin. "Thought you and I were meeting at the tower later."

"Well, plans change. I'm officially the errand boy for your father."

I creep forward until I can see Aiden's back and the corner of Sam's head. Seeing sometimes helps me hear—weird, but true. It's like when I'm going somewhere new in my car, or on the verge of being lost, and turning down the radio is my first instinct. I don't know why, it just helps.

"Errand boy," Aiden repeats. "How'd you get roped into that?"

Sam sighs. "Unclear at this point. Listen, we've got a problem."

Uh-oh.

"Those firearms that went missing?" He hesitates. "They just reappeared."

Aiden sighs. "Where?"

"Colin West had them."

"Bullshit," I say, striding out of the shadows.

Sam reels back. "Gemma. Why are you—?"

"It's bullshit that Colin has them. He wouldn't even have known—"

Aiden wraps his arms around my waist, stopping me from reaching his cousin. "Put your claws away, princess," he says in my ear.

I stop fighting, but my glare stays firmly in place. I should've *known* they would try to pin this on my brother. Again. Everything has been hung around his neck since Wilder's fake death.

"I suppose you'd ignore the evidence?" Sam narrows his eyes at me.

"I'd like to see some *solid* evidence. If you have circumstantial he-said-she-said bullshit, you can stuff it up your—"

Aiden's fingers tighten on my hips, and I snap my mouth shut. Again.

Sam brings up a video on his phone, thrusting the screen under my nose.

My brother's car stops at the curb in front of the Italian restaurant in Queens—the one Jameson forced us to go to, where he killed my father. Colin wouldn't have known that location, which means whoever set it up wanted to hurt us. Indirectly.

Another car is close behind Colin's. A stranger and my brother climb out, meeting at the trunk of Colin's SUV. The video blips, and then Colin opens the trunk door to reveal a crate. The stranger leans in, pulling out a firearm. It's barely visible in the video. It could be anything...

But then the stranger is nodding, and he slings the rifle's strap over his shoulder. He hands my brother a wad of cash and steps back. The video goes blank.

"That's it? Like none of you have sold a weapon for cash—"

"That was Hart," Sam informs me. "I don't think you met him."

I tense and glance back at Aiden, who was watching the video clip over my shoulder. He inclines his chin, meeting my eyes. "Yeah, easy guy to recognize."

"How the fuck did he get my brother to agree to that?"

Sam sneers. "Desperate men will do anything. He's probably trying to individually offload the firearms to avoid suspicion."

I shake my head again and wriggle free. "I don't suppose you inspected that weapon."

"Hart is on his way to meet me," Sam says. "It's the same caliber as the shipment the DeSantises were expecting in."

"Circumstantial." I wave my hand, my good mood gone. My attention trips over the papers we left out, on the hood of Amelie's car, and my stomach somersaults. But I can't go to grab it without calling Sam's attention, or piquing his curiosity.

It isn't that I don't trust him, but... I'm not sure I *can* trust him.

Aiden does, though.

"You're still wearing his ring," Sam comments. "Thought you would've thrown it in the trash first chance you got."

I cradle my left hand to my stomach, hiding the ring from his sight. "It's not any of your business, Sam, so fuck right off."

Aiden sighs and motions for his cousin to head back toward the street. "Are you taking that to my father?"

Sam hesitates, then says, "Not if you don't want me to. But we're supposed to be hunting, Aiden. Whether or not you're fucking her—"

Aiden slams his fist into his cousin's face.

I wince at the impact and snap of bone. A second later, blood gushes from Sam's nose. He covers it with his hand, pinching the bridge, and I can't tell if he wants to strike back or yell.

"Do not talk about my future wife in that way," Aiden says carefully. He snatches Sam's phone from his hand and types on it, then drops it to the floor. He digs his heel into the screen, shattering it. "Get the fuck out of here."

We watch Sam leave, and then my attention flips to Aiden's tense back.

I carefully pick my way forward, avoiding the bits of glass, and press my palm to his shoulder blade.

He's shaking. Barely perceptible.

"I don't know what's going on with our families," I say quietly. "Colin and Wilder and your dad. Even my father had a plan that I knew nothing about. But if you're *with* me, we can figure this out. From both sides."

A plan forms in my mind.

The way out of this.

He glances back at me and nods once, then moves out of reach. "I need to blow off steam. Want to come?"

I would've thought he'd strip me and fuck away his problems... but before I've even begun to nod, he snatches my hand and leads me around to the passenger seat of my car, opening it for me, then collects the evidence and slides it back into my hiding place in the trunk.

He motions for me to stay put, then disappears back into the house. He reappears a moment later with my keys, phone, and boots. He ducks into Amelie's car and grabs everything else, putting it in my backseat. Finally, he circles around and presents my knife to me, already tucked in the sheath and thigh holster's straps.

I gesture at myself. "No access."

"Put it on the outside. No one will think twice."

I nod slowly and do as he asks, then pause when he holds up the gun.

"You're packing heat now, princess?"

"More like a matchstick compared to what you carry."

He checks it, notes that it's loaded, and smirks. "It can pack a punch if you know where to aim."

I stop with my fingers on the straps and meet his gaze. He's still standing next to my open door, watching me. I want... so much. To kiss him. To question him.

Later.

"I don't suppose you're going to help me?" My voice comes out husky.

His smirk widens, but he only double-checks the safety and hands it back to me.

Once he's at the wheel, the rest of my belongings next to my feet, I raise my eyebrows. "What was that about?"

"Which part are you referring to?"

"Sam. Hart setting up my brother. The broken nose."

He lifts one shoulder and backs out onto the street, then puts his hand on my thigh. "He was disrespectful. He's lucky he didn't get a bullet instead."

I suck in a breath. "And the rest of it?"

"I asked Hart to look into where the firearms could've gone. He was working on it with Breaker."

The few days before the wedding were chaos—we learned information from Rubert, which obviously was only a little helpful. The warehouse seemed to be a dead end, and we're no closer to figuring out what happened after they dropped off the product. The contract...

"Who would want to target your family?" I ask. "I mean, is it Jameson's enemy? Someone he pissed off?"

Aiden squeezes my leg. "I don't know."

I tip my head back. "Dad had a notebook in his safe. And a handful of keys. I wish he could've just written out exactly what was going on. I need someone to explain this to me." More than Delia's warnings or Aunt Mary's advice. More than

Xavier looking over my shoulder, and the sensation of Colin waiting for me to fail.

"There are too many questions and not enough answers." He shakes his head. "Where has Wilder been hiding? Has this all been in an effort to invoke war?"

I sit up straighter, patting his hand. "Oh my god. Everything that's been framed on the Wests—what if that's being used as so-called evidence to move the war forward? Because despite their best efforts, you've sort of been dragging your heels on the hunt. No offense."

He rolls his eyes. "I was looking for something concrete, and all I got were whispers."

"Right, because Colin is innocent."

We turn onto a dirt driveway that winds up a manicured lawn lined with trees. The road passes a large white house, similar to Dalton and Grace's, and end up at a warehouse-sized dark-green building. The sign above the door, painted in pale yellow, says, *Sean's Weapon Emporium*.

I glance back at Aiden. "What exactly are we doing here? Buying guns?"

He grunts. "Sean runs a little fighting school, and he sells a variety of weapons."

"As the sign implies."

He nods and kills the engine. There are two other cars here and an old pickup truck. I follow him out, tucking my dad's gun in the waistband at the small of my back and tugging my tank top down over it. It's already hot, humid enough to make my hair stick to my face. New York summers sneak up on you. Calm and wonderful one minute, brutal the next. It's why so many people flee to Long Island, the Hamptons and wherever else, for the season.

Aiden takes my hand and leads me inside. A bell chimes over the door. This part seems to be about half the size of the building, running lengthwise. A minute later, the door to our right swings open. A short, squat man comes out. He's bald, but his beard is thick and trimmed close to his jaw. He nods when he sees us, gesturing for us to join him.

"Fight or shoot?" he asks. *Sean* is embroidered on the sleeve of his white shirt.

"Both, if you have a fighter."

Sean chuckles. "You're in luck. Phil is here. Training for UFC, so no funny business."

Aiden nods sharply.

"You need to warm up?" Sean's eyes flit to me. "You fighting, too, sweetheart?"

"Don't fucking look at her," Aiden growls, stepping in front of me.

Sean backpedals. "Sorry, sorry. Habit to be nice, you know? Customer service. It's why my guys keep me around."

I scoff.

Neither of them acknowledges it, and we walk into a huge room that features a raised platform in the center. There's training equipment around the rest of the room. Two men are working off to the side with wrapped knuckles, running through what seems to be exercises. Jab, move. Jab, jab, move.

One guy is already on the platform, punching the air.

He's... fucking massive. Bulging muscles, thick thighs and neck. His movements are staccato, and he dances like he's floating.

Shit.

"Let me guess, that's Phil?"

Sean chuckles and watches the fighter with a hungry expression. "My prized possession."

Ice trickles down my spine.

Aiden turns to me. "Sit over here." He pulls me to a bench and down. "Take this."

He hands his gun to me, then kneels beside me. His head

is even with my elbow as he unlaces his shoes. "Ask Sean about the weapons," he says in a low voice.

"He deals illegally?"

Aiden meets my gaze and grins. "Obviously, princess."

Ugh. "Okay, fine. I'll hold your gun and watch you play with the big guy."

He leans forward and kisses me fiercely, his tongue slipping into my mouth. I don't even have time to react—not even close my eyes—before he's stepping away. His shirt lands in my lap. I track him across the room, where he hops up onto the platform, says something to Phil, then grins.

Whatever he said must've been an insult, because Phil's face goes from blank to fury in a flash.

Aiden bounces up and down, swinging his arms in wide arcs. I watch his muscles move in fascination, anticipation crawling up my throat. I *want* to see his violent side. Crave it, really. I know this fight will be bloody. There's no other alternative, not when Phil looks like a bulldozer in human form.

Aiden says something else to Phil, too quiet for me to pick up, and the latter lets out a yell. He charges, swinging a massive fist at Aiden's head. Aiden jerks back, barely, and Phil's knuckles catch his jaw. His head cracks to the side, but then he's out of reach before the attack can continue.

They circle each other. Aiden spits blood on the floor, and his grin reveals pink-streaked teeth. He doesn't wait for Phil to make the first move again. He dives forward, getting inside Phil's reach, and hits him hard in the ribs. He hammers a few hits and retreats, then bobs in again and slams his fist into Phil's nose.

Bloody.

"Perfect, isn't he?"

I glance over my shoulder at Sean. I can't tell who he's talking about, so I just nod once.

"I tried to recruit him when he was a teenager. Jameson

wouldn't hear of it. The kid only came to me when his father didn't know what the fuck to do with him, anyway."

My prized possession. So easily traded away when something better walks into the room.

My stomach flips.

"Nice piece," he says, gesturing to the gun in my lap. "Can I see it?"

I release the magazine and pull the slide back, completely unloading it before I hand it over. "Made in Italy," I lie.

He makes a noncommittal noise.

"I've been looking for something similar for myself. Something smaller than what I'm packing," I venture. I keep my eyes glued on Aiden.

His attention keeps straying from Phil—and the fight—toward me, though. I will him to focus on the beast in front of him. Not sure it does much good, though. He gets a nasty hit across the face again, and I wince.

"Raise the stakes," Phil calls to Aiden. "I kick your ass, and I walk out of here with your girl."

My blood runs cold.

Aiden, however, goes completely still. He narrows his eyes at his opponent.

Behind me, Sean swears.

Aiden darts forward, unbothered by the hits Phil rains down to try to keep him away. Phil's back hits the ropes, and Aiden just keeps pummeling away at Phil's body. Head, torso. He grabs Phil's head and yanks him down, into his rising knee.

The fighter keels over, blood gushing from a split lip, his nose, a cut on his forehead. But Aiden doesn't stop. He climbs on top of him and keeps hitting, until Phil's face is no longer recognizable.

"Aiden, stop," I yell.

He doesn't seem to hear me.

I stand and climb up the platform, avoiding his pistoning

elbows. It would probably only take one hit to knock me flat on my ass. Instead, I wrap my arms around him from behind, pressing my cheek to his spine.

"It's over," I say on repeat.

It takes only a minute for Aiden to stop. His hand covers mine as we rise, then he peels it off his chest. He rotates slowly, eyes searching my face.

"It's okay," I say.

I run my fingertips down his swollen cheek.

He kisses me. It's rough and dominant, and he leans into me like I'm his only reprieve from the world. His tongue tangles with mine in my mouth, and I let out an involuntary groan. All my lust comes roaring back. Not that it was ever far —not after his show of force. He cups the back of my head, tugging my hair to angle me. I grasp at his biceps, slick with sweat, and will him closer to me.

Slow clapping brings us back to the present.

Sean has Aiden's gun in his hand, and a sick feeling crushes me. I left everything on the bench—his shirt, the magazine, the extra cartridge.

He makes a show of flicking the safety off, and he climbs up onto the platform with us. I spin around, plastering my back to Aiden's front, and we both back up. Sean inspects his fallen fighter with a passive stare, nudging the giant with his shoe.

Phil is out cold, blood pooling on the mat beneath him. He needs a doctor, in all likelihood. But he's breathing, and that's more than I can say about myself right now. My chest is tight, and I can't seem to take a breath.

"What are you doing?" Aiden asks.

Sean scoffs. "I'm taking what I should've a long fucking time ago."

CHAPTER 10

Gemma

H e pulls out his phone and snaps a picture of Phil, then Aiden and me.

I flinch.

"You're an asshole," Aiden says calmly. "If you think I'd ever fight for you—"

"Oh, you will. Or else every West and DeSantis in New York City will see that the two of you are oh-so-cozy out of town while your families tear each other apart. You think I don't hear the rumors? You think they don't *reach* me?" Sean's openly yelling now, spittle flying from his mouth. He cackles. "You're being fucked by your father, and you don't even see it. At least I'd let you finish."

Ew.

"Enough of that." Aiden's hand on my hip steadies me, and my shirt rides up in the back. His knuckles brush my skin as he takes hold of my gun. "How about you, Sean? You're selling stolen DeSantis firearms and you didn't think we'd find out about it?"

What? He failed to mention that was another motive for

us coming here—I should've known it wasn't just a desire to fight.

Sean stills. "Stolen? They weren't fucking stolen—your men brought them to me. I've been paying out for every sale! Same as *always*."

Oh, shit.

Aiden shoves me to the side and slides my gun free in the same motion. He fires once, hitting Sean in the shoulder. I hit the mat and roll through blood, falling off the edge of the platform as Sean blindly shoots. Bullets embed in the mat inches from where I was.

Mistake.

There's a scuffle, and then a high-pitched scream. A *thunk* of metal against the floor, then something much heavier.

"Gemma," Aiden calls. "It's okay."

Same words repeated back to me.

I pop my head up, eyes wide. He must've dived at Sean, easily disarming the man. Sean's injured shoulder is torqued back, his face on the floor.

"You see her?" Aiden says, driving his knee into Sean's lower back. "Answer me."

"I—yes, yes, I see her."

Aiden leans down, lifting Sean's shoulder up even farther. It pops, dislocating, and Sean screams.

Aiden drops Sean's arm and grabs the back of his neck. "She's my whole fucking world. And you just nearly killed her."

The fallen man stays silent, his chest heaving.

She's my whole world. That plays on a loop in my mind. I can't unhear it.

It's like when he told me he loved me. That same sort of feeling flickers through me. Awe. Disbelief... *happiness?*

"What do you want to do with him, princess?"

I meet Aiden's gaze and pull the knife out of its sheath. He doesn't blink when I toss it to him. "Whatever you want."

I check the rest of the room, the other fighters suddenly blazing to the forefront of my mind. But they're gone—maybe they cleared out when Aiden began to fight, or when I climbed onto the platform. Or Sean ordered them out.

Either way, the whole room is empty.

Aiden rests the tip of my blade at the back of Sean's ear.

"Did you sell one to my brother?" I ask suddenly, spinning back around.

Sean's eyes settle on me. "He came in here wanting to buy a rifle, said he had a buyer looking for a particular type. Wanted something clean. Punk kid was short on cash, told me he'd pay up after he collected. I'm still waiting for that money."

"Aiden," I say.

Fuck.

How does Colin even know about this guy? A clean weapon—something without history. Easy, if it's coming from Italy, or wherever the hell the firearms originated.

Another setup—this time by Aiden's crew. Albeit unwittingly.

Aiden slices off Sean's ear in one clean jerk. The flesh hits the mat next to Sean's face, and a second later, he screams. Aiden rises and slips under the ropes, hopping down next to me. He touches my face, concern etched in his features.

"You okay?"

I laugh. "I should ask you that."

He wipes my knife off on his pants and stows it back at my thigh, then smacks my ass. "We should get out of here."

He picks up his shirt, then takes my hand and threads his fingers with mine. He wastes no time in guiding me to the entrance.

We pass a door marked *Office* on the way, and I pull back. I open the door and hurry to the desk, which is chaotic—to say the least. Aiden shows me an old shoebox filled with hand-written receipts. I yank open the drawers in the desk, rifling through utility bills, fighting contracts, until Aiden says, "Here."

He hands me a yellow carbon-copy paper with Colin's name scrawled at the top, and the type of gun he took. "The same type from the video, I'd guess."

"See!" I resist the urge to cheer. "I told you he was innocent."

"He's not *innocent*, princess." Aiden shoots me a look. "But in this crime, he's not guilty."

I shrug. "I'll take that."

Aiden stops me at the door, drawing his gun and peering around the corner. I almost expect gunfire to open up on us, but it's quiet. He leads me out, practically placing me in the passenger seat and buckling me in.

It's reminiscent of the first night, when he took me from Aunt Mary's. Leading me to the car. He was a bit rougher then. Less trusting—of me, anyway. He's still on edge, his gaze never pausing. Is he going to go back inside and set the place on fire?

But he doesn't. He just takes a moment to put his shirt back on, wincing at the bruises already forming all over his body. He really let the other fighter get some good hits in.

"Is pain part of the rush?" I ask quietly, once we're enclosed in the car and barreling back down the driveway.

"Sometimes."

"Now?"

"Now, I wish I had an ice bath."

I grimace.

My phone rings, startling a yelp out of me. Aiden glances over in concern, brow raised, but I shake it off. It's my aunt.

"Hello?"

"Gemma, where are you?"

"On my way back." I glance at Aiden. He might be able to hear her, even though the phone isn't on speaker. Her voice has always had a booming quality.

He puts his hand on my thigh in response, and my abdomen tightens.

"What's wrong?" I ask her.

"Colin has called a family meeting," she says on a sigh. "And I fear if you're not there for it, he's going to try something."

"Try something, like...?"

"Take over," she responds flatly. "You know you have duties now. You cannot run away without telling anyone. As leader—"

Aiden's grip tightens on my leg, and the car picks up speed.

Shit. I never told him that Colin wasn't in charge, and I'm pretty sure Aunt Mary just inadvertently outed me.

"What time?" I interrupt.

"Eight at the bar."

"I'll be there. But I've got to go." I hang up on her and ignore the tension in the car. We make it back to his house in record time, coasting into the garage.

The door rattles down behind us.

"I have to be back by eight," I mumble.

He nods sharply, then exits the car. "I heard." He circles around and opens my door, taking my hands and assisting me out. He spins me in one smooth motion, lifting me and setting me on the counter next to his tools.

I shiver.

"Tell me I heard her wrong." He traces the strap of my tank top to the center of my chest, then flattens his palm. "Leader."

"You didn't." I grab his wrist. "My father left everything to me."

He flinches. "And you didn't tell me."

I grip him so hard, I imagine his bones are grinding together. "How could I? Up until today, I thought you knew your brother was alive. And it's safer if people think Colin is in charge. They—"

"No one takes your overeager little brother seriously," he snaps. "Least of all my father. Do you know how much danger you're in? Just staying in the city—"

"Shut up." I lift my shirt over my head, tossing it to the floor.

His mouth opens and closes, but he doesn't stop me from yanking his shirt up, too. Dried flecks of blood create patterns on his skin. I skate my palms up his chest, curling my fingers around his neck.

"You can be pissed that I kept this a secret, or you can take your pants off and fuck me," I say.

His eyes widen, but he nods and unbuttons his jeans. I undo the thigh holster, setting the knife aside, and he drags my leggings down. I lift myself, helping him slide it past my ass. My skin touches the rough wood surface. He shakes his head once and picks me up, carrying me over to the hood of Amelie's car.

Our lips crash together, and I part my legs to let him closer. The head of his cock slides through my folds, and he grins. "You been soaked for a while, princess?"

I nip his lower lip. "I want to feel you. Right now."

"How about my tongue?"

His lips trail across my skin, kissing a path straight down my chest. He latches on to one of my nipples, and I tense. Pleasure and fire war as his teeth graze me. He moves his hips, and his cock rubs my clit. I whimper.

He keeps up that motion, torturing me, until I might

burst. I run my hands up his sides, only pausing when he hisses out a breath. His injuries. Well, fuck that—he brought that fight on himself. I keep going, digging my nails into his back.

Payback.

He makes a noise in the back of his throat. "Hold on tight."

I don't have a chance. He slams into me, and my whole body slides up the car. He keeps a death grip on my hips, pulling me down into his thrusts. I arch my back. His lips return to my neck, biting and sucking. My hand slips between us and presses on my clit, rubbing quick circles.

We're both panting when my orgasm crashes over me. He stills, rotating his hips, and catches my lips again. He swallows my noises. I love this part—when my soul returns to my body and it's a moment of vulnerability between us.

The aftershocks of my climax are barely over, and he begins thrusting in earnest. I deepen our kiss, biting his lip, taking ownership of his mouth. My arms wind around his neck, keeping his chest flush against mine. The hood of the car is enough of an incline to work in our favor.

I taste blood on our lips.

Another orgasm—this one even stronger, and out of nowhere. I clench around him, and he groans my name against my lips. Two hard thrusts later, he stills inside me.

He pulls out and lowers himself.

"What...?" I reach for him, but then his hot mouth is on my clit, and two fingers slide inside me.

My muscles are jelly, but my cunt doesn't get the message. He eats me out, his fingers curling, first two and then three. Stretched and practically delirious.

"Aiden, I can't—"

"One more," he says, kissing my thigh. His teeth are on my sensitive bud, and he sucks hard.

It's the pain that does it. Like being spanked after disobeying him. I wriggle, my cheeks suddenly on fire. How do I tell him... *that* is what I'm fantasizing about right now?

He glances up and meets my gaze, going still. "Tell me."

"I..." My blush must be fierce. My whole face an attractive shade of tomato-red. "I lied to you."

He narrows his eyes.

I close mine. "I should be punished for that."

"Oh, princess." His hands on my wrists haul me upright, although I'm not sure I'm fully capable of walking. Two orgasms down, and one... maybe one on the way.

He's hard again.

I swallow.

"You're remembering the night of that inane poker game," he says quietly. "Of what transpired after."

I can't speak, my mouth is so dry. But I nod.

He nods, too, with fire in his eyes. "You did do wrong."

My body trembles, and I follow him inside. To the couch.

"Wait here."

I stand, unsure, as he disappears upstairs. He returns a moment later, hands empty, and offers me the ghost of a smile.

He sits and gestures for me to come closer.

I'm asking for this. *Why am I asking for this?*

But I'm suddenly afraid that I've made a terrible mistake —that I've awoken a predator and turned myself into unwitting prey. Still, I follow through. I stride within reach of him, and he wastes no time pulling me down over his legs.

The first strike isn't a strike at all. He runs his palm over my ass, so light it almost tickles. "Hands."

I twist my arms back behind me, and he binds my wrists with something soft. I can't see it. My hair is loose from its tie and now falls around my face like a curtain. He shifts so my torso is half on the couch beside him, but my head still hangs down. He pins my legs with one of his. Ass in the air. *Vulnerable*. Shaking with anticipation.

"Your first mistake, Gemma?"

I wait, holding my breath.

"You didn't trust me."

The smack wakes me up. He rubs soft circles on my skin again, and the second one is even sharper. It goes straight to my core, and I'm instantly wetter.

Something hard slides between my legs, touching my clit. I jerk, unsure, until his hand presses down on the small of my back.

"Trust me," he repeats.

I still.

He moves it around, then brings it up to my ass. Something cool and wet hits my skin, and then—*oh god*. He presses the object against my asshole, carefully sliding it in. I'm openly shaking now.

"You look so fucking perfect," he says. "Asshole plugged. Your skin red."

He slaps my ass again, and this time I almost choke from the new sensation. I'm going to *combust*, and I can't find it in myself to tell him to stop.

"More," I beg. "More, Aiden, please."

I've given in to insanity.

"Tell me you trust me."

Slap.

I groan, turning to bury my face in the couch.

"Gemma. Tell me you won't lie to me anymore."

Slap.

I'm going to fucking come from this. I jolt when he switches to the other cheek, his palm stinging against my skin. I cry out, the sound muted.

That unhinges him. He loses it, spanking my ass until I

yell, my core pulsing, that I do trust him, I won't lie. Tears drip down my face.

He adjusts me so my full weight is on the couch, my knees holding up my lower half. My hands are still bound, and I tug at them restlessly. He lines up behind me and thrusts into me, and that in combination with the plug sends me over the edge.

I'm a goner.

I scream his name, my climax spiraling through me, as he slams inside me. He hits a deep spot, and that orgasm just keeps rolling—until he pulls out abruptly. He groans, and his hot seed spills across my ass and lower back.

"Fuck," he whispers. He removes the plug, then the restraint, and lifts me.

My limbs aren't working.

He falls onto the couch, curling me on his lap, and maneuvers my head to fit under his chin. I stare at the object that was just in my *asshole* and frown.

"Where did you get that?"

He snorts and shifts, lying back and taking me with him. I'm completely on top of him now, but he seems unbothered.

"I bought it with you in mind."

I grunt.

"It's true. I knew I wanted to fuck your ass, and a plug is good preparation. Start small..."

"That's... honorable, I guess." I can barely keep my eyes open. "Kinda gross, though."

His laugh vibrates through me. "I love you so much. It's not gross—it's one of the sexiest things I've ever seen. But rest now, Gem. I'll make sure you're back in the city on time."

Can't argue with that logic.

But my mind has regrouped, now focusing back on Colin's family meeting. Worry tenses my muscles. I can't just sit here and pretend to sleep while my brother plots to take over. Hell, the city thinks he's already in charge. How much of a jump would it be to convince the Wests that he should be?

Aiden traces a pattern on my spine.

I don't know what he would suggest I do. Maybe kill Colin to make a point. Wouldn't that be ironic?

"I can't rest," I finally mutter, pushing upright.

He wraps his arms around me, rolling us in place so I'm tucked almost entirely under his body. Like how we used to sleep at his Manhattan apartment in the DeSantis tower. And weirdly enough, my body relaxes.

CHAPTER 11
Aiden

M y ribs are on fire. Sleep has tensed my muscles, and now everything aches. My face, too. Sean's fighter got some decent hits in—lucky shots that I didn't care to block.

Well, I regret it now.

I shift away from Gemma, doing my best not to wake her, and clean up the aftermath of what transpired. She's still naked, splayed on her back, my cum seeping out of her. She doesn't stir when I return with a washcloth and clean away the lube, gently swiping the fabric against her pussy.

My dick hardens.

She flops her arm over her eyes and shifts. "What are you doing?"

"Considering tasting you again," I admit. I set aside the cloth and straighten. "I told you I would get three from you."

Her pretty cheeks turn a delicious shade of pink, and she sucks her lower lip between her teeth. Yes, she remembers.

She sits up, hair falling around her shoulders, and reaches for my leg.

"Gemma," I warn.

She scoots to the edge of the couch, and her gaze goes to my cock. It bobs only an inch from her face.

"Three to... two?" She tips her head back and parts her lips. "You need to catch up."

I shake my head once. "This isn't a competition—"

But her mouth is on me, licking from the base of my shaft up. I hiss out a breath, automatically fisting my hand in her hair. She swirls her tongue around the head, and little zaps of pleasure shoot through me.

Gemma stops, balancing the head of my cock on her tongue. Mouth open, eyes on mine.

An invitation.

One that's hard to resist.

I guide her head toward me and jerk my hips forward, filling her hot hole. My dick hits the back of her throat, and she gags around me. It just turns me on more. Her nails dig into my thighs, barely keeping her balance, as I fuck her mouth. And then I slow.

"Hold it," I order. I spread my legs a bit, matching her height better.

Her fingers come up and cup my balls, and I groan. She stays perfectly still—a little soldier following orders.

"Now suck."

She does. Her cheeks hollow with her effort. I stay as still as I can for as long as possible, but she has skill. And soon my hips are moving of their own accord, and my balls tighten.

I pull out of her abruptly and rub the head of my cock along her lips.

"Mouth open. Tongue out." I can barely get the words out. My cum spurts out in long ropes, covering her mouth, lips, cheeks. It gets in her hair, even.

Only then does she relax her grip on my legs.

And I watch in disbelief as she collects my cum with her fingers and licks them clean. Then she rises and kisses my jaw.

She saunters away, completely naked.

Blow jobs... they seem to make her feel powerful. And all I can do is stare at the red marks on her ass from earlier.

"I fucking love you," I call after her.

Her laugh drifts back.

We shower, and she finds her leggings on the floor—then raids my closet for a t-shirt. I smirk when she picks one of the white collared ones. She ties the tails together, and it actually looks like she meant to pick an oversized shirt for... I don't know. Fashion or something.

"You're beautiful," I tell her.

She brushes out her hair with her fingers and shakes her head. "You're complimentary today."

I shrug and glance around. This space is *mine*. It feels more like home than anywhere else, and having her in my space is a heady feeling. I could keep her here.

"This seems like more your style," she comments, running her hand over the top of my dresser. It's pine, the wood almost the color of sand, and the rest of my room is similar tones. Light and airy—the opposite of the tower apartment.

I grin and press a button, and the shades along the back wall rise. I had floor-to-ceiling windows installed to have a view of the forest behind the house. And judging from Gemma's quick smile, she enjoys it as much as I do.

She flops on the bed and sprawls out, her damp hair going everywhere. "I like it here."

"Good," I murmur.

Then she exhales. "I need to get back."

I nod and crawl up next to her. "Right. Because you're the leader of the Wests now."

"Right." She winces. "I... don't tell your dad."

"I wouldn't. He's been keeping his own secrets."

Her palm lands on my cheek. "Are you okay?"

I pause. When's the last time anyone's asked me that?

Besides maybe my mother before she disappeared, but I was young. Eight or nine. Is it bad that I can't remember the exact age I was when she left? The years surrounding that *before* and *after* have blurred together.

"Aiden?"

I shake off the ghosts of my past and lean into her hand. "I'm fine."

She rises. I'm tempted to pull her back down on top of me. Her touch is a drug that I'm hopelessly addicted to. I don't want her to leave. But... we both have duties.

"This has been a nice reprieve," she says in the garage. She glances at Amelie's car and blushes again. Her handprints are visible on the paint. "Thank you."

She grabs the papers—her evidence—and tucks them back in her hiding place. Then she circles around and stops just in front of me.

"I'll see you soon." I slide my hand around to the back of her neck and draw her in, kissing the corner of her lips. It isn't enough, but if I start, I won't be able to stop.

She nods and takes her keys from my hand. She slips into the driver's seat of her car, taking a moment to fiddle with the mirrors and seat. I hit the button on the garage door, and it slowly grinds upward. And then the engine revs to life, and she backs out with a slight frown.

Almost as soon as she's gone, I go straight to my office. It's exactly as she said—a reprieve. And now, I've snapped back to the reality of what she told me.

Do I tell Luca?

Do I... fuck, what am I supposed to do?

My phone buzzes in my pocket, and I answer it with a curt, "Go."

"My, my," Dad responds. "Where has my heir been hiding?"

I resist the urge to chuck my phone against the wall. *Heir* I am not. Wilder is, wherever the fuck he's holed up. And that leads to more questions: why would he and my father plan this? Why not loop me and Luca in?

Still, I manage to bite my tongue.

"You're needed," he says shortly. "I expect you at the penthouse in an hour."

"Got it."

He hangs up, and I drop the phone on my desk.

Fuck.

Here comes a test of my poker face. Because if he finds out I know? He may as well put a bullet in my skull. Or Gemma's, just to secure his information. Loose knowledge is worse than poison in the air.

I smirk again at the handprints on Amelie's hood on my way back out. I'll deliver her car back to her, now that Gemma's regained hers. Hart has been driving mine for the past week and a half, since he came to town. Once I have a spare moment to have my bike looked at, I'll be back on it. But maybe not with Gemma. The thought of us being targeted again churns my gut. I won't be the reason she's injured.

Driving into the city, I take a few shortcuts to avoid traffic. It still takes most of the hour, though, and my phone buzzes right when I pull into the parking garage.

Where are you? He's on a tear.

Luca—referring to our father, presumably.

I stifle my sigh and head to the elevators, swiping my access card. It blinks red for a moment, then green.

Weird.

Still, the doors close, and it shoots upward without delay, depositing me on the offices level. Luca waits for me in the hallway.

"What's wrong?"

He scowls. "I'm supposed to check you for weapons."

I stare at him. "Dad wanted *you* to check *me* for weapons. To go see him?"

A stiff nod.

Someone comes out of my office—a man in all black. I crane my neck to see better, but Luca blocks me.

"Not sure what's going on with you, man, but shit's serious." He rubs his eyes. "Are you carrying?"

"Of course."

"Where?"

I grit my teeth. "Waistband. Ankle."

"Keep the ankle piece and give me your main." He holds out his hand, and I sense he's trying to plead with me to be reasonable about this.

I hand it over without comment, then follow him to the elevators in the back. If anyone saw our exchange, they sure as hell don't say anything. And as we pass my office, the door is once more firmly shut, lights off. Almost like I could've imagined that someone was inside moments ago.

We ride up in silence.

There are cameras almost everywhere, and paranoia has gotten the better of me.

Our father has two men stationed at the entrance of his penthouse. The doors, which usually have to wait for his okay to open, part almost as soon as the lift grinds to a stop. I glance at the two men impassively.

Unfortunately, I recognize both.

They're low on the chain of command, but ones who have been more than eager to prove themselves. The two have been responsible for rallying more attacks on the Wests than I can count. And I didn't think anything of it... but of course it was probably a direct order from Jameson DeSantis himself.

A man I don't really want to think of as my father right now.

He's been manipulating everyone for *months*.

"Is this necessary?" Luca snaps.

One of the guys sneers at me and gestures for us to walk ahead of him. Luca scowls, then leads the way. I follow, and the two guys walk close behind me. I can't help but feel like I'm going to my execution.

"Aiden."

I stiffen. "Father," is my dry reply.

Dad once more lounges on one of his white couches. There's no drink in his hand today, just a silver gun.

Sam stands off to the side, by the window.

"Sit." My father points to the seat across from him with the weapon, his face blank.

I comply. What else can I do?

"I received an interesting video today. And the fact that your cousin informed me that *you* knew about it... it doesn't shock me. You've always been calculating. But don't confuse my hands-off approach to your *investigation* as disinterest. I'm very much invested in who stole from us." He grabs the television remote from the cushion beside him and clicks a button.

The screen on the wall above the fireplace, to his right and my left, comes to life. And the video that Sam showed Gemma and me only a few hours ago plays on the screen. Colin's car pulling up outside that restaurant. Meeting Hart—who my father probably doesn't know, and who I *hope* Sam has left out of this fucking narrative—and exchanging the weapon for cash.

When Colin climbs back in his car and drives away, that's when my father's temper finally snaps. He lets out a roar and jumps to his feet, then flips the coffee table. It crashes on its side, barely missing my feet. But that's not enough. He chucks the remote at the television. The screen cracks, glass falling to the floor.

No one moves.

Hell, no one fucking breathes.

"You," Dad screams, pointing at me. "You have one more chance."

I lift my chin.

"Bring me Colin West's head, or I'll make sure Gemma is the one who suffers for your inadequacy." He sneers. "Is that enough incentive for you, son of mine?"

Fury flashes through me, and I grit my teeth. I will not say what I want—I will not *do* what I want. No one threatens her.

But he has—twice now.

"Luca," Dad barks. "Get your brother out of here."

I step forward. Luca and I have gone toe-to-toe before, and I'm usually the one to come out on top. Fuck this, anyway. Luca grabs my arm, and I wrench it away.

"You do not threaten—"

But then my father tips his head back, over his shoulder, and I finally see why Sam has stuck close to the window. He's disappeared into another room, but now he appears with Amelie. His gun is leveled at her head.

Luca's arm wraps around my neck, yanking me backward. I stop struggling and let him drag me all the way into the elevator. There, he releases me and shoves me into it.

I spin around, eyes wild. "You let him—"

He tosses my seized gun at me in pieces and shakes his head. He leans into the elevator, his voice angry and low. "You think anyone *lets* him do anything? He took her and won't let me near her. Again. I brought her back to New York for you— all of this is on *your* head." He was blocking the doors, but now he hits the button for the offices and steps back.

The doors slide closed, and the last thing I see is his disappointment.

CHAPTER 12

Gemma

The meeting was... inefficient.

Everyone was pleased to see Aunt Mary and me at West Bar—well, except Colin. He seemed surprised that I would show my face. Or maybe he thought I wouldn't know about it. That I didn't care enough to make it back on time.

Until I revealed that I had disappeared to check on the women, whose location only the leader of the family knew before he died. Then his attitude shifted.

"You got into the safe?" he asks me now, following me upstairs.

I spotted Xavier lingering outside the bar halfway through the meeting, and he tags along behind my brother.

"You better explain what the fuck that was," I say calmly to Colin. I take a seat behind the desk. "You want to lead? You're sure doing a shitty job of it."

He scoffs, pacing for a moment behind the two chairs meant for visitors. "What was I supposed to do? You *left*—"

"I was gone for less than twenty-four hours. Did you even call my cell?"

"Yeah, and Amelie fucking DeSantis answered." His face turns an angry shade of red.

The complexion runs in the family.

Now he sits, eyeing me like I've completely betrayed them. And maybe I have. I don't know anymore. Is loving Aiden a crime? I thought he was the enemy, but... he's not. He's on my side. He's probably the only one on my side.

I drop my phone on the desk, removing the firearm, too. When I got home, I was able to take another shower—because I refused to show up smelling like Aiden's soap—and change into my own clothes. My dress gives me access to the knife at my thigh. I've resolved to never go anywhere without it, simply because this is how I need to operate.

Like everyone wants me dead.

"He's got a price on his head," Xavier says from the shadows.

Colin jumps, swearing, and spins in his seat. "Where the fuck did you come from?"

"Maybe you should pay more attention, baby West."

I lean my elbows on the desk, steepling my fingers. It's the first I've heard of someone putting a hit out on Colin, but it makes sense. The DeSantises are behind this. Jameson. Sam. It's not Aiden, though. That much I can say for certain.

I chuckle at Colin's obliviousness. "You have a bounty on your head because you were a complete fucking moron."

He glares at me. "What the fuck are you going on about?"

"How'd that little rifle sale go?"

It's actually intriguing to watch the color drain from my brother's face. His bravado fails him, and for a moment all he can do is open and close his mouth. He seems... young. Like the seventeen-year-old boy he is, not the man he's been pretending to be.

I remind myself that he just lost his two role models in life a few weeks ago. Things have been moving too quickly for me to focus on it—on Kai and my father truly being *gone*—but he's probably had nothing but time to stew in it. Especially since I put the whole family on lockdown a week ago.

"I..."

"You were caught on camera," I interrupt. I meet Xavier's eyes. He regards me coolly, so I switch my attention back to my brother. "And the weapon you sold was from that stolen shipment. The DeSantis container."

"I got it from—"

"Sean's fucking weapon emporium," I finish. "I know."

Xavier tilts his head. "Interesting."

"What?" I snap at him.

He shrugs. "I thought I'd be bringing valuable intel to you, but it seems you already know quite a bit."

I force myself to lean back. Men can be like sharks, in a way. They scent fear like blood in the water. It brings out their worst attributes.

"I can't put all my eggs in one basket." I smile at him. "But you can tell me what you know of the bounty."

He sighs and gets comfortable against the wall. I think he likes keeping my brother on his toes, because he's in Colin's blind spot. And Colin knows the tactic, judging from the way his shoulders keep inching up closer to his ears. But he stays put, even when he could easily fix the issue and shift his chair to the side.

"It was put out by Aiden DeSantis," Xavier says. "They want you dead or alive, although the pay is higher if you're still breathing when you enter the DeSantis tower in Manhattan." He's speaking directly to Colin now. "The hit was put out to all the local small-time gangs, plus every fucking DeSantis in the city."

"Shit," I mumble. "Okay, great. Well, at least they want you alive, right?"

Xavier scoffs. "Sure, they want him alive so they can

torture him. If that's what you call *great*..."

It's not, but I refuse to backtrack.

"Okay, so, Colin. You're officially under house arrest." I meet his gaze, willing him to understand how fucking serious I am. "Xavier's men will take you to the Manhattan safe house and keep you..."

"Safe," my brother finishes. "They'll keep me safe. That's what you were going to say, Gem?"

"If you had just—" I press my lips together. I cannot play that game with him. The *what-if* game, or the *if only*. They're both dangerous and unhelpful. We can't rewind time and create a do-over. Life doesn't work like that.

I shake my head. "Aunt Mary is staying at the Manhattan house, too. I think it'll do you some good to have adult supervision."

Colin opens his mouth, but I raise my hand.

"Both of you can leave. X, take Colin to the Manhattan house and have someone stay there with him. Armed." I point at my brother. "Promise me you won't do anything dumb."

He frowns and shakes his head. "I won't."

"Good."

He rises and leads the way out the door. Xavier watches me for a moment, eyes narrowed.

I lift my brow. "What?"

"You seem..."

I shake my head and gesture to the door. A bounty. Placed by *Aiden*. I don't believe that for a second, even if Jameson wants us to think it's him. The future heir. Yeah fucking right. I'm still trying to figure out how he's going to flounce Wilder back into the city. Like, *surprise, he's not dead!*

"I'll be back to escort you home," he says.

I sigh. I don't need him to walk me home. Turner or Marius are probably downstairs, or one of the other guys. But he's gone before I can even tell him no.

Fucking hell.

I open the drawer with the safe and type in the passcode. I replace my father's gun inside and eye the notebook. I'm not remotely tired—the opposite, in fact—but the thought of settling down to read Dad's last words sits wrong. Instead, I pick up the ring of keys and flip through them.

There has to be a method to his madness.

I grab my bag and stuff the keys inside. I can test out some theories tomorrow, maybe. And find out more about this bounty. I shoot a text to Turner, telling him to heighten security around West Bar and our territories. He sends back a thumbs-up.

Leaning back in the chair, I close my eyes and try to visualize what's happening to this city. Jameson wants a war, obviously. But why the charade? What stopped him from just saying, "Hey, Lawrence, I want you gone?"

That's what he did to the Eldridges, wasn't it? It happened a while ago, but it seemed like one day, the three families coexisted peacefully. The next, the DeSantises were taking out the Eldridges by any means necessary.

Why?

Maybe that why will shed some light on his motive for this one.

His family would've listened to him if he stoked it right. If he encouraged them to expand, to be as greedy as him. To want more territory, more money.

"You're not supposed to nap on the job," Xavier says.

I crack my eyes open and smother my groan. "You're supposed to be halfway to Manhattan."

He shrugs. "I pawned your brother off on two of my guys. They know the drill." He sinks into the seat Colin occupied, seeming far more relaxed, and kicks his feet up on the edge of the desk. His blue eyes bore into mine. He'd be handsome if my mind wasn't completely consumed by Aiden. A nice jawline, tall, muscles. Those killer eyes.

I tap my chin. "We should find you a girlfriend."

"No."

I smile. "Afraid of girls?"

"I don't have time for those commitments." His brow lowers.

"Hey, for the right price..."

He snorts. "No. Sorry, not a sellout. I wouldn't ask anyone to be in my life when it's this dangerous. I have a higher risk of being killed than most other people in New York."

Eh, he's not completely wrong. This line of work is hazardous at best. Do it long enough, and you either end up in the hospital or the morgue. So, I put it on the backburner. Guy looks like he needs someone to go home to—instead of lingering at the bar and pestering *me*. But...

"Can I ask you a question?"

He smirks. "You just did."

I roll my eyes and wait.

"Fine, Gemma, ask me your question."

"Your family... why did Jameson want to take you out? What instigated it?"

His gaze immediately hardens. I should know by now that any DeSantis name brings up bad memories for him. I can't imagine how traumatizing it was to see his whole family wiped out.

Well, actually... scratch that, I can picture it.

I wait again. He holds on to silence, uses it like a weapon. A survival tactic, I'm sure.

"I think my father had bought into the tech industry," he eventually says. "And tech, as you probably know, can either be a gold mine or flop. The company he founded was the former. Too successful. He was selling outside of New York—mostly to Silicon Valley, I think—but if he put his focus on his own backyard, he'd have been able to conquer it. A billion dollar company, owned by one man." He sighs and rubs his shoulder. "Jameson doesn't like competition."

"No shit."

"Well, that's a big fucking threat. Especially since there were rumors floating around that Wilder was going to be running for office when he was of age. If my father cared enough, he could've thrown money—millions, hundreds of millions—at Wilder's opponent. So we had to be eliminated."

"And the company?"

"Broken into pieces."

I narrow my eyes. His father was involved in the scheming, sticky underworld as much as Jameson and my father. He wouldn't have built this company—which sounds clean, as far-fetched as that seems—and not had a backup plan if he died.

"Six pieces," I guess.

His eyes widen, and then the mask returns.

"Smart." I tap the arms of the chair. "I mean, it throws suspicion off of you. Especially if it looks like the company was dissolved with his death..."

"It's operating out of Virginia under new management," he says.

I nod. "Okay, so if we apply that DeSantis logic of destruction to my family..."

He shrugs. "Your father had made a deal with Rubert about weapons, hadn't he?"

A rumor. A lie.

But what if it wasn't?

"Anything that encroaches on Jameson's territory is

dangerous," he adds. "But it doesn't matter, because after my parents were killed and the rest of us scattered, your father and Jameson brokered a truce."

"Oh, shit." I leap from my chair and rush to the filing cabinet. The bottom drawer is locked—of course—and it takes me a second to realize I have a set of keys in my purse. Xavier watches me with mild alarm as I go back and forth, then flip through keys that might fit. My hands are trembling.

A stupid truce... Dad wouldn't have left it on the DeSantis word alone. No, he would've written it down. Signed it.

Finally, I get the bottom drawer open. There are deeds to the various properties we own, titles of the cars, and then—*yes*.

"Aha!" I yell, lifting the binder. It's titled *Rules of Engagement*.

I bring it back to the desk, standing beside Xavier this time, and flip through it. Sure enough, Dad and Jameson outlined their truce. That until such a time that the agreement would no longer be in effect, both parties would respect persons protected by, and businesses, operations, and properties owned by the other.

"Why get it in writing if they were just going to ignore it?"

"Wilder is alive," I tell him. "I know you heard me that first night, and you haven't mentioned much about it since then. He's somewhere, hiding, because *that*..." I shake my head. "I don't know, I'll have to read through this to see what Jameson saw. There must be some consequence for violating it, right?"

He grunts. "Maybe that's why he wants Colin. We've been spreading the rumor that he's leading the family—naturally, he would bear the consequence."

I flip through faster, trying to find words to jump out at me.

And then, miraculously, I find it.

Fuck me sideways.

The *harm* clause. The *encroachment* clause. The unequivocal proof that the truce has been violated. And the consequence: the family who breaks the truce agrees to give up all rights to the five boroughs of New York City and will vacate it immediately.

"That's why they want him," I whisper. "To get a confession out of him."

Xavier stares down at the page. "It wasn't about war, at all."

"Just about winning the city."

I flip the binder closed and tuck it into my purse, along with the set of keys. "I'm going home. You're welcome to stalk me, if that will make you feel any better."

He grunts but doesn't object when I turn off the desk lamp and head to the door. Everything's locked up tight, and I hold the binder close to my chest. I should act normal when I get downstairs, but I can't seem to loosen my grip on it.

There are only a few Wests, the rest patrons without affiliation to the family. One old-timer, a regular before we shut down, reaches out and catches my arm. I sense more than see the alertness of the Eldridge behind me.

"Glad to see you've got things up and running, girlie," the man says. "This neighborhood wasn't the same without it."

I force a smile and pat him on the shoulder. "We're glad to be open again. Enjoy your whiskey."

He releases me, and I hurry outside.

"Walking?"

I glance back at Xavier. "My car's around the corner."

"There's a parking spot in the back with your name on it."

"I let the bartender take it tonight," I say offhandedly. That's a lie—Colin was parked in the spot when I arrived, forcing me to find street parking. Another move to try and one-up me, maybe? Either way, it's done and dealt with now.

He shadows me down the street, then surprises me by climbing into the passenger seat.

I raise my eyebrows but refrain from kicking him out. I don't know why. Something in me thinks he's not the bad guy in my story.

Hopefully.

We ride the short distance in silence, and he motions for me to stay put in the car while he scopes out the perimeter, and then inside the house. Finally, he flicks on the porch light and meets me at the fence.

"You're clear," he says. "You gonna be okay?"

I smile. "Don't worry. I have an alarm system."

He grimaces. "They're unreliable."

"Even so."

His phone chimes, and he nods to himself. "Turner offered to keep watch of the place tonight once the bar shuts down."

Lovely.

"It means they care, Gemma," he says quietly. He breaks the barrier between us first, reaching out and squeezing my shoulder. His hand is hot through the thin fabric of my shirt. "You asked me for help. For numbers. For security. I'm just trying to take my job seriously. Especially if Jameson is gunning for the leader of the Wests... he'll quickly learn that Colin isn't it. Rumors or not."

I sigh. "Yeah, fine. And thank you for your insight." I hesitate, then pat his arm. He drops it away from my shoulder. "Night."

He nods and steps aside. I lock myself in the house and lean against the door. I'm grateful to just be alone. To live in the silence for a moment. To breathe.

When is the last time I've been alone? Truly.

Aiden's tower apartment.

Right, and I nearly went out of my mind in those four days.

I fill a glass with ice water and go straight upstairs, stripping out of my clothes. I could fall right into bed—and I almost do. Until someone steps out of the shadows in my peripheral vision.

CHAPTER 13
Gemma

"**D**amn you," I whisper. My heart races.

Xavier cleared the house—but I should know by now, however good Xavier is, Aiden is better.

Aiden glowers at me, stalking forward. I automatically step back, unsure. He herds me until my back bumps the door, and even then he crowds me. My heartbeat is galloping out of control, and a thrill races through me.

Earlier, I got a variety of Aidens.

I didn't get the ruthless hitman, though. That version is in front of me right now, with fury in his eyes.

"Who. Touched. You."

Not a question—not remotely. I open and close my mouth, then decide on, "No one."

He laughs. His chest touches mine, and his hands slam into the wall on either side of my head. "What's stopping me from going out to that car he's staked out in and slitting his throat? He *touched* you and you let him."

I finally shove at him. "Back off."

"No."

I tip my head back. "I'm not fucking telling you anything. Not just because I need him alive—but because you're being senselessly cruel right now. To someone who, what, put his hand on my shoulder?"

He growls.

I shift to the side, but he pushes his hips forward. They pin me even further, and now I'm caught. I slide my hands up the front of his chest and around the back of his neck.

"Your father put out a hit on Colin?"

He nods once.

"Well, he's using your name to do it," I mutter. "And if they see you here, they'll shoot on sight."

"Princess, your little guard walked right past me when he was scouting the house. Tell him next time that intruders hide in *unlikely* places." He leans down and kisses the corner of my lips, then my jaw. I tip my head to give him better access to my throat.

Neck kisses might be my favorite thing.

His teeth pierce my skin, and I jump. That's going to leave a mark—it's harder than usual, and higher up. I've been lucky that any marks he's made on my neck have been low and coverable with either creative fashion or makeup. But this one smarts even after his tongue sweeps over it.

"Don't," I warn. I'm going to have a fucking bite mark to explain tomorrow.

He bites again, lower, and anger hits me. I shove at him. He grabs my wrists and yanks them over my head.

Bite.

"Aiden, stop." I kick at him. My whole body comes alive in the struggle, but he's too overpowering. How am I supposed to stand up to someone like him in a fair fight? Ever? His lips are still on my neck, and my skin is on fire.

He chuckles, maneuvering his grip on my wrists to just one hand. His other slips down, into my panties. The last piece of clothing—and I didn't even fucking notice how naked I was once I spotted him.

"Do not touch other men." His finger ghosts over my clit. "You're soaked already. So slick. You like this, hmm? The punishment?"

"Fuck you," I groan, turning my head sharply to the side. My legs tremble, and butterfly wings fill my chest.

"Careful what you ask for, princess." One finger pushes inside me, then two.

He pulls out abruptly, and I make an embarrassing noise of frustration. The moonlight catches the glisten on his fingers, and he makes a show of tasting me. It's unbearably hot. I press my thighs together.

Fabric ripping snaps me back to reality. My jaw drops. He destroyed my panties with *one hand*. He pockets the fabric, and I catch his smirk in the low light. He already has one pair. I almost resume my struggle, but part of me is desperately intrigued by him.

By what he's going to do.

He slides through my folds, brushing my clit, and I groan.

"You're killing me."

"Not yet," he whispers in my ear.

And then his hand inches back more, and fear does kick through me. Nerves, more than anything. He traps one leg with his own and spreads my other with his knee. And then he's pushing his wet finger into my back entrance.

I close my eyes. It's a spark of foreign pressure, then—

"Oh my god," I moan.

He thrusts lazily in and out. "You feel that?"

I nod, eyes wide and locked on his face.

"That's nothing compared to my cock. I told you, princess, I'm going to claim every inch of your body. You're *mine*." He releases my wrists and withdraws from me completely.

The sudden loss of him surprises me, and I slide to the floor.

He watches me, then reaches down and hauls me up. I'm cradled in his arms now, and he places me on the bed. Crawls up next to me. His hard dick presses through his jeans against my thigh.

"I want you inside me," I say.

He chuckles, adjusting us so my back is to his front, on our sides. My head is more on his arm than the pillow, and his other arm bands over me. I want to whine that it isn't fair—that he's fully clothed while I've been stripped bare.

"And I want to rip off your guard dog's hand," he responds. His breath tickles my shoulder. That's the only warning I get before his teeth latch on to my skin there. "This shoulder is mine. Your mouth is mine. Your eyes are mine. What do I have to do to remind you?"

Fuck me, I've never been more turned on—and that includes what happened this morning. Why does this domineering side of Aiden speak to me so much?

"I slipped right past his patrol," Aiden continues. His lips move up the side of my neck again. "He may have been smart enough for a surprise attack, to get you away from my family, but he won't protect you like I will."

I roll in his grasp so I can face him. "No one can stop you. It shouldn't be surprising that he couldn't."

He hums. "Even so."

"Even so," I repeat. My hands go to the button of his jeans, pushing it down enough to free his cock. I wrap my fingers around his length, keeping my eyes on his face. "Are you going to tell me why your father put a hit on my brother?"

He grimaces. "Sam."

The betrayal hits me square in the chest, and I stop moving. My chest tightens. If *I* feel this way, how does Aiden feel? What's going through his mind?

"You broke his phone," I say uncertainly. "How...?"

His gaze shutters. "I don't know the how or the why. But Luca was helping my father—they're using Amelie as leverage."

I gasp and sit up straight. "Absolutely not."

He takes my hand, and his thumb sweeps over my knuckles. "I'm not sure we have much of a choice." Hesitation.

I peer back down at him.

"What aren't you saying?"

He groans and rubs his face. "My father has issued a threat..."

"Yeah, against my brother. *Again.*" At least this time, I know why.

"Against you, Gem." His gaze is pained. "He said if I don't bring Colin in, he'd come after you."

I grip his fingers tighter. "I discovered something... and it explains everything."

May as well be honest, right? So I explain the binder, the truce. I don't know how much Aiden would've known. His signature wasn't anywhere on it. Hell, I wasn't aware of it until tonight, either.

Aiden listens silently, then nods. "The only way it would hold up is if he got a confession from either Colin or you."

"Because it's bullshit," I say. "The death—and the stolen shipment. We didn't do that."

"I believe you."

Music to my ears.

He exhales and rises. "Sleep. I'm going to figure this out."

I stand on the bed, indignant hurt filling me. "No."

"Gem—"

"You're staying with me." I smile. "I've never had a boy in my bed before."

That hooks him. For the moment, anyway. I don't want

143

our missions to come between us. I don't want to become so goal-oriented that I forget what I have right in front of me.

A guy I'm pretty sure I've been falling in love with since day one.

He sheds his pants and shirt and flips back the covers. His little smirk is... it feels more normal than it should. Like climbing into bed with me is exactly what he's been looking forward to, and now everything will be okay.

And it might.

Or we could end in a flurry of bullets.

We resume our previous position, and exhaustion tugs at me.

"This is our bubble," I mumble.

He squeezes my waist. "Sleep, Gem."

I like that he calls me that. I don't think I've told him that before, but usually only my family calls me that—and only when they're in a good mood. He uses it freely, interchanging it with *princess*.

"You haven't been sleeping," he continues in my ear. "Even with the guard dog outside. Take advantage of this, my love, and rest. I've got you."

My heart hurts. My thoughts are sluggish, already pulled down into the black dreams that await me. Except there's a chance they might not be so bleak with Aiden here.

"Love you," I whisper. But I miss his reaction, because I'm asleep seconds later.

CHAPTER 14

Aiden

D amn my phone. I uncurl from my position around Gemma and reach for the vibrating beast on her nightstand. It's early. The sky is just beginning to lighten, allowing me enough light to see it. I hit the accept button. When I don't immediately say anything, Ford begins speaking. He's good at that—giving me information concisely, even when I can't talk.

"Sean's dead," he says. "PD got the call from the girl-friend. Luckily, the officer who discovered his body called one of our detectives, and he's locked down the scene until we get there."

I grunt and glance down at Gemma. She's still asleep on her side, gripping her pillow tightly. Not a relaxed sleep—even with me there. I tried to give her some comfort, and it kills me to think it didn't put a dent in her nightmares.

"You're in Brooklyn?"

I don't answer. He knows it's a yes—he rarely asks questions he doesn't already know the answer to. It's the part of him that would make a decent lawyer, if he had put his mind to it.

"I'll be there in ten to pick you up," he says.

I hang up and run my hand up Gemma's arm. She doesn't even stir when I kiss her shoulder. I tangle my fingers in her silky blonde hair, then stop myself. I slip from bed and use her bathroom, taking a moment to peek in her medicine cabinet and then make a pot of coffee downstairs. There's a hulking man on the couch, and I shake my head.

If he's supposed to be on watch, he's doing a shitty job.

And I may as well make myself known.

I kick his foot, then step back when he leaps off the couch in one jump. He recognizes me immediately. *Good*. I recognize him, too, as the one who hit my bike and almost killed her.

"What the fuck are you doing here?" he spits.

I laugh. "The better question is, how are you helping Gemma by sleeping on her couch?"

He stares at me, then rubs his chin. "You like her."

"Not that it's any of your concern, but I'm in love with her." I head back into the kitchen to snag a water bottle and crack it open. He's a huge presence behind me, but I'm not entirely worried about him.

"Fine," he eventually lands on. "That's..."

He pauses, and for good reason. I have a feeling my expression could kill.

"I'm going to head out," he mutters. He slept in his shoes, so all he has to do is grab his hat and slam it on his head, then strap on the gun he left lying on the coffee table. He's probably great at whatever job the Wests use him for, but he's a shitty, daft guard.

I'm going to have to fix that to keep Gemma safe.

He leaves, and a few minutes later, my phone buzzes.

Ford is down the street.

I go through and check every door and window on the first floor, just in case. When everything is secure, I head outside and lock the front door behind me. If she's anything like her dad, she probably prescribed to the theory that this *home base* house would remain unlocked at all times. And maybe it should—when she has people to protect her.

"Boss," Ford greets me. "You good?"

I grimace. "Yeah, just imagining how to beef up security in that house."

He nods. "It's a bit of a tactical nightmare to defend."

We stare at it from afar. Too many windows. Three doors on the first floor, a balcony overlooking the backyard on the second. The roof is gently sloped with a skylight—another point of entry.

Getting her out will be the best decision I make.

But until I can convince her...

"She's in charge," I tell Ford.

He appraises the house in a new light. "No shit. The old man left everything to her, not the brother?"

I shrug, dismissing that idea. "He's young. Impulsive. Even if he was raised to expect it, I suspect Lawrence always knew Gemma had what it took. It was just confirmed by her dedication—she risked everything to save them."

He sighs. "Yeah, and now look. You're in love with the girl."

I shake it off as we head back toward Sean's Weapon Emporium. "Who's on scene?"

"Just Davies, I heard." His brother or cousin served with Hart overseas, and Hart apparently saved his life. Davies offered his help if we ever needed anything. The bastard probably didn't expect us to use him the way we have. But after the first time, he became complicit. Once a dirty cop, always a dirty cop.

It only depends on their motivation.

Money? Forget it. There's always someone who'll pay

more. That's how my father works—he regularly greases their wheels. The Wests are different. Careful. I can't figure out how they keep the cops on their payroll when we've tried to outbid them.

Us? Blackmail. Or favors. Or guilt.

Manipulation at its finest—and I can't even say I *didn't* learn that from my father.

"You were up there with Gemma," Ford says. "We've got to clean it up—anything you touched. And he said he can give us an hour with the scene before he calls it in."

I nod and open the glove box. True to the name—shockingly—there's a box of latex gloves. I pull on a pair as soon as we turn onto the driveway. We sweep past the house and stop next to the unmarked police car.

Anderson Davies comes outside with a grim look on his face. He yanks off his own gloves and shakes his head. "One hour. That's the best I can give you before I've got to call this one in."

Ford and I step past him. The first room, the one with the counter and plexiglass protection, is empty. No blood that I can see, no forced entry. The door beyond has been propped open.

We pass through, and I glance around. It's... it's a blood-bath. Cleaning this up in the way that removes Gemma and me from the scene will be damn near impossible. There's blood everywhere, droplets on the floor and equipment in arches.

And then the body.

I carefully step up on the platform, ducking under the ropes.

Sean has been nailed to the center of the ring, spread-eagle. Naked.

His arm is sliced open from wrist to elbow, and his throat gapes. Blood pools around his head and neck—it's probably the cause of death. The arm wound was just his killer's way of playing with him.

"No sign of a nail gun," Ford calls. "Or forced entry."

I crouch beside Sean's body and squint at his ear. It's scabbed over, clearly an injury from prior to his brutal murder. Satisfied that it most likely won't be linked to it, I rise.

"Anything?"

Ford carries out a black rifle. "Just these."

I shake my head. "Yeah, okay. Let's catalogue everything and get it out of here."

"One more issue..."

Gemma and I didn't find this office the other day—in fact, I thought it was just a storage locker the other times I've been here to blow off steam, or to deliver a shipment of weapons... or collect payment. But behind a half-wall is an elaborate computer set up, with security feeds on the screens. There's a live one, showing Davies leaning against the hood of his car with a cigarette pinched in his fingers. But the rest of them are frozen in various states from yesterday.

Ford hits a button, and they all play at once. My fight with Phil. Sean standing over Gemma. The crazy asshole snatching the gun after Gemma grabbed me from behind, stopping me from killing my opponent.

The madness that follows.

Ford's expressionless when I slice off Sean's ear, but he hits a button to stop the video. "This is encrypted. We're going to need more manpower on this."

I nod. "Call who you need."

"Breaker is on his way." He tilts his head. "This won't be easy to clean up. We haven't found Sean's phone—and he took a picture of you, didn't he?"

"Yeah."

"If you're the last ones to see him alive..."

Fucking hell. "Is there audio?"

He shrugs and goes back to the computer. "Might be, somewhere."

I grimace. We've got our work cut out for us, or else even Davies might not be able to make this disappear. Prison isn't an option—not for me, and certainly not for Gemma.

CHAPTER 15
Gemma

I need to save Amelie.

That's really my only option.

I go downstairs, expecting to find Turner on the couch. It's still early, the sun barely up, and I suspect he would've arrived only a few hours ago. Keeping watch, for a West, generally means taking the couch or chair and dozing until danger strikes. I guess, *if* danger strikes would be the better wording. But there's no Turner—no one at all, actually.

First, coffee.

There's already a pot made, steaming hot, and I squint at it, confused. Until I see the note beside it, pinned down by my favorite mug.

See you soon.

No signature. But I grin like a lunatic all the same. There's no mistaking Aiden's blocky script. I take the note and fold it up, sliding it in my pocket. Then I pour myself a coffee and go back to contemplating my predicament.

Amelie is the key to this. Save her, free Luca and Aiden from their father's control, keep my brother out of harm's way.

Easy.

Ha.

I sit on the couch with my mug in hand and stare down at my phone. It had synced with my old one, so I still have her number. I now have Aiden's, too. It was the first on my contact list when I went searching for Amelie's information. It makes sense—he had my phone after he caught Amelie in my car. Of course he would take the opportunity to program in his own number.

I dial Amelie's number.

She could be home. Maybe they only use her when he needs... force.

I shudder.

It rings and rings, and finally the line picks up. But no one says anything, and dread creeps down my back. This isn't Amelie. It seems like I wait for eons for the person to say something. I sure as hell won't be the first to break.

"Gemma West," the man says.

If possible, my blood pressure spikes.

"Jameson DeSantis," I respond, guessing. It isn't a wild one. Who else would have her phone and play mind games like this?

"I didn't realize you were so well acquainted with my daughter-in-law to be calling her cell phone."

"I didn't realize you were so familiar with her that you *answered* her phone." I bite my cheek to keep my temper in check. Because it does flare out of nowhere on occasion. Nausea hits me. "I want to speak with her."

He exhales loudly. "So boring, Ms. West. Where's your fighting spirit?"

"I know how to pick my battles," I answer evenly. "Amelie?"

"Fine. But I'll be seeing you soon." He pauses. "The

charity event this weekend. My son informed me that you'd be attending with us."

Of course he did. That was probably before everything came to light... certainly before he realized what kind of monster Jameson is.

"I'm aware," I lie.

His chuckle grows distant, and then a lighter, breathless voice hits me.

"Gemma?"

"The one and only." I stand and pace my living room. "Are you okay? Can he hear me?"

"Conversations are rarely as private as we wish," Amelie replies.

Fucker.

"Well, I just wanted to..." I don't really have a good excuse for calling—not one that would pass Jameson's inspection. I clear my throat and rack my brain. "I have your tiara that you loaned me. Um, it survived my kidnapping."

Her laugh is tight. "Oh, good. I'd say keep it, but it's sort of sentimental value. So..."

"Tell your friend she can come return it," Jameson says.

I shudder. *Not happening*.

"He's keeping me in the penthouse—"

The line goes dead.

I pull the phone away from my ear, double-checking that she—or he—just ended the call. Penthouse. Jameson's suite, probably.

Fucking hell. That's probably the most guarded floor in the whole skyscraper. Even Luca's keycard that Amelie gave me—which is probably uselessly deactivated by now—wouldn't get me that far.

If he's as paranoid as I think, he's the only one who can get himself into his own apartment. Imagine if he trusted someone with that. *Doubtful*.

Before I lose my nerve, I call Xavier. He answers on the first ring, and I wince before asking for his help. Extra help, that is. I can't spit it out over the phone, so he arrives less than an hour later. And then I explain the situation, wringing my hands.

"No," he says. He seems incredulous that I'd even ask.

"You came with me after the wedding," I accuse. "You had no problem waltzing in then."

"Yeah... because the most important DeSantises were locked in a church."

I scoff and turn away.

"I don't work with DeSantises, anyway."

I glare at him. "She's my friend."

"And Aiden's your fuck buddy. So what? They're still are who they are." He makes himself at home in my kitchen, pouring a cup of coffee into a new mug.

I think I've underestimated how often he's been in my house—he's too comfortable. Not only does he know his way around the layout, but he knows where we keep the coffee mugs? Next, he'll probably dig around the refrigerator and help himself to the leftovers.

"Colin is pouting," he adds. "Thought you'd be happy to know he's staying put under your aunt's watchful eye. She's terrifying."

I shrug and peek through the curtains at the street. "She's just a mother figure doing her duty."

He's silent. Of course—he didn't grow up with a family. He's like Peter Pan with his merry band of lost boys. No, wait, Robin Hood had the merry band. Peter Pan was just... lost. And when I think of Xavier like that, it's hard not to pity him.

"Okay, so I guess we're not breaking into the DeSantis tower in broad daylight," I allow. "But..."

"But?"

I perk up. "The charity event! I have no idea what he was

referring to, but I'd bet everyone is going to be there. And we just need to organize another little... kidnapping."

He grimaces. "A charity event this weekend. Friday? Two days from now? Or Sunday—four days from now? Do you know how much planning it took to get you out?"

"Well, Jameson sprung the wedding on us three days prior, so..." I wink. "We can do it. Or, I guess you can do it? I should have nothing to do with it, if Jameson needs to see the Wests as innocent. You need to get Amelie and Luca to safety." Here might be too obvious. There are a few safe houses in Manhattan that aren't used much...

"She means a lot to you?"

I throw my shoulders back, doubling down on my decision. "She's my friend."

"Okay," he agrees. "You better find out about this charity dinner. I need the location, date, and time at the very least. As soon as you can." He's already pulling out his phone and heading out the door.

I nod to myself, then grab my phone again.

Aiden answers on the first ring.

"Watching your phone?" I tease.

"You have a special ringtone."

My stomach flips.

Shit. It just occurs to me that I told him the L word before I passed out last night. And he was gone before I woke up... so we haven't talked about it.

"What's up, Gem?"

A giddy smile overtakes my expression for a moment, and I struggle to snap back to reality. Now is *not* the time to be sick in love.

Gross.

"Tell me about this charity event we're going to?" I ask.

He exhales. "Right, I was hoping to be able to avoid that. It's the Children's Hospital Gala. The Pages are sponsoring it, and Councilwoman White is announcing her candidacy for governor that night. Saturday."

"Where?"

"The Museum of Fine Arts. It was a little hot-tempered of me to tell my father that you'd be joining me."

There's an apology in his tone that I ignore. I'm not going to loop him in on this game plan. Why put him in more danger? Xavier's guys can handle a simple smash-and-grab. Well, as long as they're only smashing DeSantis bones and kidnapping Amelie and Luca.

"It's okay," I say. "I tried to call Amelie, but your father answered her phone."

"What did he say?" There's movement, and then a door slams.

Yep, he's pissed. Although I can't tell if he's more annoyed that I tried meddling, or...

Well, if he's mad about this, then he'll be furious on Saturday.

"Just mentioned the gala," I lie. "Nothing monumental. I got to chat with Amelie. She sounded... okay."

"Don't lie," he admonishes. "It's just you and me, Gem. You can be honest."

I close my eyes and run through her words again. Not just what she was saying, but the emotion behind it. The lack of emotion.

"Remember when Luca locked her up? By the time Wilder's funeral rolled around, she was shut down. She sounded like that." I slap my cheek, trying to get a handle on myself. I rescued her once—we can do it again. "She hates cages, Aiden. She's suffocating."

"Luca knows that. He's going to do whatever my father wants to keep her safe."

That, I know.

"So for now, Luca is your enemy." There's murmuring in

the background, and it sharply cuts off again. "If you see him, you go in the opposite direction. He's dangerous to any West right now, but especially you and Colin."

"I understand." The thought guts me, though. That we have to take precautions against Aiden's brother.

One pitted against the other, and one completely off the radar.

"I've got some things to take care of," he says. "Sean's Weapon Emporium has been seized by local police following his murder. We're headed out to clean up."

I shiver. "We didn't kill Sean."

"I know. Someone didn't like us talking to him."

Freaking hell.

"Stay safe," I order.

His chuckle is warm in my ear. "Always, princess."

Once he's off the phone, I pass along the info to Xavier, then shower and dress. Someone knocks on the door just as I'm pulling on a new pair of boots, and I peer through the window. Marius stands on the porch, his back to the door. There's a box in his hand, and a delivery boy scurries away.

I yank it open, flipping my wet hair over my shoulder. "You work in shipping nowadays, too, huh?"

"Special courier." He shrugs and hands it over. "Want me to open it?"

I scowl. "Why, in case it's a bomb?"

His eyes narrow, like I'm not taking my own safety as seriously as I should. Which is a load of shit. I just think if someone wanted me dead, a delivered bomb would be the wrong way to go about it.

"Thanks," I mutter, then close the door. I set it on the kitchen counter and hunt for scissors. It doesn't weigh more than a few pounds, and it's no bigger than a sheet of paper. Four or five inches tall. There's no return address, just my name printed on a piece of paper taped to the top.

I slice the tape and flip open the lid. Inside is a crisp white box. That lid slides off easily, revealing a small handgun. I lift it carefully. The bottom of the grip is studded with turquoise that matches my knife's leather sheath. The dark metal is polished, shining, and under the nest of padding the gun sat in is a box of ammunition.

And a note.

It should fit under most dresses. —A

My cheeks heat. There's also another thigh holster, matching the one for my knife.

At this rate, I'll never be able to wear pants again.

I go back upstairs and change from shorts into a flowing, knee-length dress, then load the gun and slide it in its compact holster. I fit the knife to one thigh and the firearm to the other, holding my dress up to admire the way they look. They make me feel... badass, I guess. But also less vulnerable. I toss my phone and wallet in my purse, then slide flat black sneakers on my feet and head outside.

Marius leaps out of his car when I approach.

"Where to?" he asks, striding along beside me.

I glance at him, then nod to myself. I may as well use him, since I clearly have him.

"You familiar with a guy named Rubert?"

He jerks to a halt. "No."

An obvious lie.

"Well, I'm going to pay him a visit."

"Gemma, *no*. He's dangerous."

I roll my eyes. "Trust me, he's met my knife before." I keep walking, heading to my car. Once again parked down the street, because everyone says its recognizable. It is, for an older car. It isn't the flashiest thing I've ever driven, either. Amelie's Porsche takes that cake.

"That's—" Marius hurries to keep up.

I have to suppress my laugh. He's giant—easily a foot and

a half taller than me, with four times as much muscle. But he's surprisingly quiet on his feet.

"You can come, or tell..." I shrug. "I don't know, who has authority to stop me?"

"Fuck," he groans. "Fine. But I'm driving." He ducks between two cars abruptly, crossing the street. He stops at a huge white truck and grins. "Acceptable?"

"It'll do."

He nods and opens the passenger door for me, offering his hand to help me up. I actually need it—it's high, jacked up more than a typical truck. Once we're on the road, I glance over at him. "You know where he lives, right?"

Because I don't have a clue.

My plan after getting in my car was to wing it...

"I do." He grimaces. "Why are we going to see Rubert?"

"Apparently Dad struck a deal with him about weapons, which has prompted the DeSantis fury. Sean from Sean's Weapon Emporium has been selling the firearms that were stolen from the DeSantises. He said they came from the DeSantises like usual, although he couldn't give us any more information about who dropped the load off." Not to mention the still-missing marble, the legitimate part of their construction business. "He also said the DeSantises had been receiving their usual commission from any of his sales, but I can't prove that. And the other night, Colin was caught on camera selling one of those firearms to Aiden's guy. The footage was passed along to Jameson before Aiden and I could inter-cept it, because Colin stupidly bought it from that fucking emporium." I tap my chin. "Oh, and Sean is now dead."

Marius just stares straight ahead, his expression blank. Then, "What the ever-loving fuck is going on in this hellhole city?"

I snort. "Beats me. But Rubert was the one *contracted* to steal the shipment… so he should have some answers."

"Someone's been cleaning up their tracks, it seems." He glances over. "Rubert could be a target."

"Maybe."

"You and Aiden still, huh?"

My cheeks heat, and now it's my turn to keep my gaze locked on the road. "Yep."

I catch his smirk out of the corner of my eye.

"We all need to find our happiness. The rest of it is just byproducts of a good life."

Huh. Who would've thought tattooed, gangster-esque Marius would be inspirational? But come to think of it, I haven't heard him or Turner ever talk about women. Certainly never at the bars. Maybe he has someone special tucked out of harm's way.

"Our train arrives tomorrow evening," he says out of the blue. "We'll be using Benny's truck to haul it into the city, but I'll need your key."

I blink. "My key to what?"

"The car." He glances over. "Drugs are loaded into the shipping containers and then stacked on the trains, transported up from the south. We own our own containers—a few of them—and they all have special locks. Your dad used to either accompany us to make sure everything was okay, or he'd leave it to James."

I grimace. James Courier—fitting last name—is my aunt Margaret's husband. He's been in prison for years now on a bogus murder charge. Pretty sure there was something iffy going on with the district attorney's office, although Dad was never able to prove anything.

"What would you prefer?"

He meets my gaze. "If you want a full scope of the business, I say come with."

I nod slowly. "Yeah. Sounds fair." Tomorrow is Thursday. With my evening blocked off, that will give me most of the day and then Friday to prepare for this charity gala. *Ugh*. I'll need a fancy dress. Something nicer than anything I currently have hanging in my closet. The last time I went to something like that, I think I was a few pounds lighter.

Not to mention being on my best behavior around the man who killed my father.

Marius navigates into the sketchier side of the Bronx, pulling up in front of a yellow house. The small yard is sparse but clean, and nothing immediately seems amiss.

I hop out, eliciting a frustrated groan from Marius, and head up to the door. My bodyguard looms right behind me, but his hesitation doesn't last long. Once we're on the tiny porch, he edges in front of me and knocks.

We wait, and I strain to hear anything.

It's silent.

He knocks again, ringing the bell a few times for good measure.

"Hasn't been around in a few days," a neighbor calls.

Uh-huh.

"Mind your business," Marius snaps. He raises his shirt, revealing his weapon.

The woman pales and quickly disappears back inside her house.

"Great, she's probably going to call the cops." I cross my arms. "Now what? We can't wait around for him since you—"

He kicks the door open. The wood frame splinters, pieces flying forward, and my mouth drops open. I'm about to admonish him again—because breaking and entering isn't really high on my list of priorities today—when the smell hits me.

I cover my mouth and nose, fighting a gag. "What—"

"Stay here," he orders. He draws his gun and steps silently into the house.

I stand on the porch, keeping one eye on the street, until Marius returns.

"Come see this." His voice is grim.

Dead body. I know it before I see it. But he leads me through the house, which seems like it went through a half-assed robbery, and into the kitchen. Rubert hangs from the ceiling fan by his ankles.

His throat's been slit, and the floor is *covered* in blood. We can't even step foot in the room. There are stab wounds in his belly, too. It wasn't a fast death. Whoever killed him wanted him to suffer. I can't focus too much on his bloodstained face. It doesn't even really look like the man we interrogated in Aiden's little cabin.

I shudder. "We need to leave."

Marius doesn't argue. He's hot on my heels out the door, and we hurry to his truck. He helps me in again, slamming my door and rushing around to his. We peel out and hit the end of the street just as flashing cop cars screech around the corner on the other end of the block. They all stop in front of the open door of Rubert's home.

Their lights fade the farther away we get.

"This is not good," I say. I need to call Aiden. Or Aunt Mary. Or... Fuck, I don't know. I have no clue what to do. "I need to get back to my car. I..." Maybe it's the helplessness, more than anything, that tips me over the edge.

"Are you okay?"

Nope. I can't fucking breathe. My chest is tight, and my lungs are filled with lead. I unbuckle my seatbelt and try to remember how to calm down. But... I've got nothing. My vision has narrowed to just a view of the dash in front of me.

Marius pulls over and grabs my purse, fishing out my

phone. And the worst part? I can't even fucking protest. I can't speak.

"Lean forward," he advises me. "Put your head between your knees. Just breathe, Gemma."

I want to scream.

The sight of Rubert hanging flashes before my eyes, and nausea rolls through me. I'm vaguely aware of a sharp keening noise.

"Your girl is having a panic attack," Marius says. "I don't know what to do."

"Gem?" Aiden's voice fills the cab.

A broken sob bursts past my lips.

"Fuck," he says. "Baby, I'm on my way. You at your house?"

"We're on the way back," Marius says. "Be there in fifteen."

Aiden says something else, but the sound goes out. It's like I've been plunged underwater, and everything garbles. I vaguely register Marius reaching over and re-clicking my seat-belt, then being thrown back into my seat with the speed he pulls back onto the road.

White spots dance in my vision. I'm still hyperventilating, my breath ragged, when my door opens. Hands unbuckle me and turn me sideways in the seat, so my legs dangle out, and then those hands cup my cheeks.

"Breathe, Gem," Aiden says. He smooths back my hair and presses his hand over my chest. He grabs my hand and puts it on his chest. "With me."

I lock onto his face and try to mimic him. Rubert has brought back memories of Kai and my father, and I feel trauma-tized all over again. How easy was it to get him in that posi-tion? To hang him from the fan and slit his throat? I know the force it took to stab my knife into his leg. The throat is infinitely more delicate. Thinner skin.

And he wasn't even a good guy. One could argue he was dirty to the core, and his death won't impact too many people.

But that's a bit harsh, right? He was a person. He probably had family. He, at the very least, had a small-time gang depending on him.

"There you go, princess," Aiden says softly. His thumb catches a tear. "What happened?"

I glance over my shoulder, but Marius is gone. Well, not *gone* gone—he's leaning against the back bumper of his truck, studiously ignoring us.

My throat is raw.

"Rubert was murdered." My voice is hoarse. "I wanted to... follow up. We walked in, and he was..."

Aiden's gaze darkens. He lifts me out of the truck, one arm under my knees and the other behind my back. He carries me to his waiting car and places me in the passenger seat.

"Stay here," he says, gentle and soft.

He strides toward Marius, and the larger man flinches. Aiden seems spitting mad, his fists clenched at his sides. He doesn't strike him, though. He gestures back at me. Marius reddens, then nods. He says something, a long something. Maybe an explanation of what the hell happened, and now Aiden is the one nodding.

Aiden strides back toward me and climbs in beside me. He shifts into drive, and his hand lands on my thigh.

"How am I supposed to lead my family when I have panic attacks after seeing dead bodies?" I swipe more tears from my cheeks. Now that my heart rate has returned to normal, I'm frustrated at myself. I have the jittery urge to punch something. "I mean, it's not like it's my first."

He doesn't reply.

"It's just stupid," I continue. "I don't suppose Sean was tied up by his ankles, too, huh? A bloody fucking mess. He was supposed to give us *answers*."

"Rubert didn't know shit," Aiden finally says. "He would've told you if he had any clue when you had your knife in his leg, or when Breaker was working him over. He most likely did drop off the shipment at your family's old warehouse, and he wouldn't have stuck his nose out to learn more."

That does give me a tiny bit of comfort.

"Sean wasn't strung up, but his throat was slit," he adds. "So it could very well be the same person."

I exhale. "Are we operating under the assumption that this is Wilder?"

He shoots me a look. "No."

"Why not?"

"Because it's not him, Gemma."

That's just... that's just foolish. I raise my eyebrows and pivot slightly toward him. "You don't have any proof that it isn't."

"And I could say the same to you—innocent until proven guilty. We don't even know if he's in the city. He could've gone anywhere." His jaw tics. "To one of the houses in Italy, maybe."

I grimace. "He could, but why—when he'd have a better view of the West destruction from right here in New York?"

My cheeks heat, and I get the feeling that he might pull away. So I cover his hand on my leg with both of mine, simply because I like the weight of it. It's grounding. And it reminds me of the L word that I said to him just last night...

"I wonder if my father is betting on the fact that only him, Lawrence, and whoever notarized it would be aware of the contract." He drums his fingers on the steering wheel. "Colin is well hidden?"

"If he stays where he's supposed to."

"Right, then. And you and I have a gala to go to on Saturday, while avoiding the ire of my father." He smiles. "Do you have a dress?"

"That was on my list of things to do." I shift in my seat. "I'll probably go tomorrow—"

"Nonsense." He flicks his blinker on, then veers across three lanes of traffic. Brakes squeal behind us, followed by a chorus of horns. "Breaker and Ford are taking care of Sean's place."

I fidget. He's willing to just... drop everything that he had planned today to do what? Take me dress shopping? Too many questions bubble up in my head, but the first one is the one that I blurt out.

"Why are you making time for this?"

He grins. "Spending time with you trumps just about everything else."

I narrow my eyes. "What doesn't it trump?"

"Spending time with you naked."

I hit his arm, and he laughs. Soon enough, we're veering down into a parking garage. We're close to Times Square now, the traffic much more congested. The man working the booth takes one look at Aiden and immediately waves him through. Another man appears near the elevators, pulling a *reserved* cone away from a parking space. He's gone by the time Aiden and I step out.

"Preferential treatment?"

He shrugs and offers his arm. "Our construction company built it, the least they can do is give us free parking when we decide to shop. Or dine."

Ah. "Times Square. Wow. I'll keep my eyes open for that Italian marble you guys are famous for..."

He pats my hand that's curled around his upper arm. "That's the least impressive thing you'll see today."

We step into an elevator car that whisks us upward. It has glass walls, and as soon as we pass out of the garage portion, I have a clear view of the huge atrium. It slows on the sixth floor, and we walk into a dress shop that I'd never have thought to go into.

Not because it's expensive—it is, dangerously so—but because it's one of those snobby places that my mother wouldn't be caught dead in. I was raised by a financially careful woman. It didn't matter that the Wests nearly out-earned the DeSantises each year. Mom grew up in a strict, low-income family, and it shined through in how she handled our family's budget.

"We could go somewhere else," I say under my breath. "Somewhere less…"

"You deserve the best," he says firmly. "And besides, it's cute to see you embarrassed."

We enter the store, and immediately are descended upon by three employees. It's like a scene out of the movies, and my face only gets redder. Aiden quietly explains that I need *the best*, as he just said, in formal wear. And then he lists his conditions.

My mortification grows—but at the same time, I'm glad he's with me. There are some things I wouldn't have thought of until it was too late, like where I'd stash my weapons if I wore something skin-tight.

Not that I'm the skin-tight type.

One of the women takes my hand and pries me away from Aiden, leading us back into a more private room surrounded by mirrors. There's a circular platform in the center that she thrusts me toward. I climb up and eye her, but her attention is on my body. She murmurs things to herself, then nods.

"We'll be right back with a selection," she says to Aiden.

I frown.

His lips quirk, accepting my irritation. He stands before me, hands in his pockets and head tipped back to meet my gaze. I plant my hands on my hips. Close but not touching—we both have control over ourselves... for now.

A spark lights up his face, like he's reading my mind.

It's too late, though. Two of the three women return with armfuls of fabric, and they disappear into one of the dressing rooms off to the side. I heave a sigh and follow after them.

Aiden's hot stare lingers on my back until I'm out of sight.

CHAPTER 16

Gemma

I veto the wild colors immediately. I might be able to pull off bright pink or orange, but I'd rather not stand out like that. I also say no to the black dresses. It reminds me too much of death—and if Aiden wants me to act like I'm not in the room with a murderer, I shouldn't dress like I'm going to a funeral.

One of the women zips me into a tight, light-blue dress with thin straps. It barely flares past my hips, but whether I'd be able to eat *and* breathe is up for debate.

Without hesitation, she opens the door and motions for me to go out.

I walk out and climb onto the platform, then raise my eyes to see Aiden's reaction.

He's frowning.

"It's not the one," he declares. "Don't you agree? You look like you're holding your breath."

I laugh. "Because I was."

I spare a glance at myself, then silently agree. It's a nice dress. Lovely for... someone else. Someone thinner, maybe. He stands immediately and offers his hand. I grip it as I step down, my cheeks heating.

Again.

He leans in, his mouth at my ear. "I love it when you blush. It reminds me of the color your ass turns with my marks on you."

Oh Lord. I'm sure my face turns even redder at that—and that the women might've overheard him.

I rush back into the changing room.

The next dress is better, but not great. Charcoal gray and floor-length. It hugs my body, one shoulder covered and one long sleeve. The flashy part is the high slit in the side, exposing most of my leg when I stride forward.

His grin of approval goes straight between my thighs, and I glare at him. He motions for me to spin.

"Black or silver stilettos," one of the women says. "And her hair could be up or down."

"It's not the one," I tell them.

The last dress is dark emerald green. The fabric is soft under my fingers.

"This will bring out the gold in your eyes," one says. "You have little flecks of it in the blue."

I smile.

It fits like a glove. The bodice, down to my waist, is form-fitting. Long sleeves, but it's meant to be worn slightly off the shoulders and leaves my chest bare. The neckline hugs my breasts and plunges down. The back isn't nearly as scandalous. It dips down in a V, ending even with the bottom of my shoulder blades. A band of the fabric wrapped horizontally gives me the illusion of a smaller waist.

And the skirt.

I think the skirt is my favorite part.

There's so much fabric, but another high slit that ends at my upper thigh allows me to move. The skirt swishes when I walk. I do a mini twirl right there in the cramped space, then run my hands down my sides. When I'm still, it doesn't seem as voluminous.

"Show him," they tell me.

I twist my hair up in a loose ponytail and stride out.

Aiden immediately stands. "You love it."

I nod—but then I think of how much this might cost, and my stomach revolts. The smile drops from my face, and I twist my fingers. How do I tell him that I can't accept this? That I can probably find a suitable replacement at the mall?

The sad part is, I didn't even think of looking at a price tag until right this moment.

"I can't."

He comes forward and takes my hands, helping me up onto the platform. And then he surprises me by climbing up behind me. His hands on my bare shoulders elicit a shiver down my spine.

He carefully turns me toward the mirrors, then tugs my hair free. The waves tumble down my back. He runs his fingers through them, nails scraping my scalp, and I let out a sigh.

"Leave us," he orders the women. He leans down and puts his lips right next to my ear. "Whatever you do, don't look away from yourself."

I swallow.

His hand wraps around my neck, his palm around the front of my throat, and pulls me back into him. He tips my head back. My breath catches. I've become addicted to this strange sort of high—the unpredictability of being with Aiden. The dangerous undertones to our sexual attraction.

He's the first man who has touched me like this. The first one to wake up my lust. Part of me acknowledges that he's the only one I want to touch me... ever.

The hand not on my throat skims down my side, to the slit

in my dress. He brushes the straps of the holsters—which the women didn't flinch at when they saw—and then higher.

"My dirty girl," he whispers. "Are you already wet for me?"

I don't answer. I watch his hand in the mirror as it dips in the fabric, between my legs. He pushes aside my panties and swipes his finger against my clit. He groans, his teeth catching the shell of my ear. His facial expressions are more erotic than I would've thought, and I can't stop my attention from bouncing between the two.

But then he releases me and hops off the platform, cutting off... everything. My eyes follow him in the mirror, watching him circle me. And I feel more like prey in this exact moment —more than ever before. Not even waiting for him in Aunt Mary's house compares to the gleam in his eyes.

"Mirror," he orders gently when he gets in front of me.

I wince and nod.

He lowers himself to his knees in front of me and parts my skirt, exposing one leg. His breath hits my thigh, and then his lips touch my skin. Briefly.

"Aiden—"

His head disappears under my dress. I gasp, shocked, when his teeth yank my panties aside, and his nose runs along my mound. He isn't gentle when he finally makes contact. He grips my thighs, parting my legs and steadying me at the same time. His tongue sweeps over my clit.

My mind blanks.

The sight of him in the mirror, his head moving under the dress, is almost too much. I put my hands on his shoulders. He sucks my clit, then thrusts his tongue inside me.

"Oh my god, Aiden."

He hums, and the vibration is like nothing I've experienced before.

"Fuck. God, harder." I push and pull at his head. He's going to destroy me—I can just sense it.

He devours me until my legs quiver, and an orgasm sneaks up on me. For a moment, his grip is the only thing keeping me upright. Then he backs off, rocking back on his heels.

His grin is savage, lips wet from my cunt. He makes a show of licking them slowly, running the pad of his thumb under his mouth. I quiver and stare down at him, my hand over my heaving chest. Now that reality has returned, embarrassment floods back in.

He reaches out and adjusts my panties, then the dress.

"This dress suits you," he murmurs, rising. "But your just-fucked expression suits you better."

My mouth drops open.

He helps me down and undoes the four gold buttons in the back, then shoos me into the changing room. I emerge a few minutes later, somewhat more put together, without the dress.

He shoots me a look. "Where is it?"

Right. I shift on my feet and eye the floor. "I can find something similar—"

"No."

Here we go. "Aiden, I'm not—"

"I didn't fucking ask you, Gem." He shakes his head and points. "We've been through hell together, and I just want to treat you to a pretty dress. And lunch. I want to feel normal for two seconds before we have to go back to reality."

I bite my lip. "This isn't normal, though. This is..."

Dress shopping and lunch and the quick flashes of fear when we walk into rooms? That's not our normal. Before Amelie's botched wedding and Wilder's faked death, I drew and visited family, contemplated learning to play the cello, eavesdropped on my brother and father. I imagined the fall of the city, the destruction of our enemies. My thoughts ran morbid more often than not.

He cups my cheeks. "It's okay that you haven't been living since your mom died."

That's the heart of it, isn't it? She died eighteen months—nineteen, now—ago, and we haven't really been living since then. It was so abrupt. The aneurism, the hospital stay, the funeral.

"But it can't go on forever," he concludes. "So what if you don't think this is normal? It *could be*. For us. If you wanted it to be."

I sniffle and pull out of his grasp, wiping under my eyes. "Normal for us is Mafia life. People trying to kill us or over-throw us. The city bowing beneath our feet."

"It's our current predicament," he says. "We'll shelf this discussion for now... but it's okay to think about our future and what we want from it."

My brain refuses to think that far ahead. After all, life can so easily be snatched away, like a flame being snuffed out. Like my mother. Now that he's brought her up, she's all I can think about. She survived as a West. As my father's wife. She was respected... and she accepted every part of my father.

And I miss her.

The tears are still going, but Aiden leaves me in the center of the room to retrieve the dress. He doesn't push, but he doesn't take no for an answer, and I follow him back out into the main shop. One of the employees reappears at the counter from the back room, her cheeks pink, and quickly rings him out. They take the dress from him, and he reaches for my hand.

"Lunch," he says simply.

Yeah, fine. I can do lunch.

One thing at a time.

* * *

"So, is this going to be a thing?" I ask at one point. We're seated at the back of a restaurant, near windows that overlook the street. It's busy below us, bustling with activity. People trying to get places as quickly as possible. Funny thing about New York City, though: no one really gives a shit about anyone else. They all keep their heads down and truck along. Only the tourists glance up at the tall buildings surrounding them.

Aiden has ordered drinks for both of us, and now our legs are pressed together from hip to knee. We started off on separate sides of the booth, but it didn't last long. And I'm okay with that—with the view and his heat warming my chilled body.

We're far from other people, in almost an entirely separate section. That allows Aiden a small modicum of peace. His guard is still up, scanning the entrances periodically, but his expression is relaxed.

He turns toward me, his eyebrow rising. "Is what going to be a thing?"

I try to hide my smile, but I'm more than ready to put aside any heaviness from our earlier conversation. "Surprise orgasms."

He grins. "Maybe."

Something playful comes over me. We're alone back here —it's busy outside, and the front of the restaurant, but we're in our own little bubble. That just emboldens me. I slide my hand up his thigh, cupping him through his jeans.

"Careful," he warns. "Don't start something you can't finish."

I lean in and press my lips his ear, whispering, "I think I've demonstrated that *I* can finish—but can you?"

He watches me silently as I undo his button and zipper, pulling it down just enough to free his cock. It's hard now, growing harder by the second. I lean down and lick him, the thrill of it like electricity skittering under my skin. His fingers dig into the back of my neck, but there's no pressure. Not yet, anyway.

A low groan escapes his lips when I take more of him in my mouth. I love the noise. So much so that the restaurant's chatter fades away. I balance one hand on his hip and use the other to aid my mouth, gently massaging his balls.

His cock jerks against my tongue.

"Fuck, Gemma." His fingers slide into my hair, and then he goes completely still. He presses me down farther. The tip touches the back of my throat, and I fight my gag reflex. "What?" he snaps.

Oh, shit. I try to rise, but his grip is unrelenting.

A new voice says, "I didn't mean to—I'll just..."

My face flames. My jaw aches from holding this position. And yet, he's completely covered by my face and hair. I'm the only vulnerable one—unless I decide to bite his dick, which I'm strongly considering.

Especially when he adds to the man at the end of the table, "I did not dismiss you."

He proceeds to order food. He tugs at my hair, lifting my head just a bit, then forces it back down while he talks. Anger rushes through me, and I run my tongue over the ridges just under the head of his cock. It twitches in my mouth, so I do it again. I alternate sucking and doing that, until Aiden's voice wobbles just the slightest.

The waiter leaves. It seems to take an eternity, but finally it's just the two of us again.

Aiden swears under his breath. "You naughty girl." He jacks his hips up twice, hitting the back of my throat, then comes with a low hiss of breath. His hot seed fills my mouth, and I swallow around him. Some of it leaks out the corners of my lips, and I lick it away when he finally releases me and tucks himself back in his pants.

His smirk is dangerous, but my hands tremble with fury. I could kill him.

"I should've bitten you."

He leans forward and snags the back of my neck again, hauling me forward. His lips slam into mine. My heart flutters. A dangerous kiss from a dangerous prince. He takes what he wants, after all. I bite his tongue, then his lip. My hands fly up and cradle the sides of his face, keeping him still. I don't care if it hurts. Actually, that's wrong. I want to hurt him.

Blood blooms on my tongue.

Aiden bites back.

He pulls my lower lip between his teeth, and the pain is sharp. It goes straight down my spine like electricity. I'm addicted to him.

We're so tangled up in each other, it takes a long moment for me to come back to reality once our kiss-slash-bite pauses. Our lips are barely touching, both our chests heaving.

His tongue darts out and swipes across my lower lip.

"I love that you taste like me. I love that you're a little vampire when you're pissed." He presses his forehead to mine and stares into my eyes. "Fuck, that was the hottest thing I've ever seen."

I scowl. "You—"

"Come here," he interrupts. He lifts me onto his lap, situating me with my back to the crowd. I face the windows, and that somehow makes it better. He smooths my hair back.

I tentatively touch my lip. My mouth is full of the taste of *him* and the coppery taste of blood, and I can't deny that I'm wickedly turned on. I shouldn't be, though, right? Our server just caught me giving him a blow job.

"You only ordered one plate," I murmur.

He nods once, then pulls out his phone. I allow myself to zone out for a few minutes, focusing on the people on the sidewalks far below us.

"Here you are," the server says. He sets down the plate in front of us.

I turn, eyeing the food—steak, some sort of creamy risotto, and grilled vegetables. The server openly stares at me.

"How much for a turn?" the server finally asks.

"Excuse me?" Aiden grips my hip, phone forgotten.

Shame floods through me. In a matter of seconds, I'd gone from feeling powerful to dirty, slime crawling over my skin. My face gets hot, and all I can do is keep my gaze on the food in front of me.

The server clears his throat. "I've seen a lot of shit in this hellhole city, but I can't say I've ever seen *that*. Did you meet her on the street? How much does something like that cost?"

"One second, baby." Aiden's low voice curls like smoke in my ear. He sets me aside, closer to the windows, and rises from the booth. He motions to the server, whose expression has turned from curious to wary.

I can't help it—I want to see what Aiden will do. I follow a few steps behind them, through the kitchen and out into the stairwell.

Immediately, Aiden grabs the server by the collar and shoves him face-first into the painted cinderblock wall. The door has barely shut behind us when the man begins to blubber his apologies.

Aiden twists his wrist and raises it, the leverage on his shoulder forcing his face harder into the wall. "Do you know who I am?"

"What the fuck?"

I cross my arms over my chest and smother my scoff. Still, some noise slips out, because the server's eyes dart over to me. They go wide, and he struggles anew. And he isn't a small guy —it's just that Aiden's driven by fury, and the server... well, I suppose he might think his life is in danger soon enough.

Aiden flips him around and grips his jaw, turning his face

toward me. "You see that beautiful girl? She's not a slut, or whatever you thought you were implying by your crude gesture. She's the strongest person I know."

I lift my chin, a lump in my throat. He's just... saying that. Right?

"And you ruined our normal day," Aiden finishes. He slams his fist into the server's face, and he immediately goes down.

He cowers on the floor in front of us, and the satisfaction is lacking. It's disappointing, actually.

The door opens behind me, and a slim, older man rushes into the stairwell. He takes one look at me, then Aiden, before finally eyeing the server on the floor.

"Mr. DeSantis." His throat bobs with his swallow. "I am so sorry for whatever Tim—"

"He insulted my fiancée," Aiden informs him.

"He'll be dealt with," the man assures us. His gaze darts to me and back to Aiden. "I'm the owner, and I promise—"

"I don't deal in promises," Aiden says. "He'll keep his fucking mouth shut."

And then Aiden reaches down and hauls the server—Tim, I guess—up by the front of his shirt. He grips Tim's jaw and angles the man's face toward me.

"Tell your boss what you wanted her to do to you," he says quietly.

"No fucking way," he yells. He glares at me, an ounce of confidence returning now that his boss has come to save him.

Funny. I don't think the man beside me has any interest in bailing his employee out of the hole he dug.

I slip the knife from my sheath and step forward, pressing it into Aiden's free hand. He grins and leans over, catching my lips in a brief, hot kiss.

He flips the knife in his hand and runs the tip of it down

Tim's throat. One nick will cut into his jugular—and that really would be a shame.

"I wanted her to suck my dick," the server yells. "Jesus, get that fucking thing away from me, you perverted son of a—"

Aiden grabs his tongue.

His fucking tongue.

And then he slices.

I stare at the piece of free flesh Aiden holds in his hand, and then the blood that immediately begins to gush out of the server's mouth. Down his chin, spilling onto his white shirt. Aiden makes a noise in the back of his throat and rips off the bottom of the server's shirt, balling it up and shoving it into his bloody mouth.

The server gags and covers his mouth, staggering toward the owner.

"Leave," the restaurant owner spits. "I will not have you stumbling through my place of business."

He wheels away, trailing blood. It gets everywhere, a trail of it speckling the stairs he races down. Eager to get away—no wonder.

Aiden drops the tip of the guy's tongue and grimaces.

"Overkill, much?" I mutter.

He shakes his head, rubbing his hands on his black pants. "When it comes to you? Never."

I find myself nodding, transfixed at the motion.

"You..." The owner shakes his head abruptly.

"We'll be finishing our meal," Aiden informs him curtly. "And I believe we'll be needing a new server."

"Right, yes. Of course."

Aiden takes my hand and leads me back inside. He motions for me to climb into the booth first, then slides in after me. He takes his cloth napkin and dunks it into one of the water glasses, then proceeds to thoroughly wipe each finger.

Then he turns to me, and his gaze softens. "This was supposed to be a good day."

Ah. He had wanted normal—more than I did, probably. His talk of how this *could be* our normal... it wasn't all for me. It was for him, too. When's the last time he was allowed to do anything for fun? Or spend the day not threatening people?

Still, I shake my head. "That line of thinking is ridiculous."

His lips quirk.

"It's just one moment." I check my phone. "Fifteen minutes of bad doesn't sour an entire day."

His nod is slower to follow, but then he fully commits to that idea. He grasps my hips and pulls me onto his lap again, pressing his lips to my cheek. And then... well, then he reaches around me and slices off a bite of the steak and brings the fork to my lips.

I open my mouth and accept it, watching him. He focuses on the way my jaw moves as I chew, the muscles in my throat when I swallow. He takes his own bite of steak, and it's my turn to study him.

"What else?" I ask once the plate is clean. "To complete your normal-ish day."

His eyes light up, and he easily maneuvers both of us out of the booth. Impressive, seeing as how booth benches seem designed to keep people in. He readjusts his grip, one arm under the back of my knees and the other across my shoulder blades. The patrons glance over at us, but at the end of the day? This is New York City, and no one gives a shit.

He doesn't release me until we're back in his car. He leans over me, standing in the doorway of the passenger seat, and clicks my seatbelt into place.

"Safety first," I murmur.

He winks.

We ride silently until we get on the highway that heads out of town toward Long Island.

"Dad had the house in Rose Hill, but Mom sometimes took Wilder and me out here," he says. "She had a family house..."

I straighten. "Wait. Is she still there?"

"I don't know." He frowns. "Dad wouldn't have let her just... stay in New York."

What had he said about her? That she just left. *Where did she go?* I had asked him. *Away*, he'd answered. He wouldn't have known—he was just a child when she abandoned them. I reach over and squeeze his arm.

A lump forms in my throat. I don't know how he does it. I miss my mother so acutely it sometimes feels like I'm being shredded from the inside. He doesn't have the closure of knowing she did everything she could to stay with them. Some violent illness didn't rip her away from him. She chose to leave, and that has to be agony.

"Will you show me?"

He nods once, flipping his blinker on and slowing to take the exit into the Hamptons. The land of the rich and famous. I've never been partial to it. The crowds and beaches and the general rich-kid vibe.

But suddenly we're in a residential neighborhood, the water in their backyards. These aren't the giant mansions—we're on the north side of the island, and the fancy ones are on the south side—but more modest homes. A lot of them have boats on trailers in their driveways. Trees block direct views from the streets, but the flashes I get are enough to give me an impression.

We coast to a stop in front of a light-yellow house. It has a lot of glass. Big windows that look out into the tree-covered yard, a boat trailer to the side of a one-car garage. The porch is small, providing just a little shelter for visitors before the owners presumably usher them into the house.

"This was hers?" I ask.

He nods. His face is pale, and he grips the steering wheel tightly with both hands. This isn't somewhere he wants to be, and my heart hurts for him. She could be close enough to see, or talk to, but he seems paralyzed.

My strong, Mafia hitman... stuck in fear that his mother might be in that house.

Before he can stop me, I unhook my seatbelt and hop out. He calls after me, but he doesn't leave the car. I jog up to the front door and ring the doorbell.

The tone echoes inside the house, but other than that... nothing.

I wait.

"Gemma," Aiden yells through the car window. "Come on."

I glance over my shoulder and flip him off. Anger might get him moving more than concern. Fear wouldn't do it. This is just a house, after all.

Someone moves on the other side of the door, their shadow barely visible through the frosted glass. Then it swings inward, and a young woman squints at me. I stare back, trying to decide if she's anything like Aiden. She's too young—closer to my age than a woman who should be his mother. Her dark hair is swept up on top of her head, and she wears a white crop top with overalls. One of the straps is undone. I imagine without the eye makeup, she'd look like a teenager.

"Can I help you?" she asks.

"Abigail?" I pull the name out of the recesses of my mind. I don't remember where I've heard it—and I certainly don't think Aiden mentioned it the few times he brought her up.

The name triggers something, though. Immediately, the expression wipes clean off the girl's face. She clenches the door harder, knuckles white. "No one by that name lives here anymore."

I nod slowly and step down onto the top stair. "Sorry. She used to, though?"

"I can't help you."

She closes the door firmly, and I stare for a moment. I have to shake it off, though, and stride quickly back to the truck. Aiden's glower is hot enough to decimate me on the spot, but I ignore it.

I feign that everything is fine, waving my hand in his direction. "Relax. It wasn't her."

"What did you say to her?" He swings us in a sharp one-eighty, flooring the acceleration.

"I just asked if she knew Abigail, and she said she didn't live there anymore." It isn't exactly a lie. Something bugs me about it, but I can't just admit that to Aiden, right? It seems off. More than just a girl living in his mother's old family house.

"She could've sold it," I say gently. "You had good memories there, as a kid?"

He lifts one shoulder. "Yeah. It was one of the few times Wilder wasn't a dick to me."

We cross a bridge, travel through the richer side of town—it's hard to miss how drastically the financial situation changes, because the homes triple in size and so do the properties. He turns onto a narrow lane that dead-ends into a sand dune.

I raise my eyebrows. "The beach?"

He grins. "Ever fucked in the ocean, baby?"

I pause, then slowly mirror his expression.

He reaches over and takes my holsters off, dropping them to the floor between my feet. Lust roars through me.

And we can't get out of the car fast enough.

CHAPTER 17

Aiden

S he strips and rushes into the water, leaving a trail of clothes behind her. I cast aside the heaviness that lingers from this morning and follow her. *This* is what I've been craving—time between the two of us. Our phones and my keys are in the car, and the beach is close to empty this time of day.

Most of the homeowners work in the city and won't get back til later in the evening—so for now, this stretch of sand is ours.

The waves crash against Gemma's legs, and she shrieks. Her arms pinwheel. I run toward her and scoop her up, moving forward through the water until we're past the break and it comes up to my waist. She clings to me, breathless, and kicks her feet a little bit in the surf. Another wave rolls by, drenching both of us.

"Aiden!" She laughs, tucking her face against my throat. "It's so much colder than I thought it was going to be."

"Have you never been in the Atlantic in the summer?" I readjust her so her legs can wind around my hips.

She shifts, aligning herself. I have to bite back my groan—

it's a special sort of torture to be in cold water when her hot body is pressed against me. I drop us lower, and her nails claw my back.

"I love you," I tell her. I don't bring up that she said it before she drifted off to sleep, and those words sporadically replay in my head.

She draws back and meets my gaze. Her hands slide up and cup the back of my neck. For a second, I think she might say it back. We're in a bubble all the way out here, far removed from any of our family bullshit. She's not a West and I'm not a DeSantis. There's no mystery hanging over our heads, no threats.

This is what I wanted out of today.

One of her hands moves down between us, and she grips my length through my soaked briefs. She only takes a second to navigate my fly, pushing the fabric out of the way. She shoves aside her panties and lines the head of my cock at her entrance. She's slick, even with the water swirling around us.

Gemma leans forward and catches my lips. Her kiss reminds me of home. Of comfort and happiness. It unfurls in my chest, and I clutch her closer. In one thrust, I slide all the way inside her. She gasps into my mouth, and I take the opening. My tongue skims her swollen lower lip, then dips to meet her tongue.

She tastes sweet. My cock pulses, and I'm torn between wanting to fuck her fast... or drive her wild.

"If surprise orgasms in public places lead to *this*," she begins. She doesn't even go far, and her lips brush mine as she speaks. "Then we're going to be dangerous together."

I grin and kiss the corner of her lips. Another wave hits us, higher this time, and I widen my stance. "Truth, princess?"

"Always."

"I've never brought anyone here. To the island. To this beach. I've never kissed a girl in the water—" Never fucked anyone here, either, but I can't seem to spit out the crass words. The last person I stood on this beach with was my mother, three days before she left.

She cups my jaw. "Thank you. Now... Please, fuck me."

I grin, her *please* doing something to me. I pull out and slam back inside, and her eyes roll back. She arches into me, mouth parted. I repeat the motion, slow and hard, and let my gaze drift down. Her blue bra is speckled with saltwater. Smooth stomach, down to her lace thong.

If I were to commission another painting of her, I'd want it to be of this moment. Her blonde hair darkened by the ocean, her cheeks pink. Hungry expression.

"I need you to go faster," she breathes.

"I like it when you say please, baby." A wicked thought overtakes me. "You're going home with me tonight... and you won't be coming until you beg for it. Until you're so filled with my cum that there'll be no erasing me."

I run my hands down her backside and grip her ass cheek. Her eyes widen when I slip my finger to her back hole, pressing in slightly. Her pussy clenches around me.

"Aiden."

"Maybe I'll take this hole, too," I muse. "And claim every last piece of you."

"You already have all of me," she whispers. She meets my thrusts and grinds her teeth. Still, she doesn't beg for release. Her eyes are dark, and she takes in all of me. I can't tell what she's thinking—if she's thinking anything.

"Yes, I do."

I quicken my pace, catching her hands when they try to go to her clit. She's panting with need and my balls tighten at the sight. I come inside her with a groan. Only when the haze recedes do I notice how tightly she's gripping my shoulders.

I stay inside her and stride out of the water, carrying her

wrapped around me until we reach the shore. I pull out of her gently and set her down.

Her glower would kill a lesser man. I chuck her under the chin and grin but don't say anything else. We adjust our underwear and head back to the car. I find a towel in the trunk and offer it to her first. She takes her time drying off, twisting her hair over her shoulder and squeezing out the extra water.

Maybe this isn't what she had in mind, but I want her to come home with me. If she had a reason to refuse... she might've taken it.

The sun is low in the sky by the time we get in the car and head back. Our underwear is in a pile on the towel at her feet, both of us opting to go without under our clothes. I tighten my grip on the wheel and ignore her bare legs pressed together. Her dress has ridden up high on her thighs.

Frustration leaks out of her, and if I focus on *that*, we won't make it very far.

My phone blips, and I glance down at it. My brother, telling me I need to deliver Colin to them. Dad is getting angry. Luca doesn't spell it out, but his anger is probably coming out on Amelie.

I grimace and shove it back in my pocket.

"I have to go home tomorrow," she says suddenly, twisting to peer at me. "There's some business that needs to be attended to."

I nod once. I should do more: search for Wilder, try to figure out who brought the shipment to Sean. The cops are probably floundering when it comes to that customs officer. They're working with half the puzzle, after all. And I'm not exactly inclined to share *my* knowledge... With any luck, the different precincts working on different cases will slow things down. Sean was in a different county than Rubert.

"Who do you think killed Rubert?"

My gaze flicks to her and back to the road. "Probably whoever hired him to steal the weapons."

"And that person would've had Rubert drop them at our old warehouse, trying to frame us, and then deliver them to Sean to get rid of them." She taps her lower lip. "And you don't think Wilder is involved."

I shake my head sharply. "No."

"Why not?"

"Because..." *Why not?* "He's never been that type. Dad had him keep his hands clean, for the most part. He was going into politics, and you know what the media does to candidates. Any deep dive had to be squeaky clean. He was friends with Sandra White... maybe more than friends with her. He threw cash around but never his body weight."

And I just can't picture him destroying our family from the inside out.

Gemma sighs. "They're framing my family. Again. Your dad wants us out of New York—and then he's going to bulldoze every West business. And you don't think Wilder was in on that?"

"I don't." I shake my head again and grit my teeth. "It's someone else."

"What, like Xavier Eldridge?" She laughs.

I freeze, slamming on the brakes. The car skids to a halt in the middle of the road—well enough that we're still on a residential street, although I'd probably have had the same reaction on the highway.

"Where did you hear that name?" I ask.

She watches me carefully, sucking her lower lip between her teeth. And she doesn't answer.

"Gemma. The Eldridges are gone."

She rolls her eyes. "I know."

"Xavier—" I press my lips together and stare harder, trying to read her mind. "Where did you meet him?"

"A long time ago," she says, and I'm pretty sure it's a pretty lie.

Yeah, she's not fucking climaxing tonight until she's screaming. And maybe then she'll learn that the truth will get her farther.

CHAPTER 18

Gemma

"P lease."

I hate that word. Hate that it's been the only one on my lips for the past hour.

Wicked, wicked man.

He raises his head from between my legs, running his finger down my inner thigh. "Did you say something, princess?"

I jerk on the cuffs holding my wrists. They're soft, padded leather, but still vicious. I've been periodically yanking, testing their strength, and failing. We've been in this position for the better part of an hour, but he stops every time I get to the edge.

Now he climbs over my body and easily thrusts inside me.

I groan at the fullness. His hand slides up between my breasts and covers my throat. He squeezes, cutting off my breath. I go completely still.

"I love your frustration," Aiden says, hovering just above me. "I love your fight. I love the flash of fear before you give in to me." He pumps in and out of me slowly, almost lazily. His gaze is anything but lazy, though.

This is punishment—and for some reason, when that clicks, it turns me on even more.

He circles his hips, and I roll mine forward to meet him. My lips part, but no words come out. I'd beg if I could. But then he's releasing my throat, and his thumb pushes past my lips.

"Do you taste yourself?"

I nod.

"Suck," he orders.

I shiver and do as he says. His eyelids flutter, and his strokes become harder. Faster. I bite the pad of his thumb, and he comes inside me.

Again.

My cunt clenches around him, and I let out a desperate noise. He retracts his thumb—and his cock—and leans back to kneel between my legs. His gaze goes to my center.

"I love this sight," he adds. And then his expression flips to contemplative. "It would be better, though…"

"How?" I ask. My voice is hoarse.

He smirks and stands, leaving me on his bed. I close my legs, rubbing my thighs together. My arms are out wide, so taut I couldn't even touch my face if I wanted.

Totally helpless.

I trust him, I remind myself.

He returns a moment later with my thigh holster—the one with the knife still attached to it. He hops back on the bed and straddles my waist.

I eye him. "What are you going to do?"

"Something I should've done weeks ago," he mutters. He takes hold of my arm, and his thumb coasts over my birth control implant.

My stomach swoops.

"Aiden, no."

"I prefer to leave things up to fate, don't you?"

"You can't—"

"Easy, baby," he says, and then he draws my blade.

Seems fitting that the knife will be the thing to betray me. My chest is full of buzzing bees.

"Your cunt is going to take all of my seed," he says softly. Hypnotizing. "We'll make wonderful little monsters together."

"Children," I correct. "You can't call them monsters."

"Baby, they're going to be part of me and part of you. They're definitely going to be terrors." He smiles.

I can't look away from what he's doing. He drags the knife tip up my arm, raising goosebumps in its wake. It trips over the slight bump of the implant.

"You like pain," he says. "You like to be under my spell. Being spanked, your ass plugged. Ask me to cut it out of you, and I'll let you come."

My whole body trembles. I'm not even twenty—certainly not old enough to be a mother. I press my lips together and stay silent, knowing it'll cost me. My fear is more lethal than Aiden, though.

He smiles, reaching behind him and finding my clit.

I'm too on edge. I arch my back, still pinned under his weight, and yank at the cuffs. "Aiden."

"Beg, baby."

He pulls away, and a ragged sigh leaves my lips.

"Please let me come." My voice is barely audible. "I need to come. I'll do anything—"

His eyes light up. "Anything."

Mistake, something in me whispers. Like giving the Devil free rein.

And he seems like the Devil now, dipping his fingers into me and smearing his cum over my clit. His thick cock stiffens, standing up from where it's laid on my belly.

Then the prick of pain on my arm—I almost ignore it. But

I watch the blood well, and he tosses the knife aside and digs his finger into my arm. It hurts. I open my mouth and scream, bucking against him. With deft fingers, he pulls the implant out and tosses it onto the sheets beside me.

He immediately moves lower, his knees roughly parting my legs. He lines himself up and thrusts inside me, flicking my clit harder.

"Come, Gemma," he demands.

And, god, I do. It crashes into me, over my head, drowning me. I cry out and try to twist away from him, but the pressure doesn't let up. He slams into me wildly, like his only goal is to split me in half.

He pinches my nipple, and I orgasm again. My vision flickers, and finally I sag back into the bed. His hips piston faster, and he comes again with a guttural yell. He leans forward and kisses my neck. Then his teeth. Tongue. Marking a spot highly visible—just under my ear.

I let him do it, my fight gone.

My head rolls to the side, and I eye the blood seeping from the cut on my arm.

Shock worms through my chest. He just....

"You're mine," he says, a split second before his teeth catch my earlobe. "Fuck everything else, Gemma. No one will take you away from me."

I close my eyes to protect myself from his gaze. Maybe he realizes how far he went, because he pulls out of me and undoes the cuffs. They open, dropping my arms back to my sides. My limbs are jelly, and I can't seem to bring them in. I'd love nothing more than to rock into the fetal position, but I'm stuck.

Trapped beneath him.

Turns out, he's more perceptive than I give him credit— he lifts each arm, one at a time, and presses a kiss to the inside of my wrists. He folds my arms over my stomach and moves me onto my side.

"You're angry." He's right in front of me, his face inches from mine. He's never liked my hiding—demonstrated from the first instance he had me in his apartment. There's no part of me he wants tucked away.

He *likes* those parts of me I'm ashamed of. That's probably the only reason I feel able to voice my fears.

I sniff. "I am not ready to have kids."

He shrugs. "We have time to prepare."

I glare up at him. "A month, if that, for the birth control to leave my system. I don't suppose you're going to wear a condom?"

He snorts. "Definitely not."

"I'll be pregnant within the year, with the amount of sex we have," I mutter.

Aiden surprises me by chuckling. His finger under my chin tips my head back, and his eyes bore into mine. "Fearless Gemma West. I'm not afraid of this. Why are you?"

"Because..." I shove at him, even though it does nothing. "People are trying to kill us. People will probably continue to try, at the very least. And what am I supposed to tell my family?"

He scoffs. "It's not their concern."

My mouth drops. "Right."

"Don't make me turn into a caveman," he warns. "Because I will. Just say the word, and I'll sweep you far away from here..." His gaze is contemplative. "I can see why Luca left with Amelie. This city is toxic."

Would I do that? Leave everything behind to just be... us?

Hope fills my chest.

And damn it if that isn't the scariest thing about this evening. Hope is dangerous.

Hope will kill me—I just know it.

"I have to go," I say.

He shakes his head and pries my arm away from my chest. His thumb presses into the cut, and I let out a hiss of breath. It's not deep—not truly. Not as bad as the road rash from our motorcycle accident, or the burn from Aunt Mary's house fire. Not as bad as the bruises around my throat from the man who tried to drown me.

"Brave people look at things they're afraid of and do them anyway," Aiden says. He holds me close, then rolls half on top of me. "You're the definition of brave sometimes, Gemma. Other times, though..."

I shudder. "I don't want to be brave all the time."

"You don't have to be. But running from those things never gets us anywhere."

I tuck my face into his neck and war with my emotions. My brain lags, the highs and lows of the day getting to me. I can't tell if he's talking about ruling my family, running away, or... something else.

Something better—or worse.

We lapse into silence, and I concede that I'm not leaving. Not anytime soon, anyway.

Later, we'll shower and eat dinner. We'll be as normal as we can be in this house. And then I'll... I'll go back to Brooklyn. I'll devise a plan to keep my brother safe, to find Wilder, to end Jameson's crazy schemes.

* * *

HIS PHONE RINGS, jarring us from our doze. He had flipped us at one point, draping me across his chest, and he had been idly drawing patterns on my back. Now he sits both of us up, hesitates, and then reaches for his cell.

Sam scrolls across the top of the screen.

I slip away, climbing out of bed and heading toward the bathroom. He can keep his DeSantis secrets. Sam is the one who gave up Colin, who has been holding Amelie hostage for Jameson. The video didn't just fall into Aiden's father's lap. I block out the low tones of Aiden's voice, grabbing for his toothbrush. And then I freeze.

There are two in the cup. The white and orange one is definitely his, but the other seems brand-new. And it's turquoise, of all colors. My color.

At least, the one he associates with me. Like the sheath of the dagger he gave me before our wedding, or the small gun. Matching.

It *is* one of my favorite colors.

Still, I shove away that warm feeling in the center of my chest and take care of business. When I emerge, wet hair braided, in Aiden's shirt, I'm alone. I step into his closet and freeze.

He has *my clothes*. The ones from the tower, from that shopping trip. They're hung in neat rows on one side of the spacious closet. Shoes are stacked in their own cubbies, ranging from replicas of the boots I favor, to sneakers, to high, strappy stilettos. I run my finger along the pearls beading the top of one strap and have an out-of-body experience.

My main question is *why?* But it's quickly replaced with *when?* When did he have time to do this? It's sending a loud message.

He wants me here.

Probably all the time, if he had his way.

I exchange his shirt for black ripped jeans and a white band t-shirt, laying them on top of the dresser as I continue to explore. There's a drawer full of jewelry. The pieces are laid out like a store display. Another drawer of my underwear—the type of bralettes I'm fond of, and lacy panties as well as some soft, less sexy ones. Always appreciated. No one wants to wear thongs all the time.

I could just never go home, and I think I'd have everything I need.

That thought snaps me out of my awe.

I hurry to dress, at the last minute fastening on a necklace and bracelet. They're both silver, with a single pearl in the center. The bracelet easily rolls around my wrist, and my cheeks flush when I remember what was around my wrists only a few hours ago.

Stop thinking about that.

Shaking it off, I hurry down the hallway. His voice in one of the rooms pulls me in like a magnet, and I push open the door. It's an office, big windows behind the giant desk, a fireplace, pictures on the wall of his family. A painting hangs over the mantel, and I pause.

He stands off to the side, phone to his ear and gaze distant.

But I only spare him a glance, because the painting seems... familiar. It's only when I'm directly in front of it that my heart leaps into my throat.

It's *me.*

My pulse races, and I press my hand over my chest. I suddenly can't breathe. He has a painting of me in his office. The artist, whoever they are, captured the color of my eyes, the shape of my jaw. It's so very much *me* that it's overwhelming.

I have the inexplicable urge to drag my knife down the canvas.

Aiden steps up behind me. His body heat is enough of a sensation that my awareness prickles. He tugs my braid, angling my head back, then slides his hand around my throat. He pulls me flush against him.

"Do you like it?" he asks.

Off the phone, then. His attention on me burns.

"No."

He squeezes my throat very gently—a warning. "Did the artist offend you? Should I bring him in here and slit his throat for his mistake?"

I close my eyes and fight the rush of adrenaline surging through me. Always addicted to danger. To pushing him as close to the edge as I can bear it—or maybe there is no bearing it. I just want to be shoved off the cliff. "You commissioned it. That was the offense."

He leans in. His breath hits my ear, raising goosebumps along my arms.

"I like pretty things. But I love seeing you squirm." He hums. "Maybe we can make this painting more enjoyable for you."

I try to shake my head, but his hand captures my jaw. He turns my face toward him, even as his other hand presses on my stomach. Then lower, across my pelvic bone. His lips descend on mine.

We've had so many different types of kisses. Hungry, rough, brutal, sweet.

This one gives me butterflies in my belly. I feel his promises in his lips, and the taste of his mouth. The... *caring*. The hope of a future. It's all translated in a moment, in the space between our hearts.

"I have to go," I whisper, pulling away slightly.

He nods once and releases me. "I'll drive you back."

My heart aches. It's the strangest sensation—especially with how I felt just moments ago, seeing the painting. I shove down my emotions and follow him to the garage.

He yanks away a sheet, revealing a new motorcycle. This one is black, standard. Nothing fancy—nothing to draw attention. Two black helmets, the visors tinted, hang from the handles. He places one over my head, tilting it back to carefully click the buckle under my chin.

The garage door rumbles open. He mounts the bike. This one is different than his last—we will both have to lean forward. The other was more upright.

He smirks. "This one is faster."

I clench my jaw. "Right. That'll make it easier to avoid the trucks out to hit us."

His smile drops, and he takes my hand. "I won't let you get hurt again, Gem. I promise you that."

I nod carefully, but I don't trust it. The scrapes have been slow to heal. The bruising is gone for the most part, and the pain has mostly disappeared. Those injuries have been the least of my concerns.

He holds out his arm, helping me balance to swing my leg over, and then I flip my visor down and wrap my arms around him. Like last time, he gives my hands a quick pat, then revs the engine and navigates us out onto the street.

Aiden is right about one thing: this bike is a *lot* faster. We hit the city in record time, and we're constantly leaning one way or another as he weaves us between cars. He rolls to a stop in front of my house.

I remove my helmet and cast a glance at the porch. I don't know who's in there, but I would bet someone is. Turner, maybe, or Marius. From gunning us down to trusting them with my life—what a drastic twist of fate. Not to mention *Marius* was the one to call Aiden.

Not me.

Aiden swings his leg over, but I hold out my hands. Actually, I shove my helmet into his arms and stall him for a moment.

I can barely make out the surprise behind his dark visor.

"I can see myself in," I say quietly. "If you get off this bike, you and I both know you wouldn't leave."

He cups my cheek. He won't taking off his helmet—*just in case*. His thumb brushes my lower lip, and heat flares through my body. It zips straight between my legs, and I bite back a sigh. He unzips his jacket pocket and hands me two neatly presented items: my knife and gun, the straps of the thigh holsters wrapped around them.

"I can't believe I almost forgot these." I hold them into my stomach.

He chucks under my chin, a quick little tap, and I smile.

Then he nods and knocks the kickstand back up, rolling forward. He secures my helmet behind him, then takes off. I stand on the sidewalk until the roar of his motor is just an echo in my ears, and then I head inside.

The lights are on downstairs, but there are more people than I thought in my house. It's not even seven o'clock, but Turner and Marius both occupy the kitchen, one of Xavier's men stands by the window next to the front door, and my brother lounges on the couch.

Immediately, my shoulders hike up.

"Enjoying your day, Gem?" Colin asks.

I scowl, casting one final look back toward the street before I close the door. Did they see Aiden drop me off?

"You're supposed to be in Manhattan," I say pointedly.

He sighs. "Aunt Mary wanted to see you—but you were *out*."

I glance at Marius. He briefly meets my eyes, then away. It looks like he's half-heartedly chopping vegetables on a cutting board. Turner mixes a drink behind him. But it would appear that he didn't give up my secrets.

Aunt Mary comes out of the pantry with an armful of supplies. She spots me and grins. "Ah, Gemma, you're back. Get cleaned up, dinner will be ready soon."

I nod. Xavier's guy, one of the ones who may or may not

have shot Aiden—none of them admit to pulling the trigger, probably to avoid my wrath—snags my arm.

My narrowed gaze goes from his face to his hand.

He drops it, frowning sheepishly.

"Spit it out, Wes," I snap.

He shakes his head once and steps back, pressing his back to the wall. Maybe he was about to ask whose bike I climbed off of—and maybe he realized it's none of his damn business.

Or maybe he knows and just wanted the confirmation.

He's not getting that. Xavier wants to kill Jameson—I don't want to think about what he would do with the knowledge that Aiden and I are... close.

I spin the ring on my finger and storm away. Upstairs.

Colin shouldn't be here. Worry tugs at me, and I kick off my boots in my room. I drop the two weapons on my bed and consider changing, then think better of it.

Someone knocks on my door.

"Come in," I call.

It creaks a bit as it swings inward, and Colin steps into the room. He glances around, stuffing his hands in his pockets. His attention trips over the gun and knife, and his brows lower.

"Where—"

"Dad gave me the knife," I say. I sit on the edge and pat the space beside me.

He comes over and flops down, but he leaves a lot of space between us. Almost two feet.

I hand him the blade. "It's had a baptism in blood," I say. "I know you might think I'm not up for the challenge of leading this family, but I can. I will."

My younger brother sighs. "I don't *doubt* you, it's just... do you want it?"

I meet his gaze. "What do you mean?"

"I think Dad changed his mind after I tried to rescue you

from the mall. He was absolutely livid—and losing Kai nearly killed me. I can't believe I was so stupid, because I thought you needed rescuing. Dad just wanted me to see you as another soldier." He picks up the firearm, checking it over. "You weren't raised like that."

I choke on my laugh. "Colin. Seriously?"

He shrugs, eyes down. "You were off playing with charcoal while I was sitting in on meetings."

It's not a surprise that he thinks that. I never told him any differently. He didn't know I spent most of my childhood learning how to eavesdrop. To pick up on things said and unsaid. I learned from the shadows.

"I fought for every bit of knowledge I could absorb," I admit. "I wanted to be part of the business so badly. It was Mom who tried to keep me away."

He flattens his lips, no doubt wondering the same thing I did: if her death changed everything.

If she was still alive, would we be in this mess?

Colin shakes his head and removes something from his pocket. A phone. *My* phone, one that was forgotten in Marius's truck this morning.

"Where'd you find that?" I ask.

He frowns. "You left it here."

"Ah." I tuck it behind me.

"Gemma! Colin!" Aunt Mary yells from the bottom of the stairs.

"Dinner," we say at the same time. We share a smile, then rise. But before we rejoin the group downstairs, I stop him.

"Are you doing okay?" I ask. "With Kai and Dad, and then this whole shift in the family…"

He surprises me by stepping into my personal space, quickly throwing his arms around my shoulders. He pulls me tight and waits.

It takes a long second for me to hug him back.

In my ear, his voice is barely audible. "Do you remember what I told you at the mall? That you don't get to issue orders. And I keep thinking how stupid I was, charging into the DeSantis trap. Kai knew it was a trap, but he was willing to follow my lead. It's my fault he's dead."

I grip his back tightly, but I don't have words to comfort him. There's no comfort for the loss of a life—especially one stolen from us too soon. Tears burn behind my eyes. I blink rapidly. We've had too much sadness recently.

"I wish I could've been at his memorial," I say to Colin. "I miss his smiling face."

He nods into my neck. "It was sad. A bunch of men standing around trying not to cry. Even Dad was quiet." He pulls back and searches my face. "Bringing back Aunt Mary was a good idea. She's a steady presence, and a lot of us need that right now. We're heathens without the women."

I touch his shoulder. "We'll bring them all back."

Part of me wants to tell him Jameson's plan—or what we think it is, anyway. That he is hunting for Colin to extract a confession. It's so much bigger than just one life, or one death. If he wanted, he could do the exact same thing to me. Force a confession. Kick our family out—or just stomp us out, like he did to the Eldridge family.

"You okay?" he asks.

"Gemma!" Aunt Mary yells. "Colin! *Now*, please."

"Just like old times," I mutter. I loop my arm through his. The smell of lasagna has saturated the air downstairs. My mouth immediately waters—and then my chest tightens. Aiden was going to teach me how to make *pasta*, of all things, because I never learned. We had a chef, and before that, my mother.

Now, nothing.

"We were having a moment," Colin says in the kitchen. He releases me to kiss our aunt's cheek.

She shakes her head, but she can't hide her smile. "Well, next time do it when there isn't hot food on the table."

"Yes, ma'am."

I pause in the dining room. I've avoided eating here, preferring to take my meals at Dad's desk in the office of West Bar, or curled up on the couch. Sometimes just shoveling leftovers in my mouth straight from the fridge.

And it strikes me that I don't know where to sit.

Turner and Marius join us at the table, each taking a chair on the long side. They're diagonal from each other. I spot Wes through the doorway, but he remains by the front door. I motion for him, but he shakes his head. He keeps checking the window, as if something is going to be coming for us.

And who knows—maybe someone *is* coming. Anyone could've seen Colin show up, or in transit. He's the one with the bounty on his head, after all.

Aunt Mary sweeps in and sits beside Marius. Colin takes the chair next to Turner.

Anxiety moves like snakes in my stomach, leaving me with the choice of either Mom's chair, closest to the door, or Dad's at the head.

Either one feels like an ill-fitting dress.

Gritting my teeth, I slip past Aunt Mary and Marius, taking Dad's regular chair. The scrape of it against the wood echoes in my ears. I try to breathe through it.

Turner takes our plates and loads them with lasagna, salad, and garlic bread. Once everyone has been served, we clasp hands and say a quick prayer. I can't remember the last time we did that, either. It isn't like we're particularly religious— not me, anyway. Aunt Mary fully leans into it, closing her eyes and saying the words with confidence.

The fact that Turner and Marius are joining us isn't a surprise. In the past, when Dad would sit at the head of the table, whoever would turn up would be fed. Sometimes it was

Aunt Mary and Kai, other times Aunt Margaret and her husband—before his incarceration, that is. Other men who were preparing for upcoming jobs and wished to discuss it with Dad...

Ah.

I lift my chin, and my gaze settles on Marius.

Tomorrow, our shipment arrives at the train station. *That* must be why they're both here.

Tradition.

"You're coming with us," Marius says without preamble, without looking up from his plate. "So we figured we'd go through what's expected."

I grip my fork. "Expected."

"Of the night," he says easily.

Colin straightens. "Can I come?"

"No," Aunt Mary and I say.

He scowls.

I lean forward, bracing my elbows on the table. "You have a *bounty* on your head. I won't risk you."

He grumbles but falls silent.

"Okay," I say to Marius, cutting my lasagna. "What's expected?"

"Turner and I each drive a vehicle. You'll be riding with one of us. Benny has the eighteen-wheeler, which the yard will load for him. We need the key to check that everything is accounted for, then we haul it back. Easy in, easy out."

I hum. The train yard is about an hour away. "You don't think we'll be intercepted? Our route isn't a secret, I'm assuming."

Turner lifts one shoulder. "We prepare for it, but the arrival time is what we keep a lid on—that, and there are a few ways into New York from the yard. I'm not saying it'll be easy, not like this dick—" His eyes shoot to Aunt Mary. "Sorry, ma'am, not like this buffoon. Don't get me wrong. Sometimes it's easy, but with what we're dealing with... don't count on it. He's probably jinxed us."

Great.

"Well, let's hope it doesn't come to that." I'm done talking about it—what will happen, will happen.

I dig into my meal.

CHAPTER 19

Gemma

I take my time getting ready. Hair pulled back in two braids, black t-shirt, a leather jacket. I've traded out my gun's thigh holster for one that clips onto my belt, pressing between my skin and waistband of my black jeans.

I dig through my bag—one I can't quite remember bringing home with me, so I'm not sure if it was returned by Aiden's stealth or Marius—and retrieve the set of keys I kept from my father's safe. I zip them into my pocket and take a deep breath, pocket my phone, and head downstairs.

Aunt Mary and Colin should be safe, tucked away in Manhattan. Wes and one of Xavier's other men are watching. Xavier himself waits for me at the foot of the stairs.

"Planning something wicked?" he asks, nodding to the visible grip peeking out of my jeans. I pull my shirt over it and shake my head.

Still, my knife is strapped to my thigh over my jeans—that sends a message of its own.

"Blue is your color," he offers. "Do you need assistance?"

I narrow my eyes. "No, we've got it covered. Maybe you should go hang out at one of our bars. Take a night off."

He smirks. "A night off? Then I wouldn't get to antagonize you."

Ugh. He's got the antagonize part down. I push past him and grab my boots.

"Cole and Boston intercepted an attack on the Plymouth Street club," he says to my back.

I stiffen, but I don't turn around. This is why I'm keeping them around, right? To do exactly that. "Really."

"They wanted to burn the place down." He steps closer. "When are you planning to go on the offensive, Gemma? Surely you know we can't just... exist like this."

I let out a frustrated noise and face him. He's *much* closer —like, in my space, less than a foot away. I crane my head back and meet his blue eyes.

"Things are changing. I'm trying to get my footing—"

"Trying and failing, princess," he says softly.

I punch him, more surprised than anything when my hit lands. Pain explodes across my knuckles, but I ignore it. He stumbles away from me and raises his hand to his cheek. He doesn't glare, or yell, or... anything I would've guessed.

He laughs.

"Don't ever call me that," I tell him. My voice shakes.

"Someone should teach you how to punch." He steps forward again, unafraid, and snags my hand. His thumb brushes over my aching knuckles. "It wasn't bad—quick, with a good amount of power. But you shouldn't be aiming for the face."

I narrow my eyes. "Where, then?"

He curls my fingers back into a fist and lifts it to his throat. "Here, if you're fast. A quick jab to their windpipe will cut off their air." He moves my hand higher, manipulating it until it's flat. "An upward motion on the nose... that one can be deadly if you time it right."

I ignore the skittering feeling under my skin and step away.

"Both hands, cupped, slammed over the ears at the same time," he continues like I didn't just retreat.

Because I'm still listening, absorbing this valuable information.

"This knife?" He taps the hilt. "Eyes. Arms. Stomach, if you have a good angle and can get deep. Arteries. But what happens when the knife is ripped from your delicate little hand? What happens when the gun runs out of ammunition?"

"I'll be fine," I say tightly.

He sighs. "It isn't about being *fine*, Gemma West. It's about staying alive."

He... right. I hate that he's right. I am seriously out of my depth with *all* of this, but I know one thing: I can't rely on guards for the rest of my life. Right now, it's too little, too late. I'll be heading into this mission unprepared. I'll go to the gala and hope things move in our favor.

"Are you all set for Saturday?"

The fire in his eyes flickers and dies. He steps back, smoothing down the front of his shirt, and coldness creeps back into his features. I almost miss the fire—but then I don't, because *Aiden*. I can deal with cold Xavier.

"We're prepared to extract Amelie," he says. "But—"

"And Luca."

He rolls his eyes. "Yeah, that one, too."

"But?" I prompt.

Xavier hesitates. "Well, there's—"

The doorbell rings.

I jump.

No one rings the stupid bell.

In a smooth motion, Xavier rotates us so he's between me and the door. Then he pulls his gun and stalks forward. He yanks the door open, weapon rising, then immediately lowers it again.

"No one uses the bell," he tells our new arrival.

Turner.

He shrugs. "Saw you two chatting through the glass. Didn't want to interrupt."

My cheeks flame. "Nothing was happening," I mutter. "Ready to go?"

Xavier's gaze follows me out the door. I spot my car a few parking spots down, looking the same as when I parked it. Safe, in other words. Turner has a similar truck to Marius's, the only difference is the color. I hop up into the passenger seat of the black vehicle and fasten my seatbelt.

"You trust that kid?" Turner asks.

I glance back toward my house, where Xavier is still standing in the doorway.

"Eh, I'm not sure I trust anyone these days."

He laughs. "Smart."

"These are the keys, right?" I ask, holding them up.

He flips through them and then nods. "Yep. Sit back and relax, we'll be there in an hour."

We lapse into silence, the miles flying by. I chew on the mysteries that have been eating at me for the better part of the day, but nothing becomes apparent. My thoughts turn to Amelie. I don't know if I'd be able to bear the thought of her suffering.

But Wilder... if he's alive, then her suffering will be cemented either way. He put her through hell—literally faked his death to get out of that marriage—and cast her aside. The move almost condemned her family.

I shudder. If Luca hadn't been willing, Amelie easily could've been tied to Aiden.

And then where would I be?

"Here," Turner finally says. We turn off the highway, sail down a mostly deserted road, and coast into a bustling rail yard.

It isn't like a regular train station for passengers. There are countless tracks laid out parallel to each other, plus a few that cut diagonally across the lot. We pull up to a white guard stand.

Turner raises his eyebrows at the man, who just looks at the truck, then him, and bobs his head. The former glances back at me and grins.

"Track seventeen," the guard says. He checks a paper. "Should be arriving in ten minutes."

"Thanks, man." Turner hands him a wad of cash, then hits the accelerator. We bump over slightly raised tracks until we get to the correct, empty lane. There's a semi-truck idling with its lights off, and a white truck in front of it. We stop next to Marius's vehicle, so the two drivers' windows are next to each other.

"You made it," Marius says. He cranes his neck to see me. "Sup, little West. Having fun yet?"

I laugh. "I'm waiting for the excitement."

He motions for me to hop out. I meet him in front of Turner's truck, and his swift gaze appraises me. "Nice getup," he finally says. "Quite badass, if you don't mind me saying."

"Thanks."

He tips his head, and we go to the semi. "This is Benny. You met him before?"

Not a cousin—our family leans toward the smaller side—but someone brought into the family when he needed a job. I do remember him, vaguely. He's older. Bald. A cigarette hangs between his lips, and he leans halfway out his window to wave hello.

"You've grown up," he says to me.

I incline my chin.

He was at the West Bar for my father's memorial. Unless he was blackout drunk, he probably recalls the way I stood next to my brother on the bar and promised vengeance. *Smart* vengeance—that I haven't put into practice yet.

I've been too afraid to act with Amelie hostage.

How could I, when Jameson *knows* she's my friend? He'd take it out on her. It's the same reason Aiden warned me to stay away from Luca—because his love for her trumps any sort of loyalty to me. Or his brother.

I understand it.

I turn to Marius. "We need to stop hiding."

His eyebrows hike up. "Yeah?"

My attention wanders around us and finally settles on Benny. "Do trucks usually haul in their shipments from the shipyard?"

"The DeSantises? Yeah, they probably have one on hand." He takes in my expression and grins. "What do you need?"

"I want their schedule—and I want it hit. *Hard*. It is construction season, after all." If we're being blamed for the first theft, we may as well actually steal something.

Even if it goes against the truce.

But that's the thing: they need proof.

The only thing Jameson has is circumstantial, planted evidence. Conspiracies.

"Sandra White," I muse, more to myself than anyone else. "She's in Jameson's pocket?"

Benny grunts. "She's in his pants, more like."

That's a visual I don't need. I'll meet her on Saturday night—she's announcing her candidacy for governor, after all. The whole room's eyes will be on her... and that will make it dangerous enough to approach her, even for a moment.

A low horn blows in the distance, and Turner yells, "Come on, Gemma. Back in the truck."

"Back to safety," Marius says. He winks and nudges my arm.

I climb back in and mull over this new angle. Was it only a

few weeks ago that I read the article about the councilwoman? Construction, new bills, and now she's leaving all that behind for more power.

We move the vehicles closer to the huge crane hovering over the rail yard. Benny parks in position, seeming in line with a few other trucks, and hops out just as the rumble of the train reaches us. Another minute later, the headlight blazes through. It blows the horn again, entering the yard, and rumbles past us. It's louder than I would've thought, and longer, too. So many cars.

It slows, and Turner points to a black one. Unlike some of the others, it's free of graffiti. The train has barely stopped when the crane swings over and connects to our container. Benny comes back and taps my window.

I roll it down.

"Paper greases the wheels," he says with a chuckle. "Otherwise we'd be here all night like those schmucks."

I follow his gesture to farther up the line, where more trucks wait.

"Cool," I murmur. "This is how it normally goes?"

He shrugs. "Extra smooth since the boss is here."

I glance around, then realize he means *me*. He laughs louder and hops away, back into his truck's cab. The crane has secured its attachment to our container on the train and lifts it carefully. It hovers, moving sideways, until it hovers over the bed of Benny's eighteen-wheeler. The operator lowers it with a practiced eye.

"How long does it usually take?"

Turner shrugs, drumming the steering wheel. "An hour, sometimes longer. Depends who's working and if they accept bribes."

"Ah."

Finally, Turner nods. "Okay, let's go."

I follow him to the back of Benny's newly loaded truck,

where he and Marius stand. There's a lock on the container door.

"You have the keys?" Marius asks.

I nod and hand him the set from my pocket. He flips to one and inserts it into the lock, then removes it entirely. He hands both to me—the lock and key set, still connected—and swings the door open. He disappears inside, but I'm too busy staring at the lock in my hand.

"Turner," I call.

He glances over from the opening. "Yeah."

"How normal is it for the shipping container to be locked?"

"Rare, unless you're in the business of illegal smuggling. Even then, a few workers will have bump keys to get into the locked ones." A bump key—a master key with the teeth filed down. It would open almost anything it could fit into.

I nod slowly. "So... like the DeSantises?"

He gives me a weird look. "Sure, they probably have their own locks on the containers coming over, just to prevent theft. But these things are easy to cut off if you know they're there."

"Got it."

"Everything's good, boss," Marius calls, jumping down. "Looks untouched."

"What is it?"

"Coke." He grins. "We'll bring it to one of our warehouses to be cut and then dispersed to the clubs."

Easier to sell to people who already have a party on their minds... and the regular junkies who come seeking a fix. That's what I tell myself, anyway. The downside to our business: it can harm people.

But money is money, and this is just another avenue we exploit. Giving people what they want.

Marius slams the door, sliding the manual lock. Though he takes the padlock back, he doesn't reattach it. I guess it would be pointless—if we're intercepted at this point, it would be on purpose.

"Ready?" Benny asks us.

We all nod and go back to our trucks. Marius takes the lead, and we hang back while Benny turns the giant eighteen-wheeler. We follow and hang back until we get on the highway. My nerves are on high alert, and I sense Turner's are, too. He scans the road ahead of us, occasionally switching lanes to check ahead.

The DeSantises had a key to their own shipping container, just like my father had a key for ours. That thought pops back into my head, unbidden, but I go with it. There were three people who had the DeSantis container's key: someone in their family, their harbor master, and the customs officer.

See? It pays to be a practiced eavesdropper.

The customs officer was killed, but his keys weren't taken. Personally, I assumed that Rubert and his band of idiots just returned the keys to the man's pocket after they'd used them. It would've been a way to cover their tracks.

Rubert didn't tell us everything we needed to know. He admitted to killing Jimmy, the customs officer, and he admitted to stealing the shipment for whoever was paying him. But what he failed to say was *how* he got into the shipping container.

Because we assumed that's why they killed him.

But we were wrong.

They *had* keys—the DeSantis set.

My stomach revolts.

Jameson wouldn't be caught dead near the shipyard—in fact, I'm pretty sure he's been driving Aiden to find the thief for weeks.

And Luca has been out of the country.

But Wilder...

"Shit," I mutter.

My phone rings before Turner can question me.

I hit *accept* and snap, "What?"

"You need to get to West Bar right now," Xavier says. "I—"

"We're almost an hour away. What's so important?"

He pauses. Sirens echo in the background, and my heart lurches.

"I'm so sorry, Gemma, but West Bar... it's on fire."

CHAPTER 20

Aiden

M y bike skids to a halt, and I flip my visor up just to make sure I'm actually seeing this. Gemma's family bar is glowing from within, flames licking at the windows. Two firetrucks block the road, firefighters rushing around to hook up hoses and assess the area.

Patrons stand on the sidewalk across the street, seeming off-kilter. A few of them point to something, and I follow their fingers. Just visible from this angle is white paint on the wall beside the front entrance of the bar. I can't read it from here, though.

I clench my jaw. Gemma's dad's office was in there, on the second floor. It'll remain to be seen what kind of damage is sustained. Just as I think that, glass shatters from the second floor. Black smoke pours out, hiding the flicker of flames within.

The firefighters get to work, but it seems too little too late —the building is old. It's been in their family for decades.

I can't seem to turn away from the tragedy of it, though. The tracker shows that Gemma's car is still in front of her house, although I doubt she's there. The whole place was dark when I drove by a few minutes ago.

But she's not here, either.

I flip my kickstand down, venturing closer.

The writing becomes legible the closer I get. I slip between patrons. They don't notice the man wearing the motorcycle helmet winding between them—all the better. My eyes and nose are visible with the visor flipped up, but I'd prefer not to be recognized right now.

Where are you, Colin?

I stare at the question. The white paint was left to linger in a few places, and it streaks down the brick. A sick feeling roots in my chest, the singular thought that this handwriting is familiar.

My gaze lifts, and I take in the buildings around us. Where would I sit and wait? In one of the apartments? On a rooftop? Something with multiple escape routes...

A fire escape. Ironic, really. I step back into the shadows and make my way to the next alley. There's a little extra darkness well above me, on the metal grating. A person doing their best to blend in. I squint, trying to see and failing.

If I climb straight up, I'll be spotted.

I leave the alley and go around the back of the building. It has another entrance back here, locked except for residents. I turn away and throw my elbow back, shattering the glass. I carefully reach in and open it, stepping over the glass. Picking it might've been neater, but... I'm in a hurry. And the sudden spurt of violence feels good.

Ah, that's it.

It isn't my bar that's burning, but I'm furious for Gemma. For her loss.

And because I know exactly who's sitting on the fire escape, hoping to catch her brother.

I'd bet anything that Colin is locked up tight somewhere,

the threat of that fucking bounty keeping him in place. Dead or alive. Dad had to know that would entice almost everyone in the city to look out for him. That's exactly the point. The amount of money on the line, too, will put every miserable fuck on the hunt.

And why not? The future of New York City depends on this plan of his.

For a second, I contemplate that.

The whole thing rests on this *plan*—a sham, a deception. Like an illusion, it only takes one flaw to bring the whole trick into focus. Dad is smarter than this. He won't just have one card up his sleeve. He'll have several.

The fact that neither Gemma nor I have contemplated that before now worries me.

What else is there?

I finally reach the third floor, quickly checking the doors. It's a tiny building—there's only two apartments on each side. The first one is locked, but the second opens rather easily. This apartment is empty—not even furnished.

No one to walk in on him, I suppose. I creep in and set my helmet down. I check all the shadowy corners, then spot the cracked window.

I return to the front door and lock it, the scrape reverberating in my ears.

Then I go to the window, keeping out of sight.

One chance to get him off guard.

I thrust the window up and lean most of the way out, grabbing an arm, the back of the neck. I pull quickly, and he falls toward me. Off balance, his shoulder hits the windowsill, then he crashes to the floor.

His gun falls out of his waistband, and I kick it away.

I don't need to be fucking shot for this. He scrambles for it.

"Luca!" I yell in his face, slamming his shoulders back to

the floor. I'm tempted to punch his face in, but I resist. Even as he throws me off him.

I hit the floor hard, but it doesn't deter me. I grunt, yanking at his ankle. Fucker isn't going to shoot me—or Colin. Or Gemma.

Whoever fucking shows up to watch their bar turn to ash.

"Let—me—go!" Luca grits out. He kicks at me, his heel catching my jaw.

Pain lances through me, and my grip loosens. That fucking *hurt*.

"What's your plan?" Now I do rise, haphazardly, and punch him across his fucking face. I hope I break his nose.

He touches his lip and spits blood, facing me. "I'm trying to keep my girl alive."

I shake my head. "I'm trying to save *mine*."

He inclines his chin. "That's where we're at odds, then."

"Fuck off." I rush him, grabbing the front of his shirt, and we crash into the wall. At odds, my ass. "You're a coward to give in."

He hits me in the stomach. We trade a few more blows, until he spins us and my head cracks back. "I'm not a coward."

He batters me with hits, and it's all I can do to raise my arms and block my face.

"You already killed her cousin—what's one more West, huh?"

I growl and bring my knee up. Low blow—literally.

His breath leaves him in a sharp exhale, and he doubles over. I slam my elbow down on his back, and he collapses.

I press my knee between his shoulder blades, keeping him pinned to the floor.

"What would you have done if it was Gemma that showed up?" I lean down.

"I would've put her in my trunk and taken her to our father." His laugh sounds unhinged. "If he said to put a bullet in her or Amelie dies, I'd do it. I will do whatever I have to in order to keep her safe—*you* taught me that."

Shit. And I can't even throw family in his face, because Amelie *is* his family. Hard-won family, but obviously she's the kind of girl he'd die for. I won't lie—I'm contemplating shooting him in the shoulder just because.

"You can't have Gemma," I say.

He nods, his cheek scraping the floor. "I know."

"You can't have her fucking brother, either."

He goes silent. "Then we're all dead."

I rise suddenly. There's a window that faces the street, and the glow of flames reaches us. I stride toward it and watch as the roof of West Bar collapses inward.

Luca joins me, but his gaze isn't on the fire—it's on the street.

"He won't show," I tell him.

My brother shrugs. We're alike in too many ways—stubborn, possessive, smart. He knows there's a chance Colin will arrive on scene.

I shake my head.

"Are you staying, then? To try and stop me if he does?"

"I am."

He grimaces. "Fine."

"Fine," I repeat. I swipe my hand over my jaw. Now that we've stopped, I realize how much we messed each other up. His lip is bleeding, and a red mark on his cheek will probably turn into a bruise. My ribs ache, my jaw pulses.

And across the street, the firefighters are losing the battle with the flames.

"I can't believe you kneed me in the balls," he eventually says.

I laugh. I can't help it. "Desperate times."

He glances at me. "Sorry."

"Me, too." I sigh. "The writing was dramatic."

"I wanted them to know why. Closure."

Or a call to act.

The fire eventually dies. The billowing smoke slows into a trickle. It's a terrible, beautiful sight. The crowd has dispersed, but a new vehicle arrives on the scene. I lean forward, almost touching the glass, as a man walks across the street toward the black truck. He pulls open the passenger door.

My lungs seize.

Gemma lets the man take her hand and help her down, and she turns to West Bar.

Her devastation echoes from here.

No—that's her scream.

"Who is that?" Luca asks me. He doesn't make a move— probably because Turner joins her and the other man around the truck. The three of them watch the firefighters clean up, and one of them breaks away to talk to them.

"No idea."

"A cousin," Luca guesses.

I suppress my growl. If he's not blood relation, he's going to lose his hand for touching her. More than anything, I want to go down there and put my arm around her. Be her source of comfort on what might be the worst night of her life.

Luca stops me, though. Not physically—the bastard doesn't so much as glance at me. But there's some inane part of me that knows if I leave him alone tonight, he'll get into trouble. He'll look for Colin—and he might find him.

I don't know when I twisted from hunting Colin to wanting to protect the little bastard.

So instead of going out to find Gemma, I follow Luca out the back door. I grab my helmet. I can come back for my parked bike later. For now, I slide into the passenger seat of Luca's vehicle. It smells vaguely of gasoline, and I spot a red can when I peek into his backseat.

"Basic," I mutter.

He shrugs. "Got the job done."

"Their livelihood was based in that building."

He doesn't seem remorseful, and I shove that aside. Three months ago, I wouldn't have given a shit, either.

He doesn't have skin in *their* game.

"Why did Gemma show up and not Colin?" he asks me. "Is he delegating to his sister?"

Delegating—because he believes what the rumors have told him: that Colin inherited everything. I wonder when that lie is going to burst.

I shrug. "Not sure."

He grunts. "Fine. And I'm sure you're not going to let me scour the city..."

"Right."

Luca scowls and rubs his eyes. "What, then?"

I grin. "I've got an idea."

CHAPTER 21

Gemma

I rub a bit of loose charcoal powder between my thumb and index finger. My eyeshadow is bringing back flashes of the last day and a half. It was all-hands-on-deck, minus Colin, to clean up West Bar. The fire department released the building back to us after the scene was released and the arson investigator had passed through. Then our insurance company.

The media was present, too, trying to get a story.

We scrubbed over the paint that demanded to know where Colin was. I stared at those words, and even now I can see them when I close my eyes. *Where are you, Colin?* How many times had I wondered that exact thing while waiting for Aiden in Aunt Mary's house? Hoping that he got away.

What didn't burn—and there wasn't much—was completely waterlogged. There were some taped-off sections of unstable floor or walls. But daylight filtered in through the hole in the roof, and together my family cleared out the rubbish.

A construction company, one *not* affiliated with the DeSantises, will start repairs on Monday.

There was an article in today's paper about the tragedy of Thursday night, how West Bar wasn't up to code. Luckily, no one was hurt. The bar had just shut down, the closing server and bartender exiting shortly before it began. Empty.

If I hadn't been on that delivery, I might've been there, at my desk. My skin crawls. I don't know *who* did it, exactly, but the DeSantises are behind it. One of Jameson's lackeys, I assume. Some faceless man I'll never have the pleasure of sticking my knife into.

"Gemma," my aunt says, coming into my bedroom. "You look stunning."

I smile and smooth down the front of my dress. It was delivered yesterday while I was out, and I found it hanging on my bathroom door when I returned. It still fits like a glove.

It still reminds me of what happened when I put it on the first time.

I try to will away my goosebumps.

She pivots me, pushing my curled hair forward, over my shoulders. The emerald earrings peek out. Gold choker necklace, gold bracelet. I kept on the ring, even though it doesn't *really* go—the silver clashes, but I don't care. I won't remove it.

"Heels?" she asks.

I point to my bed, where the gold, strappy stilettos rest. Aunt Mary grins, tucking her hair behind her ear. She grabs one and motions for me to give her my foot. I feel a bit like Cinderella. I brace my palm on the wall for balance, and her warm, calloused hand grips my ankle. She carefully slides the shoe on, then buckles it. We repeat for the other foot, and I'm suddenly four inches taller.

"You picked a gorgeous dress."

"Thank you," I whisper.

"Aiden is waiting downstairs," she informs me.

My spine snaps straighter. "What? I didn't hear—"

"Turner intercepted him before he could ring the bell."
She chuckles. "You two will be the stars of the night."

"It's for charity," I say. "And the councilwoman."

"Right." Aunt Mary turns her nose up. "That woman
doesn't deserve support. She's hijacking a charity gala—for
children—to announce that she's running for governor."

Word travels fast, apparently. New York City is full of
gossips.

"I'll tell him you'll be down soon."

And then she leaves me alone. I cast a glance at the soot-
covered box in front of my closet. We were able to recover
Dad's safe, of all things, but I haven't had the nerve to open it.
The journal was in there, along with his gun, and other
precious items. I don't know what would be more awful: the
journal being partially destroyed, or fully. Everything in the
box might've incinerated.

Or... it could be unscathed.

Fear holds me back.

I smooth on light-pink lipstick and press my lips together.
Sudden nerves rack through me. I haven't seen Aiden since he
dropped me off at my house on Wednesday night. Three long
days have passed.

To be fair, the Wests have been keeping him busy.

I take a deep breath, double-checking that my phone is
inside my gold clutch, and go downstairs.

Aiden wheels around at the sound of my footsteps. My
breath catches in my throat. He's in all black—his signature
color. Pants, suit jacket, collared shirt. There's an emerald-
green pop of fabric tucked into his breast pocket. The black
shirt is unbuttoned at the top, and a slim gold chain peeks out.

His hand smacks into his chest.

My brow crinkles.

"Sorry, baby. You took my breath away." He grins and
meets me at the bottom of the stairs.

I stop one step above and run my hands down the front of his shirt. "That was corny."

His smile widens. "I know. But your eyes light up when you're amused, and I couldn't resist." He leans forward and steals a kiss from my lips.

"Pictures!" Aunt Mary calls, coming in from the kitchen. "You two make such a lovely couple."

I shake my head, glancing sideways at the out-of-place DeSantis. Aunt Mary thinks we're *lovely*? I seem to have missed some memo. Sure, she's been pretty accepting... I blurted out the whole story to her, after all. I didn't want to lie.

But this is almost too much.

Aiden takes my hand, and I take the last step down. My heels bring me up a bit, but he still has a few inches on me. "I once thought about kidnapping you again, just to take you to your prom," he says in my ear.

Aunt Mary clicks away, and I force my smile to remain in place. Inside, though, butterfly wings have taken off again.

"Why didn't you? I..."

"You were corrupted against me and in hiding," he points out.

Ah, well.

"This will be the same," he adds. "We'll have the popular girls and the jocks-turned-politicians. The outcasts. The ones invited because of the depth of their pockets. And everyone in between."

"And the dangerous ones," I guess.

He smirks. "Us."

I nod once, although I don't feel so dangerous. I just need to get my eyes on Amelie and let Xavier know... and then we can get her out.

"You'll be late," Aunt Mary finally says, interrupting our stare. "Go on."

Aiden offers his arm, and I curl my hand around his upper arm. His muscles bulge under his suit. Outside, he opens the passenger door and leans in. His lips press into the shell of my ear.

"It's a good thing your aunt was there, or else I would've insisted upon a repeat of our adventure at the store."

My face grows hot. "You wouldn't."

He pulls back just an inch, analyzing my expression. "Don't tempt me."

It's my turn to smirk, masking the sudden pulse between my legs. He seems to catch it, anyway, because his gaze drops. I step back and climb into the car, tucking my long skirt in around me.

He closes my door gently. As soon as he's in, and we're on the road, his hand finds the slit in my dress and navigates to bare skin. He traces patterns on my inner thigh, and I shiver. He finds the straps of my knife holster higher up.

"Keep going," I taunt. "Finish what you start."

He glances at me as his finger slides under my panties. I part my legs farther and tip my head back. *God*, three days was too long to be away from this man—not that I'd ever admit that out loud.

But my hand just hasn't had the same effect.

"Soaked," he murmurs. The car doesn't falter, which is impressive. He rubs my clit until I'm squirming in my seat, then pinches it. I clamp my legs shut, trapping his hand, and groan through a shuddering orgasm. It crawls through me like slow-moving fire. His finger dips inside me, and my muscles clench around him.

"Now you're primed and ready for the event." He withdraws.

I track his movement through half-lidded eyes. He brings his fingers to his mouth and sucks them clean. I whimper.

"Beautiful," he hums. "Be good tonight, and you'll come home with me."

I raise my eyebrow. "And if I'm bad?"

"Then you'll definitely come home with me." He smirks. "You look good trussed up in my bed, begging to come. Maybe this time, with a plug up your ass..."

I shift and press my thighs tighter together. Damn him.

We arrive at the venue too soon. I barely have time to check my lipstick in the mirror and flip my hair back before a valet opens my door. The man offers his white-gloved hand, but I stare at it blankly. A second later, Aiden is there. The valet quickly steps back, and Aiden assists me out of the car.

I press upward and kiss his cheek. It leaves a faint stain of pink against his tanned skin. I go to wipe it off with my thumb, but he catches my hand.

"Leave it, Gem," he murmurs.

We join the procession of other couples striding up the museum's wide steps. A black carpet has been rolled out, stands of flowers framing it in. On the other side of the flowers are men and women with cameras—waiting for more important people, I'm sure.

Aiden hands over two tickets at the door. The woman casts a look at them, clicks a mark in one of the corners, and waves us through. The people we followed in stand in line to go through a metal detector. A guard peers into their bags. We step around them—around all of it, actually. No one bats an eye as we coast by.

"Special treatment," I say. I glance over my shoulder. Xavier and his team will have to get by them, and it may slow them down. "Will Amelie and Luca be in attendance?"

"Probably. The Pages would throw a fit if their daughter wasn't here."

I nod.

He points out various people on our way through the

museum lobby. We enter a giant, open space. There's a dance floor at the back of the room, where a platform with a DJ stand has been erected in front of a wall of shrubbery. Standing tables dot the room. Two bars, one to our left and another to the right, that already look fairly crowded.

"I heard people paid thousands to get in here and rub elbows," Aiden says in my ear.

I nod. I can imagine. This sort of thing brings out all the socialites—and the museum clearly prepared for that. Impressive art hangs on every wall, and a few roped-off statues decorate the space. There are large doors in the far corner that lead to, from this angle, one of the galleries. The same on the other side, a different gallery open for viewing.

The ceiling is a mix of glowing lights and twisting blown glass. The lighting is warm and bright, perfect for showing off everyone's attire.

"Mr. DeSantis," someone calls.

Aiden's muscles tense, but only because he's so close am I able to tell. A familiar mask slips over his features, and suddenly he's a man far removed from the passionate one I know.

"That's what they call my father," he says to the man, extending his hand.

They shake.

"Frank, this is Gemma West." Aiden tips his head in my direction.

The man is older, probably closer to my grandfather's age than mine or Aiden's. His white hair is thin on top, but the handlebar mustache is thick. His skin is ruddy, perhaps from too many years of overindulging. Yet his suit fits impeccably, and even if I don't recognize his name, I'd bet that he has power in this city.

And that's exactly why he's here, talking to us.

Or, Aiden, as it is.

"Pleasure," Frank murmurs, taking my hand and kissing my knuckles.

I suppress the urge to yank away.

Aiden doesn't feel so inclined. He steps forward and easily moves Frank back.

My gaze wanders around. When I peek back, Aiden and Frank are discussing... I don't know. A new building just outside the city? I touch Aiden's arm and tell him that I'll be back. And then I make my way to the bar.

Let's see if I can get away with alcohol, or if they'll card me. The room is filling up quickly. On a stand next to the bar is an itinerary for the night: drinks and mingling, then a stroll through the Asian exhibit to the room where dinner will be served. Apparently we're in for a long night: the president of the children's hospital will speak, then introduce a few cancer kids, who in turn will welcome the councilwoman— and who knows how long she'll talk.

I assume there will be dancing after. Pledges for the hospital. Favors exchanged for donations.

My stomach turns.

"What can I get for you?" a bartender asks me.

"Vodka cranberry."

He eyes me. I lift my brows, and he gives a curt nod. He slides the pink drink toward me, and I open my clutch to pay him. Someone else steps up and pushes the ten-dollar bill across the counter.

I glance over and very nearly step back. Jameson doesn't so much as look at me as he orders his own drink, a whiskey sour. *Sour* is exactly the feeling I get emanating from him. He reminds me of a ceremonial dagger. The kind that's so outwardly perfect, it fools you into thinking it isn't sharp.

And that's when he'll cut you.

"Ms. West," he finally acknowledges. "Having fun?"

All I can see when I look at him is my father's death. I turn away sharply, but he snags my wrist. My drink sloshes over the rim, spilling on my fingers. I freeze, eyes down.

Don't react.

He drags me closer to him, until my shoulder bumps his chest. His voice drops low. "Disrespectful little slut. You think you can just walk away before we're done with our conversation?" He sneers. "To think, you almost tricked my son into marriage."

Chills rush down my spine.

And then he releases me, and I stumble away from him. I don't look for Aiden—all I care about is getting far, far away from his father. I spot Amelie and Luca at one of the tables and hurry in their direction. Amelie seems the worse for wear—but maybe that's just my fears overriding my vision.

I stop at their table and set my drink down. "Hi."

Amelie frowns. "He wasn't supposed to bring you."

"What?"

Luca shakes his head at his wife.

"Stop it," she hisses at him. "Gemma, you shouldn't be here. I mean, love the dress. But—"

"It's fine," Luca says. "She's probably safe here."

My gaze bounces between them. Luca's in traditional colors: white collared shirt, skinny black tie, black tuxedo. Amelie complements him in a black-and-white form-fitting dress. They feel... awkward.

"Are you two okay? And don't bother lying." I narrow my eyes at them.

Luca turns away, giving us his back. That's fine—I don't have much experience with the youngest DeSantis, and I'm not especially keen to gain any. He's the reason I had to rescue Amelie from Wilder's fake funeral, after all.

Oh, shit. I never told her about Wilder.

But, how the hell am I supposed to blurt that out? What if

Aiden told Luca, who told Amelie? What if she hates me for keeping this a secret?

"It's been a tough week," Amelie says gently, her voice cutting through my internal monologue. "I'm just hoping it's over soon. I'm ready to go back to Italy."

I sigh and stop myself from rubbing at my temples. "I'm sorry you got dragged into my mess."

She cocks her head. "Your mess? You're taking responsibility for this now?"

"Well, I was the one who wanted you to organize my escape plan. Set that into motion a long time ago." I glance over my shoulder and search for Aiden. He's being held up by more conversation, although his gaze cuts across the room and lands on me. I shiver. "And the wedding," I add. "That was..."

"Jameson," she finishes. "You can blame him. It's okay."

I grumble. "Yeah, sure."

A sudden ripple of noise moves through the space, and we both turn toward the entrance. The councilwoman sweeps inside with an entourage, but she's very clearly the spotlight. Her dress is a glittering dark red, matching her matte lipstick. Hair coiffed. Looking for all the world like a president and not just a city councilwoman.

Dress for the job you want, I suppose.

Amelie sighs. "Wretched woman."

I smile. "I read your article about her. Seemed timely..."

"Yeah, well. Mom loves it when we can get high-profile people to give quotes for her magazine. Although..." She leans in. "Word on the street is that the councilwoman's political action campaign has been receiving large sum donations from an unknown source. The company name that's claiming it is... peculiar."

I perk up. Just what I need—another mystery to solve. "Sounds interesting. What do they want?"

"Haven't said, yet. As far as I know. Jameson was bitching

about it to my father the other day. Said he wanted to get to the source and make sure it didn't interrupt their plans."

I take a large gulp of my drink. "Of course."

Luca returns with two glasses, another for Amelie and himself. He looks at me, then away. An uncomfortable feeling climbs up my throat, but I squash it. If I concentrate on the people around me, the bad feeling would never leave my skin. Appearing to be unaffected will keep the sharks at bay.

The back of my neck prickles, and I sense Aiden stop beside me. His hand slides across my lower back. "Having fun?" he rumbles. "Are they behaving?"

I smile tightly. "We're all behaving."

He leans down. "I saw my father speak with you."

"It's fine," I lie.

Not fine. I sort of want to puke. If I thought he didn't like me... I was wrong. He *hates* me. I eye Sandra White, who's making her way in our direction. She's still surrounded by people. A younger woman in a black dress, two men.

"Amelie," I say, "can you get me an audience with her?"

She mutters, then steps away from Luca. I follow her and pause a half-step behind. Aiden lets me go, his hand falling away from my back.

"Councilwoman," Amelie calls, a polite smile spread across her lips. She presses her palms into her stomach and strides right up to the woman. "So good to see you again."

"Ah, Amelie DeSantis," Sandra White greets her. "What a pleasure. Thank you for the article in your mother's magazine."

She nods tightly and motions me forward. "Have you meet Gemma West?"

Sandra White—she's not the sort of woman you can refer to by one name only—turns to me, her lips parting. True shock. "Oh, dear. No. I met your mother, though. She was a lovely woman."

S. MASSERY

I fight the urge to step back. One thing I didn't expect was to be discussing my *mother* of all people. I smile. "Thank you."

"And you inherited her beauty," the councilwoman continues.

"I heard a rumor of your announcement," I say, stepping closer. "I just wanted to congratulate you before you're inundated with them."

She chuckles. "Secrets are hard to keep in this city, aren't they?"

"Indeed." I watch her closely. "You and Jameson—"

"Gemma," someone calls.

I jerk back. My gaze goes over her shoulder to Xavier. He strides toward us, looking like... like he belongs here. Charcoal suit, white shirt. Emerald-green tie.

My eyes narrow on that.

"Oh, Xavier." The councilwoman extends her hand. "How lovely that you were able to join us."

He takes it and gingerly kisses her knuckles. He *seems* sincere when he says, "I would never turn down your invitation."

I... I don't know what to make of that.

My heart beats double-time, and I can tell Amelie is lost. She wouldn't know Xavier from a hole in the wall. How does Sandra White know him?

"Mr. Ells is friends with my son," she confides to us. "They met in college."

"Your son?" My voice is surprisingly normal, but on the inside I'm boiling. Her *son?* Please tell me—

"Here he is, now."

Xavier's gaze stays on me, even as we all shift toward the newcomer.

Another fucking familiar face.

Has this whole thing been a sick ploy to get under my guard?

"Cole, this is Amelie DeSantis and Gemma West." She smiles at her son—one of the five men in Xavier's team. "Who would've thought? A DeSantis and a West, *friends*."

And an Eldridge. The three Mafia families, reunited again. Albeit a bit... unconventionally.

Amelie scoffs. "I was married into the family, Councilwoman. I hardly think I count as a DeSantis."

She shrugs. Her eyes drop to my empty hand, then someone behind me. "Xavier, dare I say you match Ms. West's dress perfectly? Maybe you should escort her to get a drink."

He dips his head and offers his arm.

I grit my teeth and take it, more than ready to throttle him in private. He guides me away, his hand landing on top of my fingers. To anyone watching, it might seem like a nice pat. In reality, he's trying to stop me from digging my nails through his suit.

"What the fuck?" I whisper to him.

He grins. "This is Operation Rescue Amelie, is it not? You didn't leave me much time... and I doubt you wanted me busting in here, guns blazing. This called for a more subtle approach."

I scoff. "Mr. *Ells*, huh? Living another lie." I don't know why that disappoints me.

"It was to protect myself," he answers. "And something that started as a lie turned into a life."

I jerk to a halt. "You just started living it," I repeat. "Do they know who you are?"

He has the good grace to look offended. "They're my best friends, little West. Of course they do. I trust them with all of my secrets."

Interesting.

"So, um, you're not going to go all psycho when you see Jameson?"

His expression darkens. "No. I, unlike him, have a firm

grip on my emotions. I saw the way he grabbed your arm. Gemma, you should stay away from him."

I almost laugh at that. I'd like nothing more than to stay away from him—he's not just an asshole, he's a murderer. And possibly crazy.

We reach the bar, and Xavier orders both of us tequila on the rocks. "I have a drink with Aiden," I mutter. "And what's with the tie, huh? You sneak into my room to find out what color my dress was?"

His gaze lands on me again, and he shifts to face me. "I'm going to enjoy this next part."

I narrow my eyes, but I don't have time to ask what the hell he means.

Because a second later, Aiden's fist smashes into the side of Xavier's face.

CHAPTER 22
Aiden

There's a roaring in my ears.

First it was Gemma and Amelie talking to White —the latter is too slippery for her own good. She's in with the DeSantises, always has been. But I don't know if she hates the Wests on principle. Amelie making the introduction was just asking for trouble.

But then their little group was joined by a man who looked too familiar. Still, I didn't recognize him off the bat. The way he stood tugged at my memory. Body language is important. It can be a person's biggest tell.

Luca huffed. "Wasn't that the guy with Gemma at the bar?"

The night of the fire.

I eyed my brother, then the man standing beside Gemma with renewed interest. White said something to them, and suddenly he was offering my girl his arm. She *took* it.

"Easy," Luca tried to warn under his breath. "It could be nothing."

"Or, he could be trying something." I was already too

tense, and well-worn rage flooded my system. How dare he put his hand on her?

They headed toward the bar.

Now, I stride across the room toward them, distantly aware of Luca on my heels. I bypass Amelie and the council-woman, catching the latter's knowing smile out of the corner of my eye.

Bitch.

That roaring amps up, so loud I can't even think straight —I just go in for the kill.

My fist slams into his jaw, and he careens into the bar. He grips it with both hands, steadying himself. Instead of retaliating, he just straightens and sneers at me. I take another step forward, but Luca grabs my arms from behind. And Gemma slides between us, hands on my chest.

"Hey," she snaps. "What the hell was that for?"

I lift my gaze and glower at the guy. Up close, he looks even more familiar.

"He touched you."

The asshole's sneer widens into a full-on, arrogant grin.

"Incoming," Luca warns.

Gemma's face pales, and she seems to be unable to help glancing back at the man. Then me. "Get out of here," she orders him.

And surprisingly, he only hesitates for a split second before moving away.

"Should I be concerned that you're at the center of... whatever the fuck this was?" Dad asks behind me. "Luca, release him. Surely Aiden can practice a bit of self-control now that his fiancée's lover is out of sight."

I grit my teeth and roll my shoulders as soon as my brother releases me. Gemma seems startled, eyes wide. Her fingers dig into my lapel. I turn, stepping slightly in front of her.

"A misunderstanding," I answer. I'd rather he not look at

her—and certainly not talk to her. He already got his chance earlier this evening, and she left that exchange seeming frightened.

Dad pivots, analyzing the room. Those who had watched us now swiftly peel their attention away, and the noise level returns to normal.

"This is a big night for us," he says to me. "You of all people *know* that. Do not cause another scene, or I'll deal with you myself."

I stiffen, and I'm about to guide Gemma away when he suddenly leaps forward, grabbing my jaw. He yanks my face down.

"Do not disappoint me," he adds. His nails cut into my skin.

And then he releases me and strides away. We track his movement toward the councilwoman, who seems happy to see him.

Luca shakes his head at me and leaves us alone.

"Real nice," Gemma mutters.

"Who is that?" I demand. "Why has he been hanging around you—and don't give me some bullshit line about being family. He's very clearly *not* a West."

He was the one who swept her house and missed me, I realize. The one who was there the night of the West Bar fire.

Who is he?

She sighs and snatches the new drink from the bar. I follow her through one of the doors that lead into an open gallery. This long hallway curves away. It's decorated with colored glass art on the walls and on stands in the center, creating two pathways through the space.

"Where are you going?" I follow her without hesitation, but I'm fighting to hold down my temper. I just want *answers*.

"Somewhere more private," she replies. She vanishes around a corner, her green dress trailing behind her.

S. MASSERY

I round it and abruptly stop.

The man I hit is in front of her, fixated on one of the glass objects. His profile is sharp. Strong jaw. Strong overall, I'd guess. He's only an inch shorter than me, and leaner. The type of body built from a lot of running.

"Xavier," Gemma says.

My stomach drops. "Eldridge." Suddenly, her mentioning his name the other day makes sense. New fury spikes through me, and I ball my fists at my sides. She's been hanging around *him*?

Both of them tense. And I *hate* that. I hate that they share anything at all. If we weren't in the middle of a fucking gala, I'd be tempted to just strangle him to death. No bullets—that's too quick. Maybe Gemma's knife. It would look pretty decorated with his blood.

"Aiden," Gemma begs. "Please."

"Explain," I snap.

Xavier rubs his jaw, still smiling. Fucking bastard.

"You didn't fight back," I say, reining in my calm. "You just let me hit you. To make me look bad?"

"Nah, I figured you owed me one, seeing as how I shot you."

My jaw drops, and if Gemma wasn't between us, I'd kill him. No questions asked.

"*You?*" I try to keep the fucking surprise out of my voice. "You kidnapped my fiancée."

He doesn't respond, but his glee says it all. He's enjoying this.

And Gemma seems... worried. Her attention bounces back and forth between us, although she's a lot closer to me than him. Her hand is out, extended in my direction. Stopping a charge before it's even begun.

"You deserve a lot worse than one punch for that," I finally answer.

Damn. He got the upper hand on my family. Bested our guards. And got Gemma out without hurting anyone except... well, me.

"If you listened to directions—"

"There was zero chance I was doing that." I fold my arms over my chest.

She relaxes a hair. Perceptive little thing—I wouldn't cross my arms if I was still contemplating attacking him. I'd want my hands free to move quickly.

"Listen, I'm sorry I didn't tell you," she says to me. "It just... didn't seem like the most important thing we were dealing with."

"That, and your girlfriend promised I could kill your dad." Xavier pulls out his phone and types something, then returns it to his breast pocket. "Not tonight, though."

"Dandy." My voice comes out through clenched teeth. "His life isn't yours to barter away, Gem."

Now it's her turn to seem shifty. "He's leaving one way or another. I had to guarantee him the shot for their help."

But will Dad be leaving in a body bag or... by choice? I can't see that happening.

"You can do it, though," she whispers to me. "You can take over the family once he's gone. The DeSantises and Wests can be in a *real* truce."

"Over fifty years of anger, forgotten with the drop of a hat," Xavier adds. "Sounds like a daydream."

Sounds like hope.

I finally shake out my limbs, releasing my tension. I step away from them and move farther down the hall, staring at the twisting pieces of glass. I'm not supposed to lead this family. I never was.

"Dad didn't prepare me for leadership," I say under my breath.

It's more than true, isn't it? Wilder's been groomed his

whole life to impress. Politics, charm, swagger. Confidence but not arrogance. He walked that thin line and dazzled everyone he met. He would've gone far—maybe all the way to the White House.

Now he's a dead man walking.

"Gemma could say the same," Xavier says. "Yet she's risen to the role."

I shake my head. She *has* risen. Beautifully. And on the inside, I couldn't be prouder. Frustrated, but proud. Because how am I supposed to keep her safe when she's off doing dangerous stuff? Like transporting drugs and meeting with people who wouldn't hesitate to shoot her if their meetings didn't go well?

"Can you give us a minute?" Gemma asks.

I glance over my shoulder. Xavier's buddy, the council-woman's son, stands in the shadows. And Xavier Eldridge stares at her for a long moment, seeming to contemplate something. Finally, he nods and leaves. He takes Cole with him.

She comes up behind me and lifts my arm, sliding under it. I grip her shoulder, pulling her into me.

"He and his team broke me out of your wedding," she starts. "It was put in motion before you even took me."

I twitch, but she hugs me tighter. These are the secrets she's been keeping from me, the ones I never imagined hearing.

"I texted Amelie the night you came to Aunt Mary's house," she admits. "If she didn't hear from me after a week, she was to put a plan into motion to get me out. I didn't know what it would be, of course, but she was familiar with the DeSantis tower and how you operated.

"And I lied. I did see Colin in the mall. I told him what floor your apartment was on, because at that point I still regretted my decision. You hadn't stopped hunting him, and my sacrifice was for nothing."

A lump forms in my throat. *God*, I drove her to do all this.

"Xavier's team was hired by Colin—probably once the mall thing failed, and also after Dad died. He only knew him as X—not Xavier, and certainly not as an Eldridge." She's quiet.

My gaze drops to the top of her head. I put my finger under her chin, forcing her head up. "Keep going."

"The DeSantises have always outnumbered us," she says on a whisper. "Your family was hitting us where it counted, and even though we're in a better financial position, it still doesn't help us recover when our restaurants and clubs are targeted. So I asked Xavier to stay on and help us. Intercept DeSantis attacks."

I nod. It's not surprising that they were able to do it so efficiently—they got in and out of the chapel and avoided all our security. Even Hart on the sniper across the street was ineffective. But one thing stands out to me: she *wanted* to leave. She had an exit strategy ready to go from the moment I found her.

She didn't know if it would succeed, but does that matter?

Gemma flattens her palm on my chest. She might be able to feel my erratic pulse, because she frowns.

"I don't mean to tell you this to hurt you," she says quietly. "Honestly, I wasn't sure if I ever thought I'd talk about this. I pushed through the anger and betrayal *I* felt when you continued to hunt my family. I put my emotions for you over them, and sometimes it still guts me. But just because I had an escape strategy, and I hate your father, and I *did* leave, doesn't mean I would leave you now."

"Now that you have a choice," I finish.

Except she doesn't have a choice—I'd kidnap her again if I thought it would work.

But maybe there's something to be said about free will.

She rises up on her toes and kisses my jaw. "Aiden. I don't

261

think you have to worry about my choice, because I will always choose you. I'm in love with you. It terrifies me—"

She's in love with me.

Those words bounce around my head, and then I'm on her. My lips touch hers, gentle and then decidedly not. She immediately parts her lips and lets out a soft moan. The sound travels straight to my dick, which hardens in an instant. I walk her back, pressing her to the wall between the art. We might get caught here—but the insane part of me doesn't give a shit.

The part of me that's desperate to find our happiness doesn't care, either.

I slide my thigh between her legs, and my hands grope her ass. She presses into me, nipping at my lips, hands in my hair. That dress slit comes in handy now, and I grind against her core.

Her hands slip between us and moves her dress, then frees my cock from my pants. She holds aside her panties and meets my eyes.

"Fuck me," she orders in a whisper.

I angle my hips forward, sliding the tip of my cock across her slit. That feeling alone is too good—even now. Even though we've had sex almost too many times to count, it never gets old. It's better every single time.

I don't understand it.

"I can do that," I give in. I lower her onto my shaft, and we both groan.

"Probably should make this fast." Her voice comes out breathless.

"No shit." I move inside her, biting back my groan of pleasure. Her pussy is heaven.

She claws at my neck, pulling my face toward hers. Our wet, open-mouthed kiss fuels my lust—and hers. She rubs herself as I thrust, the force slamming her spine into the wall. Whether it's the exhilaration of being in public or just *us*,

Gemma is soon clenching around me. I swallow her noises, keeping my lips sealed to hers.

Her release triggers mine. I come inside her, stopping fully buried. I keep her pinned there and run my hand up her side, to her arm. She had bandaged it after I went full-on caveman and ripped out her birth control.

This stuff takes time, I know, but my blood sings in triumph. She can get pregnant with my baby.

She shudders, moving her arm away, but I ignore it. I pull out of her with a slick noise and drop her feet back to the floor. There's no one around, so I kneel before her and slide two fingers into her.

"What are you doing?" She pushes at my head. "Aiden."

"Making sure your cunt takes my seed." I kiss her bare thigh, then remove my fingers. I carefully replace her panties and straighten her dress.

"I like you on your knees."

I look up to find her staring down at me, eyes dark. She's a siren in this dress, with that just-fucked expression. The caveman feeling comes roaring back. Forget the gala. Forget our families.

She's in love with me.

"You're more than anything I'd ever hoped for," I tell her quietly. "I'd kneel for you and you alone. *Me*. A man who has bowed to no one. Just you."

She smiles and cups my cheeks, urging me to rise. "In case I didn't make myself clear before... I love you. Dark, possessive, angry bits and all."

I smirk. "Those are my best qualities."

Instead of a smile, though, a worried frown slides over her features. "You're not mad at me? And don't get me started on how dumb I sound even asking that. I kept some pretty big secrets."

She's right—she did keep secrets.

But haven't I?

My family has put her through hell. Not just us versus them—it's been the DeSantises versus *her*. She alone has carried the weight of their hate. Guilt punches me in the face.

"I'm not mad—I'd never be mad at you."

She cups my cheek. "Good," she whispers. "Because Xavier and Cole aren't here just for the hell of it."

Great.

CHAPTER 23

Gemma

A iden doesn't interrogate me about Xavier and Cole. I'm still irritated that Xavier's friend is the council-woman's son. That bit of information might've been helpful. But I can understand his need for secrets. Haven't I been grappling with that same thing?

We reemerge just as the bell for dinner is rung. A man in a suit holds the bell with white-gloved hands, and as soon as it's quiet, he announces that dinner will be served through the doorways he blocks.

Guests migrate his way. They'll have to wind through another exhibit, which was probably the museum's fine idea. Expose these rich people to more art.

I catch Cole's eye and raise my own.

He just smirks at me.

Aiden's grip tightens on my hip, signaling that he didn't miss the exchange. I lean into him, sighing. After dinner, then? When people are distracted by dancing and alcohol?

I keep waiting for them to grab Amelie, but no. Jameson sat her and Luca at his table with Sandra White and her son. Xavier is off at another table, and Aiden and I find our places at another. I glance at the name beside me and immediately smile. Then frown.

"Hey there, girlie." Mac, Jameson's brother and my poker friend, walks up and sets his drink down at the table setting beside me. "You survived."

I grin. I've developed a soft spot for the man, although I have no idea why. Maybe because he mentioned playing cards with my parents. Or that he seems the opposite—in terms of personality—from his evil brother.

"Uncle Mac," Aiden says, surprised. "You know Gemma?"

"We became fast friends," I tell him. I turn back to Mac. "And yes, I did survive."

He winks. "Good. I've never seen a better match for my nephew, as much as his father thinks otherwise."

We sit, and Aiden's hand is immediately on my thigh. I keep my attention on Mac and ignore the goosebumps traveling up the backs of my arms. Aiden's hand slides between my legs, hidden by the tablecloth, and runs along the hem of my panties. His cum has slowly been seeping out for the last few minutes, and I shift at the new sensation.

Mac is asking how my family is—a tricky question.

"We're managing."

He's all sympathy, though. "I heard about the fire at West Bar. I'm so sorry, Gemma. I'd been there a time or two, and it was always a great place."

I stiffen. "It's... it'll be rebuilt," I finally say. My mind trips over the unopened safe in my room and whether the journal survived. I lost the picture of our family at Coney Island. I lost everything in that office that reminded me of my parents.

Those things can't be rebuilt.

We paid off the arson investigator to pass along any leads to us. One of Aunt Margaret's sons is handling it. I want answers for who burned our bar down, but in the back of my head I *know* it was a DeSantis. Maybe no one important.

Or maybe it was Jameson himself.

Wouldn't that be some sick sort of justice? Take his truce contract and throw it in his face.

"Excuse me," I murmur. I extract Aiden's hand and rise.

Mac and Aiden both stand, too.

"I'm just going to wash my hands before dinner," I tell them, fighting back a smile. They both nod, Aiden slower than his uncle, and return to their seats.

I stride away, glancing one more time at Amelie's table. She's... gone. Her chair and Luca's are empty. Cole, however, remains. He's deep in conversation with Jameson and his mother.

My phone chimes. I pull it out and stare down at the text from Xavier.

Got them.

He put up a hell of a fight, though... at first.

I shake my head and delete the messages. He'll take them to one of our safe houses. We have a few hidden throughout the city under different names, some more recently purchased than others.

I sweep through a different exhibit.

This one shows off African history. The long hallway is dark, only the spotlights on the art providing visibility. There are large tapestries on the walls, statues of animals and masks in cases, ivory objects. It's a beautiful collection.

A discreet sign for a restroom points farther down, and I tuck my clutch under my arm. I find it easily, and the gold-and-white marble bathroom is completely empty. I pass through the little powder room and pause at the row of sinks.

My hair is a bit more wild than it was when I left the house. My lips are plump, my pink lipstick gone. Aiden had given me a moment to straighten up, but it wasn't enough. I *look* like I just had sex with him.

Mac must've seen right through us.

My face heats, but I ignore the redness blooming on my cheeks. I swipe on more lipstick and run my fingers under the water, trying to tame my hair into submission again. Only then do I consider my new predicament: using the toilet without dunking my dress.

The door opens around the corner. I close my clutch with a snap and move toward the last stall.

But then I catch a flash of black in the mirrors. I whirl around, startled to see two men.

"This is the women's—"

One lunges for me. He's no one I recognize—not that it means much. I fight him off for only half a second before he gets control over my arms. He slams me back into the wall, and my head cracks against tile. I see stars for a moment.

"Knife," the second grunts. He moves up beside me and slides it free. He doesn't release it but instead steps back and inspects my blade.

Loathing and panic war for space in my chest. I thrash and try to ignore the wave of dizziness. I bring my knee up sharply, aiming for anything soft—a groin, stomach—but the one who holds me blocks it.

He flips me around and smashes my cheek to the wall. He yanks my hands around, keeping them against the small of my back. I face away from the mirrors, so I can't see what comes next.

Something sharp pricks into my neck.

"What—" Almost immediately, a fog descends over my thoughts. I blink and try to keep my eyes open. I kick out at them. I won't give up. A shriek builds in my throat. A *scream*. Why didn't I scream earlier? Surprise kept me silent. And now I open my mouth to let it out. To call for someone to save me.

Fabric is shoved past my lips, my teeth. It touches the back of my throat, and I gag.

"It should be working," one says.

My mind spins, worse than that dizzy feeling from a moment ago.

Just let go. My mother's voice, strange enough. She's front and center in my vision, her face a mask of fear.

I try to hold on, but I don't have a choice. That fog becomes cement, and I sink like a stone...

But I don't lose consciousness—not yet. I lose control.

My body slackens. The man holding me releases his grip slowly and catches me before I hit the floor. I try to scream again, feeling it like glass in my throat, but no noise comes out. New fear bolts through me at this level of helplessness.

"Do something with that."

I catch sight of the second man wrapping my knife's blade in fabric and slipping it into his pocket. He's going to die for that. It's *mine*—made worse that it was re-gifted from Aiden. That knife holds too many memories.

And when it counted? I didn't even get a chance to use it.

Colin would've fought better.

Aiden would've killed them without hesitation.

I was overwhelmed in under ten seconds.

The bladeless one hooks my arm around his shoulders, then scoops me up. It's too similar to how Aiden has carried me before, except my head falls straight back. The world is upside down.

I manage a sluggish blink. By the time my eyes reopen, we're crossing through a different exhibit. A stark-white room with colorful portraits on the walls.

I take in as much detail as I can, but those colors—all the colors—are bleeding together. I can't keep my eyes open for longer than a few seconds. The world around me is blurring into soft shapes. I try to claw at the person holding me and only manage to get a weak grip on his lapel.

We exit out a side door and into the cool night. A car idles at the curb, and it beeps as the trunk opens. I get one look at the dark interior before I'm deposited into it. Tossed in, really, like a sack of grain.

I can't move to fix my position, I can't even make my muscles work to roll onto my back. God, it's like I'm being pulled down a drain. Everything is heavy.

They adjust my legs, then grab my arms and zip tie my wrists in front of me.

"She's good," one says. "We might've underdosed her, but there's no use adjusting it now."

Then the trunk slams shut over my head. For the second time.

This is different, though. I had a thread of trust in Aiden not to kill me when he tossed me in his. Now, I have to actively try not to freak out. I've retained enough control to keep breathing, although it's hard. It takes most of my focus, and I'm on the edge of hyperventilating.

The car jets away from the museum, and I slide a bit as they round a corner.

It'll be okay, I tell myself.

But my eyes still fill with tears. I close them, but it doesn't stop the waterworks pouring down my temple, into my hair.

Sometime later—I lost track, I might've lost consciousness —the car engine dies and the trunk pops open. Dull, artificial light floods into the space, and I'm hauled upright. One of them shoves a black canvas over my face—not unlike the one Xavier and his men put on me when they took me from the church.

Breathe, Gem.

I inhale loudly. The noise is ragged in my ears. I'm lifted, this time thrown haphazardly over a shoulder, and the man begins to walk.

My face burns with shame. I can't even move—how am I supposed to escape this? How will Aiden find me? I should've taken more self-defense lessons. I should've... I don't know. Prepared better for this sort of eventuality.

We go up a set of stairs, then into an elevator.

A maze of turns, another elevator. I'm counting steps, but in a matter of moments I'm lost. My brain can't keep up.

The man drops my legs, then lowers my torso. My ass hits the seat of a chair. They quickly undo the zip ties and reattach my wrists to what I imagine are the arms of the chair. Then my ankles, one to each leg. The plastic tightens against my bare skin, just above the straps of my heels.

"She's lost her fight," one of them comments. He taps my cheek through the cloth.

Instinctively, I snap at his finger. I catch the tip between my teeth and clamp down hard, even through the canvas. He yanks free, grunting, and a second later something strikes my face. My head whips to the side, and pain blooms across my cheek and temple.

They share a chuckle, then yank the bag off my head.

I train my gaze on one of them—the one holding a phone up. He leans forward and waves at me. His flash turns on, and it's blinding after the darkness of the trunk and the bag over my head.

"Proof of life," he explains. "Say your name and what day it is."

I lick my lips. "Fuck off."

The other one hits me again, and I see it coming—but I don't have time to flinch away from it. His open palm strikes my cheek. I stay in the same position—head turned, face throbbing—for a moment. Too slow.

"Say your name," the slapper orders, grabbing my hair and wrenching my head around.

I ignore the phone and glare at the man behind it.

"Gemma West," I finally say. My voice is low and rough. "It's... Saturday. The night of the Children's Hospital Gala."

The man lowers the phone and leers at me. "You're lucky we have orders not to touch you, Gemma West. Enjoy your stay."

The bag is shoved back over my head. A minute later, the door slams.

Alone... but for how long?

CHAPTER 24
Aiden

G emma is gone.

My brother and Amelie are gone.

Even Xavier fucking Eldridge has disappeared without a trace.

"Looking for something? Or, someone?"

I wheel around and glare at my father. He seems unperturbed, leaning against the wall of the museum. I came out here because it's obvious she's no longer in the building. I searched every exhibit, I called her cell... nothing.

How can someone just *vanish* like that?

Dad tosses me something. I catch it, then immediately wish I hadn't. It's Gemma's gold clutch. Something inside it is making noise, and I open it. On her phone's screen, a video plays. Gemma sits on a wooden chair, her arms tied. Her dress is askew, hair everywhere. Her lipstick is smudged.

"Proof of life," a man off-camera says. "Say your name and what day it is."

I scowl. "Proof of life, Dad? Seriously?"

He shrugs and watches me closely.

It's her eyes that get me. She can't keep them open.

"Fuck off," she slurs.

"What did you give her?" I demand.

Someone moves toward her, and then another man slaps her. Her head whips to the side.

I grip the phone tighter, anger churning my gut. I'm going to be sick—he *hit* her.

She stays in that position for too long, and he manhandles her again. The view drops, then comes back up. "Say your name," the one who holds her head snaps.

Her blue eyes crash into the camera. "Gemma West." Long pause. "It's Saturday..."

I end the video and stow her phone in my pocket. I've never felt so fucking helpless.

"Here's how this is going to go," Dad says casually, striding up and stopping beside me. He faces the street, I face the museum. "You're going to bring me her brother. You've been dragging your heels, and the family needs to see some loyalty."

"And if I don't?"

"Then she's going to be fucked by every DeSantis with a dick, then tossed in a pit to die." He pats my shoulder. "Better hurry on finding Colin, son. Can't promise she'll stay safe if you continue to pretend you don't know where he is."

He strides away, his laugh floating back toward me.

Fuck. *Fuck*. *FUCK*.

CHAPTER 25

Gemma

A grinding noise wakes me up. I jerk upright and startle myself. For a split second, I forgot I had been kidnapped and that I'm still tied to a chair. It reminds me of our interrogation of Rubert, alone under Aiden's cabin. That sort of sick anticipation he must've felt, knowing something bad was about to begin.

My head pounds, and my mouth is dry. I roll my wrists against the plastic ties to try to get some blood flow back into my fingers. My legs are numb from sitting in the same position on the hard seat.

And then I sense another person in the room, and I go completely still.

Who is it?

One of the gangs desperate to find Colin and collect the bounty? Maybe Xavier has double-crossed me. Or Luca.

My heart thunders. If I were an optimist, I'd be glad that my breath comes easier. There's no more weight—from whatever they injected into me—pressing down on my chest.

Moment of truth, I suppose.

The bag is yanked off my head, and Jameson DeSantis leans down in front of me.

"Hello, little West."

Well... shit.

"Did you think you could get away with your schemes?"

He taps my cheek, but this time I don't even try to bite him. Something tells me he'd do worse than slap me. And then my mind turns to Aiden. *Shit*. Did Jameson do something to his son? I wouldn't put it past him—he's an evil fucking bastard. Clearly.

His tap turns into a strong grip on my jaw. "Answer me when I speak to you."

I can't stop my hoarse chuckle. "I didn't think I'd get away with anything more than you've tried."

He narrows his eyes, contemplating my word choice. My mother's face flashes in my mind again. She was so panicked when Aiden stole me away three years ago—but the true monster is right in front of me now.

I yank my head away. "So, what's the plan this time?"

He's too close, leaning down in front of me. There isn't any room to move—and certainly no room to breathe He's completely in my space, and I think he likes it that way. His gaze falls to my chest, and the way it rises and falls with my erratic breathing. He pulls something from his pocket—a folding knife. The blade springs out inches from my collarbone.

"The *plan* is for you to motivate my son," he says. "I'd hoped Luca and Aiden would be working on this together, but... alas. My bastard son has disappeared along with his pretty bride."

Hope swells in my chest. Xavier wasn't lying—he got them out.

But then Jameson takes the front of my dress in his hands and drags the knife down. He slices straight through it, gaping the front open. His hungry eyes take in my frame, and then he moves away from me. Disgust takes over his features.

"You're going right where you belong," he informs me.

He crosses to the door and bangs on it. A second later, it opens and Sam walks in. His bland expression doesn't change when he takes me in, and my anger surges.

"You traitor," I growl.

"Oh, oh, Gemma," Jameson coos. "The only traitor here is my *son*, working with a band of misfits. And you. To think, you were going to marry into my family. You would've taken my *name*."

Sam crouches beside me and cuts the ties. He hauls me up, gripping both of my upper arms, and pushes me out ahead of him. I stare at Jameson. My open skirt tangles around my legs, tripping me up. My feet scream in the heels. He seems gleeful about all of this, his finger tapping the glinting metal of the knife. Like maybe the only thing that could make this better for him is a little bit of blood.

"You're trying to force us to leave the city," I spit back. "But it won't work."

He smiles. "I welcome the challenge. Your brother's forces... they can't compare to mine. You have hired minions. I have *family*."

Sam's grip tightens, and he shoves me through the door ahead of him. Jameson follows, his footsteps unnervingly light. We go down a long, dimly lit hallway, and out into an elevator lobby.

We've been in the DeSantis tower the whole time.

My attention halts on the floor number.

And Jameson begins to laugh. "Yes, you're familiar with this floor. Aiden took you here to try and teach you a lesson, didn't he? How did that work out?"

I grit my teeth.

We enter the pool room. Memories of Aiden dragging me

in here after he caught me in Jameson's office surge to the forefront of my memory. He had them touch me. Hold me in the water. And now Jameson seems ready to throw me to the wolves.

There are only a few women here. I haven't been able to get a feel for what time it is. They sit in little bits of strappy clothes on the edge of the pool. One rises and makes her way toward us.

"Mr. DeSantis, an honor."

He smirks. "You have a new one to train."

Sam releases me, and Jameson shoves me forward. I take a few stumbling steps and only manage not to faceplant because of the woman's steadying grip on my arms.

"Of course," she says smoothly. She pulls the green dress away from my body. Her gaze takes in my face—and whatever damage she sees on it—then the rest of me. Finally, she nods. "She'll do."

"Everyone earns their keep." Jameson's attention lingers on me, and then he turns abruptly.

Sam pauses for a second, watching me. His stupid gaze is blank, like a perfect, plastic mask. I raise my hand slowly, making sure he sees it coming. He follows it until my fist is extended toward him. And then I raise my middle finger.

He shakes his head and follows his uncle out the door.

"Coward," I yell after him.

"Shh," the woman chides me. "Provoking them will only make it worse."

I grimace and rip free from her grip. "I don't..." I almost say I don't belong here. But none of us do.

"We know you, Gemma West," another girl calls. She goes to a far door and opens it, gesturing for me to follow her. Unlike the woman who caught me, she wears a t-shirt that hangs to mid-thigh.

I don't want to stay in the pool room. And if I were to attempt to leave...

Shaking my head, I give in and trail her. I try to pull my dress closed in the front, but it's pointless. And I keep stumbling, although she doesn't wait to see if I'm keeping up.

The hallway has many doors, some open, some closed. They reveal private rooms lit up with sconces on the walls. Soft lighting. Discreet. A man would feel comfortable cheating on his wife here, or even just handing over cash.

Wait.

"Do you get paid?"

She laughs. Full-out belly laughs, right in the middle of the hallway.

Someone yells for her to shut up, but she ignores it.

"We do, but not directly." She doesn't elaborate. She leads me up a set of stairs and into a large bedroom. There are a dozen bunkbeds, some with bodies inhabiting them. It's dark in here, just a faint glow from another room farther down. Soft snores fill the room. I imagine others are working...

She glances back. "Welcome to Hell."

I swallow. "Right. Um, what..."

"I'm Ali." She extends her hand.

I shake it.

"Listen, I hate to break it to you, but your situation is pretty unusual." Her expression veers toward sympathetic. Or pitying. "Let's get you a bed and new clothes. Jameson will probably come back in the morning."

I shudder. "He doesn't expect me to..."

"Maybe not right away." Definitely pity. "You look like shit, though. What happened?"

"Um..." I hesitate. I don't trust her. I don't really trust anyone right now, but I think I'm too worn down. Like, some part of my brain is saying, *Yeah, talking to her is normal.* It isn't. This whole situation is fucked up. "What day is it?"

There's a kitchen beyond the room of beds. She tosses me a bottle of water from the fridge, the seal unbroken, and watches as I unscrew the top and guzzle most of it. I close my eyes, the cold water soothing my throat.

"It's Saturday," she says. "Well, technically Sunday morning. Four-oh-seven."

"Thanks." I set the bottle down. My thumb brushes my ring finger, but it's bare.

My gaze falls to my hand. No ring.

No jewelry of any kind, but especially *no ring*.

"You okay?"

I flinch. "No. I was abducted from a freaking party and drugged and hit and then told I'd be *earning my keep* in here." Aiden has to find me.

She softens and takes my hand. She's pretty. Young, maybe just a few years older than me. "He must have plans to release you, or else you would've been drugged with something a bit more... addicting."

I shiver.

"They keep those girls in the back, high on H. There's no escaping their fate."

"And you? The girls who sleep out here?"

Her gaze shutters. "We have our individual reasons. Come, Gemma West, I think it's time you sleep. Morning will arrive soon."

She gives me a bed close to the kitchen and bathrooms. I guess I thought my day was going to be a lot worse than it's turning out to be. I mean, am I once again trapped in the DeSantis tower? Yes. Is there a chance I'll be forced to have sex with someone against my will? Maybe. I'm not ruling it out—but I'm not ruling it in, either.

My faith in Aiden finding me is solid, and the hopeful part of me isn't smart enough to know whether I'm being naïve.

"Thank you," I whisper to her when she slips a few Aspirin into my hand.

She smiles, and it's just a little ruthless. "Don't thank me yet. Get some rest."

It should've been impossible to sleep, but it isn't. I close my eyes, and in a matter of seconds, I'm gone.

* * *

TWO DAYS PASS. Two days where every second feels like a year. Time scrapes by, and so does my patience. I keep waiting for something to *happen*.

For the shoe to drop.

Ali and a few other girls took me under their wing, and Jameson has been scarce. These girls protect me. They steer potential clients away. And guilt racks through me each time one of them disappears with a man who had been aiming for me.

It's midday, as best I can tell, when the outside door opens again.

Every time someone walks in, I try not to make eye contact. But I peek nonetheless, afraid that Jameson has come to make good on his promise. Or maybe Aiden will be the one breaking in. Instead, it's a different familiar face.

Jack.

He scans the room and picks me out. One of the girls steps into his path, but he brushes her off.

Then another.

The room goes quiet when he stops in front of me.

"Here for a piece of me?" I ask.

He grimaces. "Tempting, but no. You have to come with me."

I raise my eyebrows. "Now?"

"Jameson's orders," he replies with fake cheer.

Then his expression falls, and he takes in what I'm wear-ing. It's a complicated piece involving a lot of straps, the mate-rial similar to a bathing suit. It covers the important bits and not much else. He glances around and points to another girl. "Bring me... shorts. And a shirt."

She nods and scrambles away.

I appraise him. "You don't really care for this scene, do you?"

"Trapping girls with debts, then only giving them one option to pay it off? Not particularly my style, West."

I grunt. Fair enough. "You were right, by the way."

He cocks his head.

"About Rubert and my father. I guess they did have a deal going."

He shrugs. "I wish I had never discovered that..."

"You found out a lot earlier than when you brought it to Aiden, right?" Why didn't that occur to me? *Jack* is probably the reason Jameson found out in the first place, thus kicking off his insane plan. The day he came into the office and mentioned it... it's burned into my memory because I was so angry that he'd even insinuate it.

But he probably had already claimed as much to Jameson, and the information was only then circulating back to Aiden. Framed as new information.

"Yes," he admits. "Jameson needed—"

"Jameson killed my father for that," I interrupt.

The girl returns with clothes, and I pull them on quickly. Then we're off, my bare feet padding across the smooth concrete after him. We get onto the elevator. It immediately drops down, lower than the parking garage level.

It opens onto a lower garage level, but there aren't any cars. Just a ramp leading upward.

"Ready, Ms. West?" Jameson asks. He steps out of the

shadows. "I've been waiting for this moment. My son does like to do things dramatically."

I roll my eyes. "He must get that from you."

He only smiles.

"So, what? Did you threaten him to keep him in line? Did you expect him to be like Wilder?" I hate this role I'm playing. Egging him on. When he snaps... it's just us down here. Him and me. Even Jack has disappeared.

I glance around, though, because the shadows are deceptive. It isn't just us.

We're surrounded by guards.

DeSantis men, armed and ready, linger along the fringes of the garage.

I gulp. This can go bad *very* quickly.

"What's your plan?" I ask again.

His smile is purely manic. Like he's been waiting for this moment for a *long* time.

"I'm going to enjoy ruining your life," he says. He tilts his head, something catching his attention, and grabs my arm. He hauls me against his body and presses a gun to my temple. "Feel familiar? This is the same gun that killed your father."

He chuckles.

I flatten my lips and stand there, more vulnerable than ever. I miss my knife, my ring, my life. It's been two days and you'd think I was held captive for a year. Aunt Mary must be worried sick. Colin, too. He would've had to step up and lead the family.

Xavier...

Would he still protect my family if I wasn't around to enforce that? Would he honor our agreement?

"Are you going to blow my brains out?" I ask.

He nudges the muzzle harder into my temple, forcing my head to move to the side. "A quick and easy death? You don't deserve the honor."

S. MASSERY

I shiver. "What did I do to make you hate me?"

A black SUV comes down the ramp, stopping twenty feet away. The headlights make it impossible to see who has arrived.

Anxiety pricks at my skin.

Jameson doesn't answer me. He's suddenly on alert, although his posture doesn't change. It's more of an attitude shift. He goes from manic to cold.

The headlights flick off, the driver door opens, and Aiden steps out. He leaves the door open and strides toward us.

"Ah, ah," Jameson tsks. "Not so fast."

Aiden pauses, taking me in. Relief and fear fight in equal measure in my head. His father has already demonstrated that he'd happily shoot his son to make a point. And he knows Luca can be controlled through Amelie.

But he has neither Amelie or Luca...

He just has me.

Finally, Aiden shakes his head and returns to the vehicle. He drags someone out of the backseat and leads them toward us. Aiden's victim has a bag over his head, a giant orange sweatshirt, and hands bound behind him. He stumbles on the slight decline in the floor, and Aiden roughly keeps him upright.

They stop halfway between the SUV and us.

"Give me Gemma," Aiden says.

Jameson grins and shoves me in his direction. Suddenly, twenty red dots align on Aiden's chest.

"Make one wrong move, and you're both dead," Jameson says.

I don't have to look to know they're probably illuminating my chest, too.

Aiden focuses on me, motioning me forward. I walk slowly toward him, terrified that the *one wrong move* will be simply moving too fast. I reach him and pause.

"Keep going," he says. "Get in the car. I love you."

I spare a glance at the man he has captive. More than a glance, really. A bad feeling takes root.

"Aiden. Please tell me—"

He releases his hostage and grabs my arm, towing me to the SUV. He shoves me into the passenger seat and slams the door. The driver's side is still open, though, and their footsteps —plus my harsh breathing—are the only things I seem to be able to hear.

His expression tells me he's sorry. All I can do is watch him lead his hostage closer to his father.

"Gemma," Jameson calls.

I flinch.

He turns the man around and yanks off the hood.

My brother blinks in the sudden light. There's a cloth tied around his head, cutting through his parted lips. He couldn't have warned me if he tried. His wild eyes find mine, though, and he immediately thrashes.

Jameson raises his gun.

I scream. The sound echoes.

But he doesn't shoot him—he just swings the butt of it, clipping my brother's temple.

No one catches him as he falls.

I scramble for the door handle, but suddenly arms wrap around me from the backseat. I flail, still shrieking. My heart is going to fracture. Aiden just gave up *my brother*.

"Please stop," a familiar voice says in my ear. "You're going to make me deaf."

I crane around, meet Xavier's eyes, and punch him in the face.

He drops back, hands on his nose, and I make it out of the car. I don't have a plan. Save Colin? Throttle Jameson? Or better—Aiden?

But a second later, I register what has happened in the precious few moments it took me to escape Xavier.

Jameson's gun is now trained on Aiden.

"What are you doing?" I yell.

"What I should've done when you first entered the picture," Jameson replies. "You are my fucking *son*, and you will act like it." He jerks his gun toward the elevator. "Pick up Colin and bring him in. You're not leaving with your precious little fiancée."

I freeze.

His words register for Aiden at the same time they do for me—but he's resigned to it. Instantly. His whole life, he's had to follow his father's orders or face his wrath. One week of Aiden's life being turned upside down hasn't changed his core.

"She leaves here unharmed," Aiden tells him.

Jameson makes a noncommittal noise. "You're not in a place to be making demands. *But*—she'll be unharmed if she's out of my sight in the next two minutes."

Xavier doesn't give me a chance to argue. He drags me back and practically throws me into the passenger seat, then hops in beside me. He slams it into reverse, and our tires squeal on the concrete as he makes a fast getaway.

I stare at Aiden as we go, until Xavier hooks the wheel and we curve out of sight.

Now I have nothing, and Jameson has everything.

CHAPTER 26
Gemma

W ar council.

It's something my mother used to talk about. "Sorry, honey, Dad won't be joining us for dinner tonight. He's meeting with the war council."

I didn't know what it meant until I was a teenager, and I realized it was his way of plotting revenge. Just because there was a truce didn't mean our family didn't feud with the DeSantises. Quite the opposite, actually. Everything was just disguised under mysterious happenings. Cops hassling us. Bribes getting lost. Permits not being passed, or held up in red tape.

But the truce has clearly gone out the window.

Do you recognize the view? Aiden had asked me, the night he brought me to the tower. We stared out at the building across from us, and I had no idea what it was—I didn't even know where *I* was.

Now, I pace the glass-walled office that looks out onto the DeSantis tower. We're twenty stories up, and I have a clear view down into the restaurant. And straight across, into the empty DeSantis offices.

I imagine I'm looking into Aiden's, but I have no idea.

This floor was used as a law office owned by Aunt Margaret. Funny how she can run a firm of defense lawyers, but she failed to keep her husband out of jail. She doesn't practice law—she just has an interest in business. And when this business suffered the scrutiny her husband's trial brought her, she closed it down.

I should've recognized it. My father and I would visit her sometimes for lunch. I'd sit on the floor and play with dolls while they talked business.

But now, I've assembled my own war council.

Two of Xavier's five friends have agreed to join me: Cole, the councilwoman's son, and Wes. Xavier insists that the other three are working, although I'm not quite sure what that means anymore.

My trust is a fragile thing.

Amelie and Luca sit at the table, as well.

And Aunt Mary. I'd like to think Kai would be with me if he was still alive.

Turner and Marius are working. As good protection as they've been... I don't need them in my war council.

And now, everyone is digesting what I've told them. I'm mostly concerned about Luca and Amelie. Apparently, Aiden didn't tell them about Wilder. I can appreciate his tight-lipped nature, but my worry is fraying.

I'm barely holding it together.

Jameson played his trump card. He has Colin, and it's only a matter of time before my brother is tortured into admitting he killed Wilder. And he has Aiden.

The one I love.

Who turned my brother in... to save me.

I can't imagine a worse scenario.

Oh, and we don't have Wilder. Don't know where he is, if he's even in the city. If Jameson gives a shit about his eldest son at all. Because there's another chance that Jameson doesn't care—that he'd be fine if Wilder's head was mailed to him.

"Gemma," Xavier says, snagging my arm. "Please sit."

Amelie is pale across the conference table. She leans into Luca, who seems equally stunned. "I just don't understand it," she whispers. "Did he really want to get out of marrying me?"

"I..." I shrug helplessly. "Who knows?"

"That's why the death certificate took so long," Luca muses. He's jumped to the same conclusion Aiden did. "Because Dad probably had to bribe someone to fake it."

"Right."

Amelie checks her phone, then sets it back down. "I warned Mariella."

I stare at her. "The girl Wilder had a fling with?"

She frowns. "It wasn't a fling. Not to her. And yes, I warned her because we're friendly, and him being alive is a major upset." She turns her glare on me. "How could you not tell me?"

I open my mouth to retort, but there's no excuse. I *should've* told her.

"Sorry," I mutter. "The stakes are too high on this. Jameson had Luca bent under his thumb because you were in his control. What would've happened if—?"

"And Colin knows," Wes adds. "Did you show him the proof?"

The papers from my car are spread out on the table. Each of them read everything, and I hoped something would come of it. A clue Aiden and I missed, or... *something*.

I shake my head. "Never. We didn't really talk too much these past few weeks."

"Could work in our favor," Wes says. "Maybe Colin won't focus on that. Or if he does, Jameson could brush it off without proof."

I shudder. It's time for a plan.

"If you were trying to hide from the world, where would you go?" I get up again. I can't sit still—not when Aiden and Colin are *right there*. Right across the street. And yet, unreachable.

Amelie's phone chimes, and her eyes narrow. She rubs her hands over her face.

"What is it?" Luca asks.

She glances at her husband. "Did you know…?"

He shakes his head and takes her phone, reading the message. He frowns. "Wilder has a sister."

My mouth drops open. "Excuse me?"

He slides the phone across to me. It's from Mariella. Amelie told her that Wilder was alive, then asked if she had any ideas of where he might go. A long-shot question, considering I'm not sure that Mariella has ever been to the United States.

But there's Mariella's response, clear as day.

Maybe with his sister?

I slide the phone back to Amelie. "Get me more information on that." Then I turn to Xavier. "If you were hiding, where would you go?"

He's the expert at hiding, after all.

"Somewhere no one would expect," he answers.

Shit.

"And if Jameson's biggest embarrassment was letting his wife leave, and she got pregnant with someone else's child… He wouldn't breathe a word of that to anyone." I find myself pacing faster behind my chair. "I mean, why would he want anyone to know? He has a reputation to uphold."

"He cheated on Abigail with my mother," Luca points out.

"Right, of course. Misogyny at its finest. He can do it, but no one can do it to him. And she might not have even cheated —she just wanted out. He let her leave?"

Luca nods. "Yeah, I was pretty young."

I chew on my lower lip, thinking. My gaze lands on Amelie, who has raised the phone to her ear. A moment later, she puts it on speaker.

"You're here with Luca and me," Amelie says. "And my friend, Gemma."

"Hello, all." Mariella's English is clear, although her accent is thick Italian. Her voice is like a song, though. I can immediately see why Wilder would've been drawn to her.

"So, this sister?" Amelie pries. "Please, anything you might know."

"She's probably fifteen or sixteen by now," Mariella says. "I don't remember much. We were teenagers in love, with other focuses. They shared a mother. He didn't find out about her until the girl was already born and tucked away from Jameson."

A teenager.

Did... did Abigail DeSantis leave Jameson *because* she was pregnant? To protect her child?

"I hope that was helpful," Mariella says. "After our first encounter with Luca and Amelie, we searched her parents' villa in France. I always thought it looked more lived-in than it should for a summer home that wasn't in use, but my brothers brushed me off."

Amelie's shoulders jump up.

"Thank you," Luca says. "You've been helpful, and we appreciate it."

"If you find him, tell him to eat shit." Mariella laughs, then hangs up.

"What is it?" Cole asks Amelie.

"I... um..." She grabs her water and takes a shaky sip. "After Wilder's funeral, I went back to Sanremo. But I flew through France... we stopped at the villa."

"And...?" Xavier taps his fingers on the table.

She sighs. "There were just a few things off about the house. A cup in the sink, the kitchen chairs not stacked on top of the table like we normally left it. And... oh god." She visibly pales. "There was a noise upstairs. I didn't investigate. I didn't —what if it was him? Hiding?"

Luca wraps his arm around her waist and lifts her onto his lap. She curls into him.

"If it was, you probably were smart to avoid him." I try to get her to look at me. "Seriously, Ames. If you discovered him, he could've killed you."

She shivers violently.

"It's okay," Luca says into her hair. "It'll all be over soon."

I sit heavily. "It could be over for you now," I offer. "Get on a plane, get the hell out of dodge."

"You need help finding Wilder and Aiden's half-sister." Amelie sniffs.

"About that..." Aunt Mary finally stirs. She's been so quiet, it was easy to forget she's here. "Last I heard, Abigail still owned a house out on Long Island. It was in her family for generations."

My heart drops into my feet.

And all at once, my little field trip with Aiden comes rushing back. I'm a fucking *idiot*. I met Wilder and Aiden's sister. Looked her in the eye on the step of *her mother's house* and asked if she knew an Abigail.

"Fuck," I whisper.

"Language," Aunt Mary admonishes, although it's definitely halfhearted.

"I think I met her," I tell the tale. "And... yeah, I can definitely see Wilder being there."

Xavier meets my eyes. "How sure are you?"

"If I gave you a number, I'd be guessing. Maybe ninety percent?" I shake my head. "But Xavier... I need to know: even if you don't get a chance at Jameson, are you still willing to help me?"

Twice now, Xavier has stared down the man who decimated his family.

And twice, he hasn't done anything about it.

Maybe he's biding his time... or maybe he's scared of going through with it.

But he just lifts his chin, and an easy, cocky grin slides into place.

It's a mask. Just the same as the one I wear when I'm out of my depth and trying to be strong. The same one Aiden wears when he's dealing with ugly things.

"I still want my shot at him," he finally says. "But you've grown on me, little West."

Cole nods.

And something *else* occurs to me.

"Wait a second. *You.*"

"Me?" Cole grins.

I wag my finger between both of them. "You both... *you're* the mystery donors, aren't you? You wanted to hurt the DeSantises in more ways than one."

Xavier laughs. "She finally figured it out. I only told you about our companies *eons* ago."

Cole joins in, and it's infectious. He's right: I could've put it together a lot quicker than I did. Part of me wondered if it was Aiden... But, no. Positioning himself as someone the future governor had allegiance to is much more up Xavier's alley.

The whole room laughs, mostly at my expense, until my phone's shrill ring stops everything.

"I'm getting sick of phone calls," I say to the room.

Aiden's name flashes on the screen... but I somehow doubt it's him.

"Hello?" I answer. I put it on speaker, because I'm pretty sure Aiden wouldn't call to instigate any sexy-time talk. I am more expecting Jameson to be on the other end of the line, anyway, to threaten me.

Or to deliver the news that Colin confessed.

"Gemma." It *is* Aiden. "I'm so sorry."

My throat immediately burns. I haven't decided whether what he did is forgivable yet, but his voice hurts. He sounds... defeated.

Did he know what kind of choice he was making?

"I don't think I should see you anymore," Aiden continues.

My muscles lock up, but I still manage a weak, "What?"

Aunt Mary reaches out and takes my hand, and I latch on to her.

"I won't put you through a lifetime of misery."

I scoff. I can't help it. "That's ridiculous."

He's quiet for a moment. "You'd be miserable because I've killed every last person you loved. Because I used you to find your brother."

Lies.

"I might not have pulled the trigger, Gemma, but I put everyone in those situations. I put *you* in them. I killed your father. I killed Kai. I'm going to kill Colin, I knew I was going to kill him even when I decided to take you home with me."

I stare at my aunt and will her to lend me strength. Because this declaration...

"You don't mean that," I whisper.

"I do." He makes a noise of exasperation. "Stay as far away from me as you can, West. So I don't put a bullet in you, too. Everything you know was a fucking lie to get in your head— and it worked."

A joke. A mean trick by his father.

Does he have a gun to Aiden's head? Is he watching his

son talk and laughing to himself? Tears prick the backs of my eyes, and I only blink once before they're streaming down my cheeks.

"Fine," I say, keeping my voice even. I don't know how I do it. "If that's the way you want to play it, go fuck yourself."

I smash the button to end the call and shove my phone away from me.

They watch me in silence, but only Luca is brave enough to break the quiet. "He wouldn't say that to you. Not unless there was a reason for it."

"If he kills Colin, there's no going back. But besides that, he was...." I can only hope that he was lying. That his love wasn't some imagined thing. I nod to myself and brush away the wetness on my cheeks. "I need to find Wilder. And after that, we need to arrange a meeting with Jameson."

I take a deep breath and spare another glance toward the DeSantis tower. Before, it seemed like a place that held two people I love. Now, it seems darker. More twisted.

The only way we're getting Colin out is if we receive a miracle.

I take inventory of my war council. We all seem more strung out, more exhausted, than we did even an hour ago. My attention lands on Amelie, still on Luca's lap. "Amelie, are you in? Or do you want to join my family upstate?"

"I'm in," she answers quickly. "No fucking way am I missing this."

I nod once. "Luca?"

"In."

"Aunt Mary?"

She squeezes my hand again. "I'd never abandon you or this family, dear."

"Xavier?"

He leans back in his chair. "I already told you I'm in."

"Cole?"

"In."

"Wes?"

"I follow where you lead," he answers.

I roll my eyes and clap my hands, doing my best to wrangle my emotions. "Okay, let's get to work."

CHAPTER 27

Aiden

I did it to save her.

That's the lie I tell myself.

I did it to save her.

But my heart is ripping itself into pieces.

I watch my father try to break Colin, but the boy is stubborn. He's fueled by the hate his father force-fed him, but even then, he won't admit to something he hasn't done. He laughs in my father's face.

I turn away when Dad strikes Colin. The latter is already bloody, one of his eyes swollen shut. He probably has a cracked rib or two, as well. There's a camera mounted in the corner of the room, ready to pick up any confession.

But so far, the only thing that's spilled are Colin's blood and my father's confessions.

Things that would never see the light of day.

I told Gemma to get out of the city. To leave before it's too late.

Jameson DeSantis has won: he has Colin. He'll get a confession. And then he'll take it to whoever the fuck he thinks is in charge of the Wests after Colin, and they'll have to leave. Or be stamped out like a dying fire.

Dad makes a comment about the leader of the Wests, and my shoulders hike up.

"Not my rodeo," Colin wheezes on a laugh. "So go ahead and fucking kill me, old man. It wouldn't dent our family. And I certainly won't admit to a murder I didn't commit."

I turn back to the screen. And the way my father straightens with realization.

He had the West leader in his grip... and he let her go.

I smile with grim satisfaction, knowing she might be out of the city by now. Away, to wherever the West women were hiding. Away with Amelie, perhaps, to Sanremo. Anywhere is better than this blood-drenched city.

I did it to save you, Gem. But I can't save everyone... I'm not even sure I can save myself.

CHAPTER 28

Gemma

We stole a car.

Well, *steal* might be a little... no, it's accurate. We jacked it off the curb in the Bronx, and no one batted an eye. It's early morning, barely light out, so naturally there wasn't really anyone around *to* bat eyes at us. The borough is still fast asleep.

I smother my own yawn.

Xavier and Cole ride shotgun. Amelie and I are in the back. Wes and Luca are scoping out the DeSantis tower, although they're under strict orders to remain out of sight. Still, we needed to know if Jameson was leaving.

The last thing we want is to plan this whole thing on an assumption.

The car's the important part, though. We couldn't roll through Long Island's fancy neighborhoods in a blacked-out SUV. So we picked a late model BMW. Silver. It shouldn't stand out in the upper-middle-class neighborhood. That's the hope, anyway.

"Are you nervous?" Amelie asks me.

I shrug. Wilder has been this phantom in my head for the

last two and a half months. Before then, I didn't really register him. It was only after Amelie's wedding, and his death, that I was forced to pay attention.

Being framed for murder will do that to you.

"I should be asking you this," I say. "I mean... there's history."

She sighs. "Yeah. *History*. Like, I thought I was going to marry him and then he faked his death to get out of it."

I wince. "It's probably not that."

"I want to smack him as much as thank him. Luca is everything to me, and I know that was hard-won. I just... I don't think Wilder ever really cared besides what my parents were bringing to the table."

"Which was what, exactly?" Xavier asks.

It's a sly question—maybe he doesn't know the involvement of the Pages with the DeSantises.

"Money in exchange for protection," she murmurs. "We had debts out on the street, and the DeSantises were willing to help with that, too. Our union was supposed to be good for both families. I came from a rich family and would've made a nice trophy wife to stick on the shelf. Wilder would've... I don't know."

Cole scoffs. "I'm never getting married."

"Because you don't think you'll find love?" I inquire.

He's handsome—light-brown hair with streaks of natural blond highlights, hazel eyes, a nice face. He towers over everyone. He'd have no issue getting a girl if he wanted one.

"Any girl I bring into the family would be a political pawn for my mother." He meets my eyes in the rearview mirror. "You think Jameson is power hungry? That woman wants the presidency."

Amelie hums. "Wilder was heading there, too."

"Yeah, and she wasn't keen. Secretly, of course. She does

what Jameson wants because of the donations and his influence—"

"And probably the orgasms," Xavier adds.

Cole punches his arm. "Gross, dude."

Xavier laughs. "Come on, we all know they're boning. If he wants her on the hook, he's gotta make it good for her—"

Another punch, this time hard enough to make Xavier wince. He shakes his head, still chuckling.

"Well, there's that," Cole finishes. "The mystery donor has opened up some other opportunities for her. Financially. Although she's waiting to act until the time is right. Maybe she thinks the DeSantises' days are numbered, anyway. It's only a matter of time before another predator claws its way up the food chain."

I lean back and smile. "That time is now. Us."

We turn onto the street and coast to a stop. Xavier puts the car into park and twists around to look at me and Amelie.

"Who's doing this?"

"He's probably not going to recognize me," I offer. I purposefully dressed very differently. My hair in an over-the-shoulder braid, and my eye makeup is dark. Instead of the innocent dress, I opted for black jeans, a white t-shirt, and a black vest.

Luckily, I didn't take my gun with me to the gala. It was waiting for me in my nightstand when I finally got home, and I haven't parted with it since then. I pull it from the hidden holster at my hip and check that it's loaded.

Not that I plan on shooting anyone, but you never know.

"Is anyone else creeped out by the fact that a grown-ass man has been living with a sixteen-year-old?" I voice. "Just me?"

Cole grimaces. "They're siblings."

"He could've rented an apartment," I retort.

"Focus," Xavier snaps. "You're going to the front. Your one job—"

"I'll go with her," Amelie finally says.

Xavier nods. "Fine. Your one job is to not let him get by you. Cole will disable their vehicles, and then we'll cover the back doors."

Since all we could find was a shitty satellite photo of the neighborhood, we don't know exactly what we're dealing with.

Cole raises a little device. "This will jam their cells, and probably the neighbors' phone lines, too."

I take a deep breath. "Got it."

"Where are we putting him?" Amelie asks. "Like, um, should we have brought another—"

"He's going in the trunk." I nudge her. "It'll be fun."

Her eyes widen. "You're devious."

"I've spent too much time in trunks." I unclick my seatbelt and lean forward. "We parking here or moving up?"

"You drive up," Xavier says.

He and Cole slip out and move into the trees. The houses here aren't too close, and hopefully the brush will give them enough cover to go undetected.

I check my gun again, secure it back in its holster, and take the driver's seat.

"You okay?" I ask Amelie.

"Peachy. Might puke, but..."

"I wonder if Aiden knows he has a half-sister," I muse. "He probably would've mentioned it."

She's quiet. "Do you believe him? What he said on the phone?"

"No." I grip the steering wheel tightly. "Well, there's a small seed of doubt, but he's going to need to repeat it to my face to convince me. Until then, I'm just assuming he's his dad's pawn."

"Okay."

"You believed it?"

She shrugs. "You know how I feel about them, Gem. I *like* Aiden. He wasn't a bad guy. But yeah, it sounded awfully convincing."

"Lies," I repeat, more to myself than her.

I pull into the driveway and park in front of one of the cars. There are two out front beside that same boat trailer. More company isn't quite what I had in mind... or maybe one of these vehicles is Wilder's. He could've been out the last time I was here.

I snatch a baseball cap from the floor and toss it to Amelie. "Put that on."

"Why?"

"In case he spots us before we spot him." My throat is tight. I can barely swallow. I need this to work.

She doesn't say anything, just wrinkles her nose at the red, stylized *B* on the front. "No one will believe I'm a Red Sox fan," she says under her breath. Still, she follows me out of the car and lingers behind me when I climb the steps to the front door.

I ring the bell and step back.

This is insanity.

The door is pulled open faster this time, the girl glancing around before her gaze lands on me. She doesn't seem to recognize me, though. Her expression is only wary.

I bet Wilder—and probably her mother—drilled *stranger danger* into her head.

"Hi," I say.

"Can I help you?" She cranes to the side and peers at Amelie.

"I think you can." I go back up the steps, until we're face-to-face. It draws her attention back to me. "You're Abigail's daughter, right?"

She stiffens, and *now* she realizes who I am. She tries to swiftly closes the door, but I block it with my foot. I grip the door and force it inward, then hold my hands up. Don't really want to shoot a teenager.

"Listen, I don't really give a shit about Abigail. I'm hoping you know where your brother is. Wilder."

Fear flashes across her face, and she spins around. "They found you!" she screams.

I push her aside and dart forward, but Amelie suddenly grabs me and hauls me back.

A crack of gunfire cuts through the air. The wall beside me catches the bullets, drywall flying everywhere. Amelie and I fall back onto the porch. We scramble to press ourselves to the wall beside the door.

"He can't escape," she mouths.

I nod sharply. Obviously he can't—and he sure as hell can't die, either.

Shit.

"Wilder," I call out. "It's Gemma West. We met once, remember?"

Silence in the house, then, "Show yourself."

I grimace. This is the part where I get shot in the fucking head for being stupid, I just... I know it.

But before I can move, Amelie rises. She gives me a look and steps into the doorway before I can stop her. Her cap is still low, blonde hair loose around her shoulders.

"What's stopping me from killing you?" he asks her.

She must reveal herself—the cap, maybe, or she just lifted her head.

"Amelie."

Fucking hell.

"Put down the weapon, Wilder. We don't want to kill you, just talk."

He laughs. It's loud, with the same sort of confidence it

316

takes to command a room's attention. He hopefully has Xavier's and Cole's guns trained on him from behind, with any luck. But they won't shoot him... not if he's pointing his at Amelie.

Wouldn't risk it.

"My dad put through our marriage certificate," she tells him. "Did your dad relay that to you?"

He pauses. "We're married?"

"That's what was supposed to happen."

I fumble for my phone and swipe to my video, pressing record. Then I tuck it, camera pointing out, into the front pocket of my jeans.

"We were never going to get married," Wilder tells her. His voice is like whiskey. A bit smokey, and its heat curls in the back of your throat. "The wedding was the start of a war."

"The war you wanted to start," she finishes. "To frame the Wests for your death."

I peek around the corner. He stands halfway up the stairs, looking... *fine*. I don't know what I expected, but it wasn't this. Navy-blue swim trunks, a white tank top. His hair is still perfectly cut. No facial hair. The gun is lowered, at his side. He has a fascinated expression on his face that gives me a bad feeling.

To the right of the staircase is a wide hallway that leads to the rest of the house. I catch sight of the sliding door opening, and Xavier slips in.

The sister, whose name I still don't know, is on her ass pressed up against the wall. Tears streak down her face.

"Gemma West," Wilder calls. "Come on out."

I grit my teeth and walk into the open. "You rang?"

"Are you the brains behind this..." His lip curls. "Operation?"

I smile. "Why, are you impressed?"

"Hardly." He raises the gun.

"You pull that trigger, I'll put a bullet in your brain," Cole says. He descends from above, stopping on the stairs just above Wilder. He bumps Wilder's head with the muzzle of his weapon.

Wilder's eyes go wide.

"Surrender," Xavier says, striding quickly down the hallway. His gun is pointed up, at Wilder from another direction.

"Well, shit." Wilder laughs. "You brought backup."

I lift one shoulder. "I'm the brains, remember? I'm not an idiot."

"Yeah, you're just a cu—"

Cole smashes his gun across the back of Wilder's head.

And you know what? It's a sweet sort of payback to see his eyes roll back in his head.

CHAPTER 29
Gemma

S uicide mission.
 I don't know who first mentioned those two
words, but they've been ringing in my ears on repeat
ever since. *This is a suicide mission.* I brought my family in on
the plan—not just some of the Wests, but all of them.

The women have returned to New York City, and the rush
of relief from those who stayed behind has been palpable.
They've been gone for almost two months, and I should've
recognized the strain it was putting on couples.

I recognize it now, feeling Aiden's distance in my chest.

Colin has been in DeSantis possession for three days. He
hasn't cracked—not completely. Jameson would've called.

But part of me fears that, if Colin doesn't break, Jameson
will do worse. He'll give in to whatever demons are in his head
and let out everything on my brother.

So I called Jameson.

Told him Colin would admit the truth if I asked him to—
and I'd only do that if I could see him. Face to face.

My family didn't agree with that. They thought I should
string Wilder up by his ankles outside of the DeSantis tower

and let him bleed out on their front step. That's the sort of retribution *they* wanted.

That won't save my brother.

Or Aiden.

I've been searching for a way to bring them both home to me. It's all I've been able to think about. And this is the only solution I see.

"You ready for this?" Xavier steps into my bedroom and glances around.

I'm not quite sure when he decided that he was, in fact, my personal bodyguard. It was something I had insisted I didn't need. But imagine if he had shadowed me to the bathroom at the gala instead of escorting Amelie and Luca out?

When my thoughts veer down that path, I try to stop it. I tell myself that it would've happened anyway, no matter what. Maybe not that night, but at some point I would've been vulnerable.

With Xavier's question lingering in the air, I kneel beside the unopened safe. I type in the passcode and hold my breath.

It flashes blue and unclicks, and I twist the handle.

It's still there.

The journal, right on top, untouched.

My exhale is loud in my ears, and I meet Xavier's stare. "Did Amelie get her chance to talk to him?"

He nods once.

"Then, I'm ready."

"Good. Let's go." He holds out his hand, and I let him pull me up.

The safe's lid slams closed and automatically locks back up. He gives it an inquisitive glance, but my bet is that he already tried to open it when I wasn't around. Maybe the night of the gala, before he showed, or long before that.

I lead the way downstairs. It's crowded down here, everyone wanting... I don't know. A slice of the action?

Besides stealing DeSantis shipments in some fucked-up, guerilla-warfare-style fight, I've sidelined them.

Cole and Wes stand in front of a converted police SUV. It has the plastic back seats, complete with a divider and doors that won't open from the inside.

That's where Wilder waits for us.

"Good to go," Cole says.

He's second-in-command, I've come to realize. Their structure is fluid, one stepping up when another isn't there, but the subtle pecking order is solid. A captain, a lieutenant, and then the rest.

Xavier and I take this one, while Cole and Wes join the other three guys in a different SUV. That one is less conspicuous, and hopefully it'll slip under the radar.

I turn around and meet Wilder's gaze. He's been quiet for the past twenty-four hours. Refusing to talk.

Shame.

"Were you behind the stolen firearms and marble?" I ask him.

He sneers—and that alone is different. He's given me something for the first time.

"And probably killing Sean, too. You know, Aiden didn't believe me when I told him it was you." I tap my lips. "Oh, and framing the Wests. But maybe that was Daddy DeSantis's idea? He seems to be the mastermind. You're just a puppet."

"Gemma," Xavier says under his breath.

"I'm not a fucking puppet," Wilder spits. "Where are you taking me?"

I smile. "It's a surprise."

He lunges forward and batters the divider.

My smile widens. "Am I detecting fear? Dear Wilder, you're *dead*, remember?" I pull out his death certificate and hold it up. "No one would believe me if I killed you outright."

He's come unhinged. I almost wanted him to remain ice cold.

"How much communication did you have with your father?"

Xavier side-eyes me, but my attention is fixed on Wilder.

"Nothing," he says. "I was left to my own devices after I got back into the States."

I wonder if Jameson actually *knows* Wilder is back from France. I don't bother confirming if he was hiding out in the Pages' villa. It's one of those details that doesn't really matter. And the sister—she's with Aunt Mary for the time being.

Apparently, Wilder and Aiden's mother died almost five years ago, leaving the house to her then-pre-teen daughter. The girl, Melody, was raised by an aunt and uncle until she filed for emancipation, got a job as a waitress, and took back the house.

Then, her half-brother showed up on her doorstep.

"Coming up," Xavier mutters.

I nod and face forward again. We pull onto a side street, and Xavier steps out. He yanks open Wilder's door and grips his wrists. He snaps on metal handcuffs, then secures them with zip ties. Wilder watches him stoically, but he winces when Xavier reveals a black bag.

Xavier grabs the front of Wilder's shirt to keep him from throwing himself backward. He sticks a strip of duct tape over his mouth, then shoves the bag over his head. Muffled yells come from under the cloth, and I can practically taste Wilder's panic.

I know how that feels, too.

Cole's vehicle arrives, coasting to a stop behind us.

He hops out and comes to my window.

"What?" I ask.

"We have a problem."

I raise my eyebrows. "Okay...? I love problems."

Wilder makes a muffled noise behind us. I motion for Cole to step back. I hop out and slam my door, then cross my arms. Xavier meets me on the curb.

"Aiden's guys—the sniper and the other two—are in position."

Ugh.

"Where?"

"Rooftop across the street." Cole looks down the road. We're still a few blocks away from our final destination, but I imagine he's picturing the layout in his head. "Not sure who they're fighting for."

"Aiden, of course," I reply. "But they probably don't know that's what I'm doing, too."

"What do you want to do?" Xavier asks.

I want someone else to decide.

I want to crawl in a hole.

I *want* my brother and Aiden back in one piece.

But only one of those things is doable right now. I glance at my watch and frown. We don't have time—not if I don't want to be extra late and "Proceed as planned and hope they don't shoot us."

Aiden's guys probably won't shoot me, but Jameson will.

We get back in the car, and Xavier takes us down the last stretch of road. We round the corner and pull up to the front of the Italian restaurant. We're in Queens. The place my father died.

It seems like Jameson is already here—and he's brought an entourage. DeSantis guards stand at the doors, and I'd bet anything that more are inside.

Good.

I take a deep breath and hop out of the car. I retrieve Wilder, who is clumsy on his feet, still blind, and shove him in ahead of me.

The guards open the doors for me. They don't meet my

gaze, instead keeping their eyes outward. Maybe Aiden's sniper will come in handy if we need to make a quick exit.

Inside, Jameson sits at the same table as before. The whole place is empty except DeSantis men, and for that I'm grateful. No civilians should be caught up in our mess.

As soon as he sees me, he rises and claps.

"My, my," he calls.

I jerk Wilder to a halt. He grunts, low enough that only I can hear him.

"Gemma, I must say," Jameson continues, "I didn't think *you* would be the one Lawrence entrusted to run his family's businesses. Are you drowning under the pressure? Perhaps that's why you've come to make a deal for your brother? And you've brought a hostage with you... how quaint."

He'll think it's quaint until he realizes who I have in my grip.

My gaze goes past Jameson, to where my brother stands. Sam, the traitor, is at his back with a knife to my brother's throat. And Aiden... Aiden stands off to the side. Unrestrained. His eyes burn, but I don't want to focus on that.

All I can hear is his lies, telling me everything between us was in my head.

I *know* it's false. Knew it as soon as he spoke it... but he said it. He created those words, and now they live between us.

Jameson slams his hand on the table, and silverware rattles.

"You know how I treat disrespect, *girl*."

I nod slowly. I do know, intimately. I take in the other people in the room: Mac, his gaze impassive. Another man, who I have to guess is Sam and Cat's father.

"I guess we should get on with it, then," I answer.

Jameson sneers. "Are you calling the shots?"

I shrug. "If you won't, sure." My gaze moves to Colin again. His face is so swollen, but his eyes are steady on me. "Are you okay?"

My brother grimaces. "Dandy."

I glance at Aiden again. He's moved his attention from me to the hooded man beside me. A deep scowl mars his brows, pulls his lips down. Worry tugs at him, too. He probably is of similar opinion to my family: that this is my suicide mission.

And he's probably debating how to prevent it.

"So, Jameson, what am I telling my brother to admit?" I tap my fingers against my chin. "Remind me, it seems there's a long list of complaints."

The leader of the DeSantis family rises swiftly. "You *mock* me?"

"Just want to make sure I have it right the first time," I reply drily.

Mac glares at his brother. "Is this a waste of our time?"

"Your *brother* killed my son!" Jameson yells at me. "He's going to pay for his crimes."

His acting skills are off the charts. Spittle flies from his lips, and even his hair has come free from its gel. He yanks his gun from his waistband and points it at me for a second, then swings it around and aims at Colin.

"Tell her, Colin," he goads. "Tell her how you snuck into the church—"

"Stop," I order. "You know as well as I do that Colin had nothing to do with this. The one at fault is in this room—but it isn't my brother."

Colin trembles against the blade, and it's already begun to slice into his skin just from the contact. A trail of blood runs down his throat, into his shirt.

I kick at Wilder's leg, and he crashes to his knees beside me.

Jameson wheels back around to me, and the gun comes with him. I stare down the barrel—even though he's ten, fifteen feet away—and steel myself to be shot.

"Who is at fault? You?"

"You," I say.

Aiden flinches.

I yank the hood off and reveal Wilder. His wide eyes take in the room, and he struggles against the cuffs. With my free hand, I slip their shipping container key from my pocket. Wilder had it in his possession, and I now toss it back to Aiden.

"I solved your theft, by the way."

He catches it and stares down at his palm.

I yank my gun free of its holster and press it to Wilder's temple, gripping his hair. The room has fallen silent.

"Tell them, Jameson." My voice comes out light. Casual. The opposite of how I actually feel. "Tell them how you and Wilder schemed to fake his death in order to start a war and get rid of us."

"Ludicrous."

I rip the tape off Wilder's mouth. "Let's see if you break faster than a West," I say in his ear. I direct his attention to my brother. "Do you think you could take those injuries?"

He's been mostly untouched in our possession, unlike Colin.

"Poor little Wilder," I continue. "Raised to be on the frontlines of the family. You were going to run for *president* one day. And now..." I drop his death certificate at his feet. "That's what *your* father has done to you."

"It was Dad's idea."

"You stupid son of a bitch," Jameson says. "You were supposed to stay out of the country."

Wilder glares at him. "I came back because you said I'd get my *life* back once the Wests left."

"And you broke into your own shipping container," I finish. "Hired Rubert to frame us. Delivered the shipment to an old West warehouse, not realizing we'd shut it down months prior."

His expression wipes clean. Ah, see? That's the rub.

"All these crimes, Jameson, are just fabrications. *You* murdered my father in cold blood in this restaurant. You broke the truce."

The color leeches from Jameson's face.

"Excuse me?"

I lift my shirt and retrieve the file I had tucked there. It would've been destroyed if I was shot, but... a girl's got to take risk sometimes, right? Mac walks forward and takes it from me. He flips through it, his face going from wary to downright outraged.

"You broke this," Mac tells his brother. "And the consequence—we have to leave New York."

Murmurs break out around the room.

"Fuck this," Jameson says. He raises his gun and aims it at me.

With a roar, Aiden lunges forward and tackles his father. The gun goes off, and a burning sensation tears through my shoulder.

The whole place promptly explodes into chaos.

"He's mine!" someone screams.

Xavier.

His guys help him bulldoze a path through the DeSantis guards, but everyone seems to be unsure about who they're fighting. More gunfire peppers the air, and I fall backward. I land flat on my back, clutching my upper arm. Pain radiates in waves down my arm and across my collarbone.

Wilder falls to the side, then scrambles up. He casts one look at me and immediately orders a guard to follow him. They rush out the back.

Aiden and Jameson grapple for only a moment before Jameson's gun flashes.

I scream.

Blood.

There's blood this time, following the shot. Jameson shoves his son off him and sprints toward the back room, but Xavier blocks his path. The two glare at each other for a moment, and I'm sure Xavier will kill him.

But there's no gun in either of their hands. Jameson must've dropped his or ran out of ammunition.

"Eldridge," Jameson finally says. "I should've recognized your face at the gala—and you should've stayed in your hole."

Xavier stares at him, and it seems he's frozen. I watch him through blurry eyes, and Jameson simply strides past him. Sam steps forward, shoving Xavier out of the way, and chases after his uncle.

My chest hurts.

I stagger to my feet and rush to Aiden, falling to my knees beside him. He's bleeding from his chest. A hole up high. The tendons in his neck are strained, and his chest rises and falls unevenly.

"Help me!" I scream at Xavier. Or Cole. Someone.

I lean over Aiden and try to cover the wound with my hands, but only one of my arms is working. It's easy to shove aside my pain and lean into the adrenaline, the panic.

The shooting has stopped.

The fight's over as fast as it began.

The room tilts, and light spots burst like white fireworks in front of my eyes.

"You're going to be just fine," I tell him.

His eyes are closed, and his face is pale.

"Just fine," I repeat.

"Gemma." Colin skids to a halt beside me. "Holy shit, they shot you."

"Colin, get someone to fucking help Aiden *right now*."

I'm going to pass out. It's one of those things you know just before it happens. My skin goes from cold to impossibly hot, like I'm burning from the inside out. My heartbeat feels sluggish in my chest. And those white spots intensify until my mind quits.

There's no Aiden.

No me.

No blood or pain.

Just... absolutely nothing at all.

CHAPTER 30

Xavier

I failed in every aspect.

  Jameson got away.

  Wilder, too.

  I wanted the DeSantis family to pay for hurting my family. Jameson killed my father and got away with it—and now I've let him slip through my fingers.

  I cast one look at Aiden and Gemma, bleeding together on the floor, and my stomach turns. I'm a coward compared to them. I had a shot and I didn't take it. I didn't pull my weapon. I just...

  Let.

  Him.

  Go.

  "Come on," Cole says. An ambulance's sirens wail in the distance. "X. Move your ass."

  I snap out of it and let him lead me away. If he's caught here, his mother would murder all of us. If *I'm* caught...

  There would be no resurfacing.

  So I follow him outside, let him shuffle me into the car

next to Wes. Boston sits in front of me. The other two are in the repurposed police SUV.

I lean back and close my eyes, and I acknowledge that I'm abandoning Gemma. Arguably when she needs me most of all.

Just another thing I'll have to live with.

CHAPTER 31
Aiden

I wake with blind panic.

Hands push me down, restraining me, and I automatically fight against them. I can't breathe. I can't see. I can't *think*.

My muscles are lead, but I rebel anyway. My fist connects with someone, and they curse.

"Easy," a familiar voice whispers.

Her body collapses into mine, her hair fanning across my arm.

"We're okay."

I hug her tightly, cracking my eyes to make sure she's real.

Gemma is curled into my side, her arm in a sling. I automatically loosen my grip, fearing causing more injury. She tips her head back and meets my gaze.

"I knew you were lying."

A hoarse chuckle escapes me. "Sorry, baby."

I drift off again after that without taking inventory of my injuries. There's no pain, just a heaviness moving through my blood. A sedative and painkiller concoction, maybe.

Either way, Gemma is with me. And wherever we are, we're alive.

CHAPTER 32

Gemma

TWO MONTHS LATER

A resounding *boom* echoes through Manhattan, and a moment later, a building shudders. Well, the frame of it does, as another piece is lifted off and dropped to the ground. Over the past month, it's been dismantled slowly. Now all that's left is the metal skeleton.

They're taking down the DeSantis tower today.

It comes on the heels of the last DeSantis leaving New York City—officially, anyway. Once the dust settled from the restaurant's chaotic meeting, Mac and I met to discuss the truce. It had been signed by Jameson and my father, and notarized. There was even a clause that said it would have to be upheld even if one of the signers had died.

It didn't bind my father and Jameson—it bound our families, our businesses, our properties. Everything was at stake. It's unclear if Jameson knew what he was risking. He might've just been arrogant enough to think he'd get away with it.

But Dad had thought to close the loopholes.

Aunt Mary pops a bottle of champagne behind me.

The DeSantis construction business declared bankruptcy.

The Pages slunk away, pretending to not be involved with either Mafia family. And the Wests are celebrating.

"You did it," she says, handing me a glass.

I nod.

On the other side of the city, in Brooklyn, West Bar is also celebrating. After two long months, it's reopening.

Construction moved at double their usual speed in time to catch the last tourist rushes before winter sets in. Colin supervised it. He needed a project, and West Bar kept him busy. Plus, there's something about manual labor that settles nightmares—at least temporarily.

Some of the girls who were trapped as unwilling prostitutes in the DeSantis tower have been helping him. Others have moved to my clubs across the city as waitresses and barkeeps. The sex appeal sells but keeps them safer than their former occupation.

If you can call it that.

Debts wiped clean.

Fresh starts all around.

I sip the champagne and glance around the war council room. It's back to being an empty level of this giant skyscraper, although that will change. I'll find someone to lease it out, as the other floors are. And on the illegal side, we've broken into the weapons business, taking over the demand from Sean's Weapon Emporium *and* Rubert. Turns out, their small gang was made of lesser men.

And they didn't want to go up against me.

"You ever think of getting away?" I ask my aunt.

She smiles and shakes her head. "No. Kai's spirit is in this city, and in Colin. Even if I had wanted to leave, nothing could separate me from it now."

I nod. The cranes are lowering giant metal shafts to the ground, and the process is hypnotic. Every so often, the *boom* repeats. Another layer down.

"Do you want to get away?"

I shrug. "Sometimes. I'd like to know more than just this city."

Amelie and Luca returned to Europe.

"Honey." Aunt Mary stops at the window beside me. "You're twenty years old, you—"

"Nineteen," I interrupt.

She gives me a *look*. "Your birthday, Gemma?"

"Is next week..."

My aunt bursts into laughter. She cups my cheek. "*Today* is September nineteenth, my darling niece."

Crap. How did I miss that? I exhale. This is a red flag that I've been too caught up in West business.

"Well, no time like the present for a present," she adds. "Come with me."

I drain my glass and set it down next to the bottle, then follow her into the next room over. It was once Aunt Margaret's very impressive office, but now it's bare. Except for a small, round table in the center of the room that holds a bouquet of roses...

And a clothes rack with one garment bag hanging from it.

"The last two times I put on fancy clothes, I was kidnapped." I eye her. "What's going on?"

She just smiles. "Note on the table. See you downstairs."

I stare after her, but she doesn't look back. I'm wishing I had refilled my flute, but instead I bypass the note and unzip the black bag. Inside is a gorgeous silver halter top dress. It has thousands of little silk tassels hanging from it, giving it movement. There are silver sandals, too—no heels.

Dinner, maybe?

I backtrack to the table, leaning down to smell the roses. That's what the saying demands, right? Sometimes you just have to... well, you know.

The envelope is in Aunt Mary's handwriting, and I exhale.

I don't know what I was thinking it could be, but if it's from her and not some secret ploy... then it's safe.

I slide my finger under the lip and take out the folded paper. It's creased heavily, and it seems vaguely familiar.

It isn't until I smooth it out that it hits me: it's my father's handwriting.

Damn it.

Tears well up in my eyes before I can get a grip on myself. I blink rapidly, take a shaky breath, and then read. It just... starts. No introduction, no greeting. I don't know who he's writing this to, or why. There isn't a date on it, either.

GEMMA DESERVES a life outside this family. Outside this city. I hope you're the one to give that to her. I look at her and I see hope. Not just for herself—for everyone she comes into contact with. She's the bright light in my life.

She was a brilliant star in Faith's life, too.

And her dying wish was that Gemma not experience the heartache my wife has suffered. A Mafia woman is strong. Courageous. Able to stand up to her enemies and her husband in equal measure. But with strength comes an infinity for loss. Her brother. Her parents.

I lost her before she could lose us.

Take Gemma away from here. Give her a life of passion.

That's my condition.

And love her. Always, always love her.

I SHOULD'VE PUT the dress on first.

Now, I feel like an idiot crying my brains out and pulling on the silver dress. I slip my bra off after the dress is secure and drop it on top of my clothes. It doesn't really matter, does it? Modesty and all that.

My hair is a wild mess, and I quickly tame it with two little braids that twist around the crown of my head. No makeup—no solution for that, though.

The note would've been to Aiden...

And now it's in my hands. Another connection to my father. I run my thumb over his signature at the bottom of the paper. I locate Aunt Mary downstairs, leaning against the passenger side of my car. She grins and opens the door.

"You look fantastic."

"Thanks." Am I blushing? My face is hot.

I slip in, and she circles to the driver's side. We go through the city and out. I eye her, but she seems content to let me be surprised. I finally raise the note.

"Did you read this?"

She glances at it. "Nope."

"You don't know what it said."

"Not a clue. Did you read it?"

I roll my eyes. "Of course I did. Are you... Are you taking me to Aiden?"

Her lips tip up, but she doesn't respond. My stomach somersaults. Another few minutes, and we're coasting to a stop at the gate to Aiden's neighborhood. She types in the code.

I glare at her.

In truth, I've been avoiding him. It was hard enough in the following week after we were both shot, and his family was essentially served an eviction notice by yours truly. But harder still for us to grapple with the major events of our lives.

Wilder had been alive and pulling strings—specifically, *Aiden's* strings. That didn't hurt nearly as much as Aiden's phone call. There was a small part of me that believed him in that moment, and that small part grew bigger and bigger.

So, no, I haven't seen Aiden in weeks.

"I don't want to be here," I murmur.

She scoffs. "Gemma West. Do not be a coward."

I look away. Too soon, we're turning into his driveway. I want to tell her that I'm not a coward, that I'm just a realist. We could go our separate ways from here. There are no more obligations to fulfill.

"Get out of the car," Aunt Mary prods.

I stifle my sigh and unbuckle my seatbelt. My shoulder has been healing well, but the muscles are still sore. When I reach for something too quickly, my body reminds me that I'm not infallible.

Oh, how I thought I was.

Then again, two months makes a big difference.

"Happy birthday," she says quietly.

"Thank you. But I'm not sure I like you right now." I shove the door open and step out.

As soon as I close the door, she puts it in reverse and rolls away. I turn and watch her speed out of here, and it does prevent me from chasing after her car. Not that she'd let me back in. My mood has been a fractured, black thing. Even doing good things, groundbreaking things, didn't lighten it.

Or stitch me back together.

The garage door rumbles open, revealing Amelie's Porsche. She probably gifted it to him when they left for Italy —he's obsessed with the thing. And, I heard she found out about our little sex adventure on her hood...

Aiden isn't there. The door into the house is open, though. An invitation.

It gives me déjà vu. A waiting elevator. Another beginning.

I shake off my impending shiver and stride inside, hitting the button to shut the garage door, then softly close the house door behind me.

I am Gemma West. Ultimate badass of New York City.

Squasher of tyrants and freer of prostitutes. I cannot be afraid of entering a house.

A house I know rather well, in fact.

Once I'm in, it's a game of hide-and-seek, it seems, because Aiden is nowhere to be found. Not upstairs, in the bedroom or his office. Not downstairs or out back.

I stop in the middle of the kitchen and plant my hands on my hips.

Huh.

This isn't what I expected.

A motorcycle revs outside, and my heart jumps into a frantic beat. I grip the counter, and all my nerves come pouring back into me.

The garage door rumbles open, and the bike roars, then goes quiet. Silence fills the house, and my legs tremble.

I wonder what Aiden is thinking.

Maybe... maybe he doesn't know I'm here.

A month ago, I removed the tracking device he planted on my car.

A week ago, a doctor informed me that I was definitely, absolutely, *not* pregnant.

That was its own fear, a twisting beast that lived in my abdomen for weeks before I caved and went into a doctor's office. It kept me up at night. I'd lie flat on my back and stare at the ceiling, pressing my fingers into my stomach. I would imagine it swollen and not be able to breathe.

Aiden walks in, his head down. He's looking at something on his screen.

But my silver, shimmering dress must catch his attention, because his head jerks up. And his eyes land first on the dress, then my face.

My body tingles.

"Are you a ghost?" he asks me.

I tilt my head. "Do I sound like a ghost?"

He slowly steps toward me. He looks worse than I do—as he should. The bullet that tore through his chest collapsed his lung, and he had a chest tube for days. Then a surgery to fix a complication. Then another surgery that brought him back from the brink of death.

He was out for all of it.

Aiden stops in front of me and lifts his hand to my face. His palm cups my cheek.

I shudder against him.

He almost died.

We both did—but he *really* almost died. A few times.

"How did you get in here?"

My gaze drops. "Aunt Mary."

His head swings around, and he nods to himself. "And Ford, probably. Co-conspirators."

That makes sense.

"Why did you stay away from me, baby?" he asks.

"I—" I touch his chest. "You were covered in blood. In that same forsaken restaurant that my father died."

"A restaurant that's been demolished, I hear," he says.

I sniff. "Right." I bought it outright—the owner was more than happy to sell after not one, but *two* disastrous DeSantis encounters—and ordered its demolition the next day. Needless to say, it came down a lot faster than the DeSantis tower.

"Gemma."

I turn away. "I don't know why my aunt brought me here."

"Because you need to face what you're afraid of."

I'd left the note on the counter. Carried it with me all through this damn house, and I couldn't seem to release it until I discovered he wasn't here. And apparently, didn't know I was coming.

"Dad wanted you to love me." I point at the now-crumpled paper. "And you told me on the phone that it was all a lie."

His gaze softens.

Damn it.

"I wanted you to save yourself," he says.

I shake my head. "That's not how this works. That's not how it's ever worked. It was supposed to be *us* versus *them*. Why didn't you fight? Why did you bring my baby brother into the DeSantis tower?"

No amount of projects can keep Colin's new nightmares away.

Three days.

Three days of torture by Jameson, and whatever happiness was in my brother's personality has cracked and leaked away.

I can't stop my tears from flowing—and *this* is why I didn't want to see him. I'm so terrified to start to cry, because I don't think I'll ever stop.

It took a toll.

Not in the moment, but after. In the quiet.

When I'd wake up to my brother screaming and felt like screaming myself.

When nightmares gripped me by the throat, even in broad daylight.

Noises that sound an awful lot like gunshots make me hit the ground—and I know I'm not the only one to suffer like this.

A few times, I woke up to find Colin sitting at the foot of my bed, his head in his hands.

Just wanted to make sure I was really here, he would say.

"My heart is broken and it keeps breaking," I tell Aiden. "I don't know how to make it stop. I can fix my family's bar or destroy another one. I can erase your family name from the

349

city. But I can't stop myself from dreaming of you being shot, or seeing you intubated in the hospital, or—"

He wraps me in a hug. One arm bands across my back, and his other hand slides up my neck, winding through my hair. I rest my cheek on his chest and bite the inside of my cheek. The sobs are racking up in my throat, blocked by a lump.

But as far as hugs go, it's a fucking good one. I wrap my arms around his waist and hold on for dear life.

He shushes me, just a noise that someone makes to comfort another, but it unlocks everything. I grip his shirt and break again.

I barely register him lifting me. But then we're moving, and he sinks carefully onto the couch. I'm in his lap. I keep my face pressed to his chest and let out all the horrible feelings I've been keeping back. His hands move up and down my back lightly.

"I kept waiting for you to show up," he says in my ear. "The time in the hospital, after I woke up the first time and you were there? That was the last time I slept easily. I kept *waiting* and you didn't come. But it's more than just the two months, Gem. I've been waiting for you for three years. The only lie I've ever told you was that I didn't love you. And I'm so sorry I did that to you. I wanted you to get out of here and save yourself for once."

"You knew I would sacrifice myself a hundred times over to save my brother." And quieter, "And you? A thousand times over."

His fingers flex against my scalp. He tilts my head back so he can meet my burning eyes.

"I love you, Gemma West. Now. Always. I loved you before your father wrote that silly little heartfelt note and practically ordered it." His eyes gleam. "You know I don't take orders well—this is all *me*. And you."

I nod and adjust my position, swinging one leg over so I'm straddling his thighs. My dress slides up, and his hands land on my bare skin.

"I was terrified," I admit. "That everything I had put into motion was going to fail. And then he shot you, and I couldn't stop the bleeding, and no one would help me—"

He nods, absorbing my words.

"I just didn't want it to end like that. On two different sides of the fight."

He leans forward and presses his lips to the corner of my mouth. His tongue darts out, catching still-falling tears, and his mouth moves to my ear.

"I wanted you to succeed."

I roll my eyes. "Your guys were staking out the restaurant."

"Who do you think helped Colin when he went rushing out of the place, screaming for help? He looked like hell warmed over, Ford said. They were the ones who called the ambulance."

"And Xavier?"

Aiden exhales. "No idea."

"Me neither." He didn't return to any West establishment, although we'd been on the lookout for him and his crew. "He didn't go through with it. All his talk of wanting to kill your father..."

"He froze," Aiden says simply. "It happens. Sometimes we create monsters in our heads, but when they're in front of us, we realize they're just people. And my father is a sick son of a bitch, but he can seem deceptively human."

I grimace but nod. It would've been a weight off my shoulders for Xavier to pull the trigger. Jameson and Wilder both got away in the end. And... that's something Aiden and I will have to live with.

"Kiss me," I demand.

A smile graces his features for a quick second, then a more serious expression takes over. He leans forward and catches my lips more fully. His hands, still on my thighs, immediately move up to grip my ass. They slide under my dress and under my panties, keeping the skin contact.

I tremble.

The kiss, though, is sweet. He doesn't rush parting my lips or taking ownership of my mouth, like he has all the time in the world. My heartbeat is a frantic thing, but it slows when he doesn't hurry this moment. I roll my hips forward. His erection brushes my core through my panties and his jeans, and I groan into his mouth. I repeat the motion, grinding on him.

He lets me without trying to take anything more. Just kisses.

I'm wired tight, and it only takes me another minute of rocking against him, humping like a teenager, for it to tip him over the edge. He jerks his hips up, giving me firmer friction.

My climax takes me by surprise. I stop kissing him, our mouths just millimeters apart as I frantically gulp air. And then he grunts, my name on his lips, and comes. I fall forward, my forehead pressing to his, and giggle.

"When's the last time you came in your pants?"

He groans. "When I was twelve, probably. Good thing I was going to change, anyway."

He sets me aside and swiftly kisses me again—a hotter, wetter version of a peck—and rises. I only have to wait a few minutes for him to come back with a glass of water, which he hands to me, and new black slacks.

New outfit entirely, actually. Black collared shirt, the top few buttons open and exposing some of his tattoos, the slacks. A gold watch. A gold chain around his neck. His hair, too, is slicked back. Although I can't tell if that's water or gel.

Still, he looks too good—I clench my thighs together to suppress any outward reaction. Like getting wetter... *again*.

"We're fancy," I accuse. "Why?"

He smirks. "I thought your aunt was going to have you meet me out, but this was the better order of events."

I take his offered hands, and he pulls me up.

"Ready to celebrate your birthday, my love?"

CHAPTER 33
Gemma

B y the time we reenter the city, darkness has fallen. The days are getting shorter, anyway, and the nights chillier. We pull up in front of one of my family's clubs in Brooklyn. I shoot Aiden a weird look, but the bouncer—trained to know and reject DeSantis faces—doesn't bat an eye at him. He does, however, wish me a happy birthday.

Weird.

Aiden leads me inside, skipping the line, and up to the VIP section. The bouncer there nods to both of us, grinning at me. He removes the rope and allows us to pass. We round the corner, and suddenly a crowd is yelling, "*Surprise!*" at me.

I nearly jump out of my skin.

And then I realize who they are, and my jaw drops.

My immediate family, who I hold near and dear, plus a whole lot of Wests. Amelie and Luca. Cole and Wes. And Aiden's sister, Melody, tucked halfway behind Aunt Mary.

My opinion? Aunt Mary needed someone to fill Kai's void, and Melody came along at the perfect time. No family to speak of, except her brothers. One she's never met. One took advantage of the situation. Even though she's emancipated doesn't mean she doesn't need a mother figure.

So they're working things out, although I haven't seen the girl in weeks.

I've been busy.

So busy, I forgot my birthday.

"Happy birthday, princess," Aiden says in my ear.

Goosebumps rise on my arms.

He runs his finger just above the back of my dress.

And then I'm swarmed, although he stays close to me. It's probably because I find his hand and refuse to release it, even when accepting hugs. Colin eyes Aiden, then throws his arms around me.

In my ear, he whispers, "I hope he makes you happy, Gem."

I tighten my one-armed hold on him. "He does," I promise.

Better yet—he *will*. Once we're away from this summer.

I nudge Aiden and drag him aside once the greetings have ended. Melody, I noticed, hung back with my aunt, and I've got an introduction to make.

But not without a warning.

"Um, there's something you should know." I shift. Maybe Luca told him—damn it, that would've made life so much easier. "Your mom had another kid."

His eyes go wide. "Excuse me?"

"That's where we found Wilder, living with her in your mom's family's house on Long Island. Her name is Melody, she just turned sixteen, and she's right there." I gesture to her. "So, um..."

"Holy shit." He rubs his face. "Okay. I'm going to..."

He strides across the room, stopping just short of her.

"Happy birthday," Amelie says in my ear.

The music seems to be getting louder, because I have to lean in to hear her. She flicks one of the tassels on my dress and grins.

"I have news," she shouts.

I eye her. "Yeah?"

"I'm pregnant!"

Whoa. I grab her arms. "Really?"

Luca catches my expression from behind his wife and grins. His arms sneak around her waist, hands on her abdomen. I shake my head in bewilderment. I mean, *yeah*, a baby. Aiden's going to be an uncle.

"Are you happy about it?" I ask.

She laughs. "Yeah, Gem. We're thrilled. Paloma is already threatening us with a home birth in her house."

Paloma—Luca's aunt on his mom's side. Everything I heard about her reminds me of an ideal parental figure. They were helping her out with her restaurant in Sanremo until they got diverted—twice now—back to the States.

"I'm happy for you." I squeeze her hands. "Feel free to name her after me."

Amelie rolls her eyes. "We'll definitely consider it."

"Gemma."

I turn and find Cole and Wes behind me. They each carry drinks, seeming more relaxed than I would've given them credit. I narrow my eyes. "Well?"

Cole has the decency to look sheepish. "I'm sorry for how things panned out."

I scoff. "Really."

"We just came to wish you well," Wes says. "And apologize on behalf of X."

I make a show of glancing around. "I don't see him here to apologize for leaving Aiden and me to die. But, honestly? It's fine. He choked and ran away."

Cole's gaze hardens. It might not be the nicest interpretation of what happened, but what does he want from me? To say, *oh, sorry, these things happen*. Aiden and I can be sympathetic on the inside—but not to Xavier's friends.

I lift my chin. "If I see him again, just know he owes me."

They nod and slip away.

I let out a breath and try to shake it off. It's my *birthday*, after all. I don't need two of Xavier's crew throwing a wrench in my night.

So I do what any newly twenty-year-old would do...

I order myself a drink.

Hours later, most of our party has dispersed. Colin dances with a girl in a throng of bodies, Aunt Mary and the older folks have left us to our antics, and Amelie and Luca sit in a booth, *very* close.

It's cute, but it also sort of makes me nauseous.

Aiden and I dance, too, but we stay away from Colin. I don't need to see my brother in compromising positions.

Eventually, Aiden takes the drink from my hand and leads me away, into a quieter hallway. He presses me against the wall and runs his hands down my sides.

"I can't get enough of you," he confesses. "You're so goddamn beautiful."

I smile and slip my hand into his pants, cupping his cock. It twitches and hardens in my hand. His lips crash down on mine, and he sucks my lower lip into his mouth. I groan at the sting of pain. He shoves me harder against the wall, and I unzip his pants. I don't care that anyone from the dance floor could wander this way and see us. I just need to feel him—for real this time.

He lifts my leg and yanks my panties to the side, then slams inside me. I feel his groan vibrate in his chest and mirror it, the fullness almost too good to be true. Each thrust rocks me back against the wall.

I drag my nails up his neck, into his hair, and raise my hips to meet him. His fingers dip into my panties, rubbing rough circles on my clit. I clench around his dick, the orgasm exploding through me. It seems to go on and on—because he doesn't stop touching me. He prolongs it, the aftershocks coursing through me, and only stills when he jerks to a stop inside me.

His lips leave mine, and he bites down on my neck. I shriek, the sound lost in the music, and spiral away. I swear, my soul leaves my body for a minute. Only his grip on my leg, and the way he pins me to the wall, keep me upright.

Movement at the top of the corridor catches our attention. A couple have stopped, their eyes locking on us.

Without hesitation, Aiden reaches back and draws his gun. He points it at them, and they turn and rush away.

"Holy shit," I mumble.

He chuckles and pulls out of me. I straighten my dress and panties, ignoring the cum seeping out. It sort of gives me an adrenaline high, in a way.

"One more thing," he says in my ear.

"Sure."

He kisses me quickly, then reaches into his pocket.

In the darkness, it's almost too hard to see it—but then it registers.

My mother's ring.

"Marry me, Gemma. For real this time." His hot breath on my ear, and then his teeth chasing it. He nips the shell, his tongue darting out to soothe the spot.

Marry Aiden.

Who would've thought I'd ever get a choice in the matter?

I grin at that thought and hold out my left hand. "Absolutely."

He presses his forehead to mine and carefully slips the ring on my finger. "I should've waited," he admits. "Should've made it romantic. But I couldn't wait. And I want everyone to know you're mine."

I cup his cheeks. "Pretty sure they already do."

Xavier

Down falls a king.

I follow Jameson DeSantis from the courthouse to a hotel, then a bar. He seems unconcerned about his surroundings, although I know that's another lie he puts out into the universe.

He's slippery.

I've tracked him for the better part of a year and a half with nothing to show for it.

He may as well have been a ghost—and just as trapped. If I was sure of anything, it's that he wouldn't leave New York City. Too much pride, too much arrogance.

This is the first time he's ventured back into public.

He exudes that arrogance now, sitting at the bar drinking a whiskey sour.

I enter the bar, which is nearly empty. The bartender takes one look at me and disappears. The only patron besides the man I'm here for stands, striding out without a backward glance.

Yeah—I have a reputation of my own.

I slide onto a barstool two down from Jameson, facing him.

He meets my gaze with a blank expression, but then the recognition dawns.

"The boy who couldn't kill me." His lips curl up in a sneer. "Tell me, did your father roll over in his grave when you failed?"

My smile is hard. How *dare* he bring my father into this? And he does recognize me—this confirms it. But I need him to say my name. "That was a long time ago."

He spreads his arms wide. "And here I fucking am. What do you have to show for it?"

A ledger, written in red.

A lifetime of anger.

He pauses, then nods to himself. He snatches his drink and downs it quickly, slamming the empty glass onto the bar top.

"So, what's the plan, son?"

"Say my name."

He keeps his focus on his empty glass. "Sure, sure. Xavier Eldridge. The last survivor. The inept son."

They're just words from a scared man about to meet his end.

I slide my gun out and carefully twist on the suppressor.

"I won't freeze this time," I promise him.

My soul is black. It's eroded from what I've done.

Killing Jameson DeSantis will not be my worst offense—or my last.

"You don't have the nerve." His eyes go from the gun to my face, and that sneer comes roaring back. "I never wondered about you. The scared boy who watched his daddy die. But I should've just put you out of your misery—"

I squeeze the trigger.

It isn't out of anger. Or passion. I've long since let go of those things.

Only loathing.

The noise is muted, but still seems to echo in the small space. Maybe that's just my imagination. The bullet tears through his throat, and he chokes on blood.

Good.

He slumps to the side, clawing at his neck. There's too much blood to stop it, too much damage. He bleeds out in a matter of seconds. The choking, gurgling noises stay with me.

I sit and watch him die.

When he finally goes still, I shove him off the stool. His body crashes to the floor.

I circle behind the bar and run a rag under cool water, dabbing at my face. It won't help with the blood on my shirt and in my hair, and a part of me selfishly wants to savor this quiet that follows his death.

Mission completed.

And then, out of the corner of my eye, I catch someone staring through the glass in the kitchen door. She ducks, but it's too late.

I step away from the body and stride toward the kitchen. As soon as I open the door, a frying pan flies at my face. I duck, the metal hitting the frame above me with a crack.

The girl stands in front of me with one of the chef's knives extended out in front of her. The tip of the blade trembles as if caught in a bad windstorm.

She's unusually pretty. Big, dark eyes. Dark hair. Red lips. She's tiny and startling. I stare at her, at the horror behind those eyes.

Something shifts in my chest.

And... I'm in the mood for something new.

Perhaps a chase. To play with my food before I devour her.

I lift my brow. "What are you waiting for, little bird? *Run.*"

THE END

Download Aiden & Gemma's bonus epilogue at
smassery.com/desantis-bonus

Acknowledgments

Hey friends! I hope that ending was satisfying. This duet—actually, the entire DeSantis Mafia series—was so much fun to write. I loved bringing Amelie back from the Fallen Royals, and then fell even harder when I met Luca, Aiden, and Gemma.

Thank you so much for supporting this series. It means the world to me that y'all join me in fangirling over the DeSantis guys, despairing over the bad stuff that happens, and cheering (or wincing, I suppose it depends on the situation) when things get a little bloody.

Special thank you to my reader group—a truly supportive collection of people, I love y'all. My alpha readers, Rebecca and Ari, and other early readers (Amber, Tara, Erica, Jolie!) with their valuable insight and feedback. Editor, Emmy at Studio ENP and Paige Sayer Proofreader. And for the beautiful cover photos, Wander Aguiar and Michelle Lancaster—and to Cassie for turning those photos into the gorgeous covers.

Much love!

Xoxo,

Sara

Also by S. Massery

Dark Bully Romance

College Hockey

Brutal Obsession

Devious Obsession

Fallen Royals

#1 Wicked Dreams

#2 Wicked Games

#3 Wicked Promises

#4 Vicious Desire

#5 Cruel Abandon

#6 Wild Fury

Reverse Harem Romance

Sterling Falls

#1 Thief

#2 Fighter

#3 Rebel

#4 Queen

About the Author

S. Massery is a dark romance author who loves injecting a good dose of suspense into her stories. She lives in Western Massachusetts with her dog, Alice.

Before adventuring into the world of writing, she went to college in Boston and held a wide variety of jobs—including working on a dude ranch in Wyoming (a personal highlight). She has a love affair with coffee and chocolate. When S. Massery isn't writing, she can be found devouring books, playing outside with her dog, or trying to make people smile.

Join her newsletter to stay up to date on new releases: http://smassery.com/newsletter

Made in United States
Troutdale, OR
01/10/2024

16870394R00235